Bayou Savage, Guitar Ghost Fighter

Book III

Attack on the Institute

Dean Russell & Chase Walker

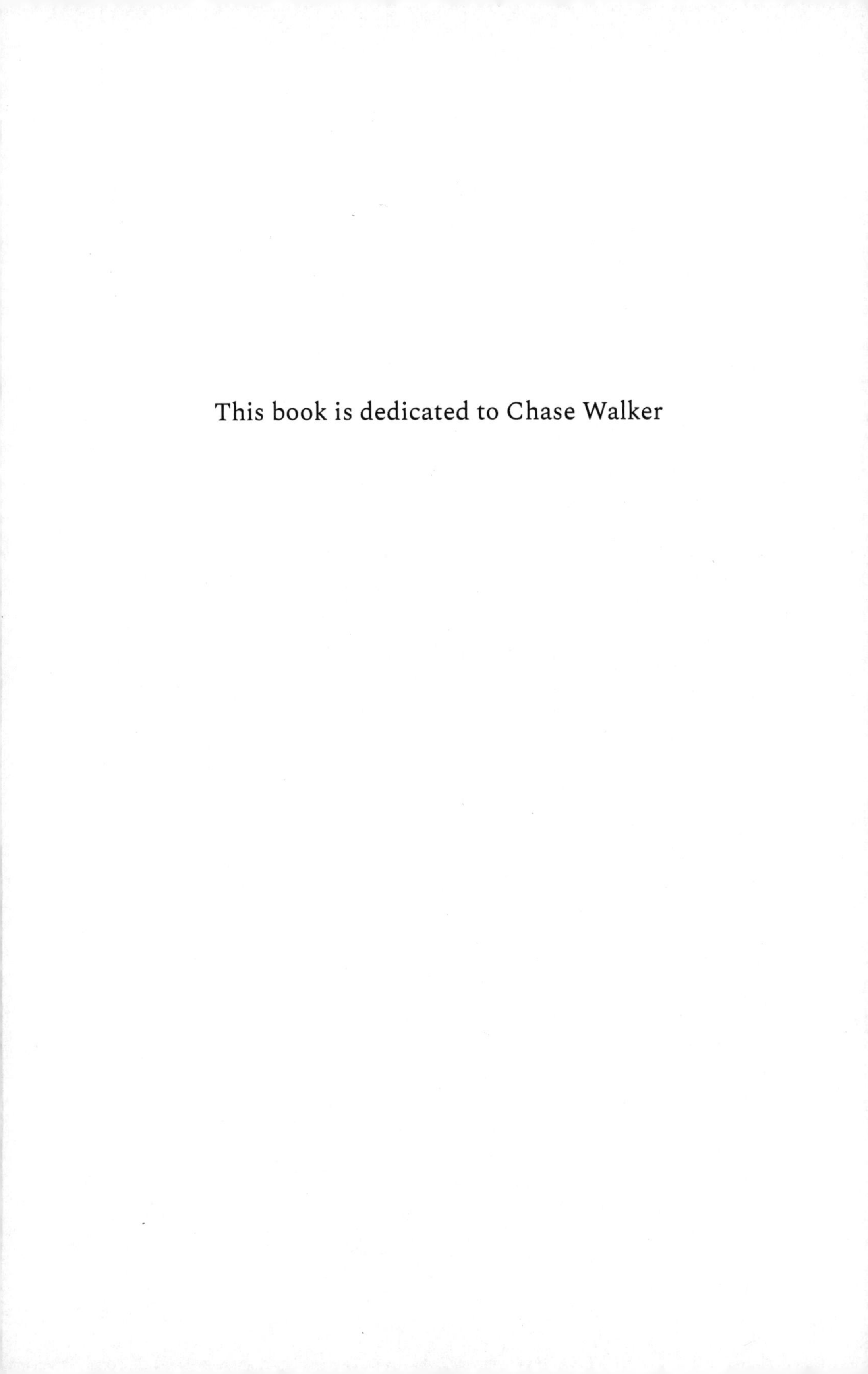

This book is dedicated to Chase Walker

Contents

1. Chapter 1 1
2. Chapter 2 6
3. Chapter 3 13
4. Chapter 4 17
5. Chapter 5 20
6. Chapter 6 29
7. Chapter 7 32
8. Chapter 8 36
9. Chapter 9 39
10. Chapter 10 42
11. Chapter 11 46
12. Chapter 12 49
13. Chapter 13 51
14. Chapter 14 58
15. Chapter 15 60
16. Chapter 16 64
17. Chapter 17 74

18. Chapter 18 76
19. Chapter 19 87
20. Chapter 20 95
21. Chapter 21 113
22. Chapter 22 117
23. Chapter 23 118
24. Chapter 24 123
25. Chapter 25 127
26. Chapter 26 137
27. Chapter 27 143
28. Chapter 28 146
29. Chapter 29 150
30. Chapter 30 152
31. Chapter 31 154
32. Chapter 32 162
33. Chapter 33 167
34. Chapter 34 172
35. Chapter 35 182
36. Chapter 36 187
37. Chapter 37 190
38. Chapter 38 198
39. Chapter 39 202
40. Chapter 40 204

41. Chapter 41 208
42. Chapter 42 222
43. Chapter 43 225
44. Chapter 44 227
45. Chapter 45 229
46. Chapter 46 232
47. Chapter 47 234
48. Chapter 48 242
49. Chapter 49 249
50. Chapter 50 252
51. Chapter 51 254
52. Chapter 52 257
53. Chapter 53 259
54. Chapter 54 272
55. Chapter 55 276
56. Chapter 56 280
57. Chapter 57 281
58. Chapter 58 283
59. Chapter 59 285
60. Chapter 60 287
61. Epilogue 297
62. One Year Later 301

Chapter 1

Bayou looked around the smoldering carnage through the bruised slits he used for eyelids. His body was covered in blood and demon phlegm. He felt a hundred miles beyond exhaustion and was surprised he could still breathe. Bayou sensed the battle was finally over. His lanky six-foot frame contorted with an excruciating spasm. Charred, shredded clothes loosely shrouded his almost well-built, nearly naked, and now mostly useless body. Bayou Savage, the world's most famous guitar ghost fighter, was in rough shape—even for him. The spasm subsided, and he caught another unexpected breath.

His blood loss dwindled to a trickle, unlike the hordes of ghosts and demons he'd spent the last few hours killing—if that's what you call sending malevolent beasts back to the fires of Hell. Bayou's mind wandered. "How did we get blindsided? And so damned easily? What's the opposite of a well-managed battle? Oh yeah, that's it, a well-manured battle. They knocked the shit out of us! Do these sons of bitches keep dying more than once? The Magi damn sure did."

Somehow the Magi—or some version of him—failed to cooperate and die like the rest of the demons. The son of a bitch wouldn't die or stay dead. How many of these stinking behemoths could there be? Bayou was certain they'd decimated at least two of the sulfur-reeking degenerates. They were resilient. They came back. And another tier from the depths of Dante's imagination followed each time.

Bayou contemplated recent events through battle fatigue, even as it smothered him in miserable debilitation.

"Why couldn't the bastard just stay dead?" His head hurt. "I'm not crazy; I've killed that bastard twice. I know I have. This one was different, no doubt...different the second time. The second time? How many of these assholes are there? But dead is dead."

He'd filled out the report and submitted the details just as he saw them. If ever there was a situation where **"you had to be there"** was a prerequisite, this one qualified. Without Quirk and Mist to verify the sequence of events, they'd strap him in one of those funny white coats that tie in the back.

"They'll probably send me to an Institute shrink for this one." Bayou faded in and out, as he randomly parceled information through the wreckage in his head.

He scraped himself across the splintered floor, closer to Leslie's cooling, lifeless body. Leslie had died moments ago in this latest battle with the Magi. Leslie, his half-sister—a revelation come to light only moments before she died. The shock still rolled over him, through him, like sour notes of a poorly tuned guitar, invading and infecting the inner ear.

Her beautiful face was covered with the remnants of his shirt, not enough cloth left to hide the gaping puncture where the curve of her hip joined her rib cage. Sobering evidence her warrior spirit was permanently removed from the land of the living.

Bayou wished he had her gift of clairsentience. Leslie could feel emotions from the living and, sometimes, even the dead. He sensed nothing from her. He struggled to hold on to his own senses, let alone reach out to others.

"Focus!" he commanded himself, wincing in pain as he looked to Leslie. Bayou was at odds with his recollection of the horrific battle which took place nanoseconds in the past.

He and Quirk had arrived first and took the early brunt of the fight. Already weakened from previous and recent days of battle, neither of them was in the best of condition.

Bayou bent the strings on the guitar, shooting blue-light magical energies harder than ever before. The two were barely holding their ground as the remaining ghost fighters arrived and began turning the tide of battle. He and Quirk had been at death's door many times...but never closer than today.

There were too many demons, too many ghosts, too many banshees from across the River Styx. The ghost fighters knew it would be bad, but none expected the magnitude they encountered here. The Magi came for a bloody finale, to kill with no remorse, and, this time, Leslie was his victim.

Bayou panicked. He desperately searched the carnage for his guitar. The mystical talisman no longer hung across his neck and shoulders. Had the magical "Smith and Wesson" survived? Was the guitar still intact? Would it still work? He remembered the guitar blasting its magic, slashing legions of ghosts and demons in the last stormy minutes. He didn't know how many he'd killed; he really didn't care. The miscreants numbered in the hundreds, maybe thousands. Bits and pieces of memory surfaced, drowned, and resurfaced again as he slipped in and out of consciousness. He could still feel the piercing claws tearing and ripping his flesh.

Shaking his mop of sandy hair to clear his head, he wondered if this last battle with the Magi had inflicted any damage on the guitar. He didn't feel the talisman reaching out for him as in past encounters. He tried to resurrect his supernatural tether to the guitar. Nothing happened. He tried again, holding his shaking hands out before him, fingernails glowing with power.

Weak and scattered, the flashing neon "Out of Order" sign inside his head blistered his mind, and he knew focus was an urgent requirement.

His thoughts were fuzzy as he fought against the vertigo creeping into his melting speculations. A distant voice whispered, "It's all right; surrender to the darkness." He didn't know if the suggestion belonged to the Magi or his overdrawn mind requesting much-needed sleep. He was fading quickly towards the beckoning, seductive darkness.

He wiped the blood and sweat from his eyes and squinted through the smoke and steam. He spotted the guitar a few feet to Leslie's side. He remembered. Leslie had harnessed the energy from both guitars and the Bloodstone to give the ghost fighters her final message: She was Razor's daughter. Armageddon arrives in three days with an attack on the Institute. Cornelius is coming.

"There's just not enough going on right now," he thought. "let's throw in some cryptic frickin' messages. Who the hell is Cornelius and what's he bringin' to the party?"

He reached out slowly and painfully, trying to will the blood-spattered guitar to his side. He was too weak. Bayou thought of his father, the old, tough-as-nails, guitar-playing, ghost-fighting father, Razor Savage, who abruptly walked out in the instant the battle was finished.

"Razor, damn you! Why'd you quit?"

Bayou knew the answer.

"You old bastard. You quit because you couldn't protect Leslie. She took the Magi's death blow meant for you. She died saving your ornery ass and you can't live with it."

Anybody dying for Razor broke the old ghost fighter's rules of engagement. Razor did his best to keep Leslie alive, and he'd failed. Failure was a foreign experience to the elder Savage. She died absorbing the Magi's blast intended for him. In her dying moments, Leslie revealed herself to be the old man's daughter. The impact of the revelation devastated the great warrior.

Razor announced his retirement. "Damn her, and damn this guitar." He allowed he was headed for the nearest watering hole. The best idea anyone within earshot could have would be to leave him alone. His voice filled with cold steel and hot iron. The piercing wolf's gray eyes spoke, "Don't fuck with me," and Razor turned on his heels. The six-foot, 220-pound legend hurled the Fender Esquire clear across the room, a final exclamation point to a very short speech. The guitar slid to a stop within inches of his dead daughter.

Chapter 2

Razor hadn't thrown in the towel because he thought he was too old for the Institute's stringent regimen. Bayou knew that much. We all have a tipping point. Razor had found his and gone a good ways past. Pissed and moving fast, Razor's backside passed through what was left of the door jamb and onto the cobbled streets of old Charleston. He didn't even notice the collateral damage left in the wake of his personal carnage. He moved as any man on a mission...quick and determined. Razor said he quit, and that was the end of the conversation.

He headed to the nearest saloon to vaccinate the insanity. Taking on the Magi turned into a suicide mission, and the medicinal booze would provide a temporary raincoat, protecting him from the flooding memories of Leslie's death.

Razor walked out and left Bayou to clean up the mess.

This was a first. Razor never quit. Never! Razor's resignation left Bayou alone to take on the next battle, maybe the last battle, and Leslie had forecasted the beginning of the end in three short days.

Mulling the logistics of the next few days, Bayou added Razor's guitar to his growing inventory of talismans. Two guitars, a Bloodstone, and his own daughter fleshed out the elite group Quirk started two hundred years ago.

Bayou had no idea if he could use twin guitars like Leslie did or if they would even make a difference. The word "damn" was invented for situations just like this. Of course, there had never been a situation like this before now. If the prophecies were even partly right, there never would be again.

He groaned, rising to his feet. The ionized air weighed heavy in his lungs and hung on his skin like a jousting knight's armor. He fought to maintain equilibrium. He tried to focus and forced himself to look at Leslie. The aching in his heart was far more devastating than the misery coursing through his battered body. Waves of grief washed over him as he howled against the hurricane of sorrow. Why hadn't she told him sooner?

"Damn her!" Leslie carried too much of the Savage DNA and too much of it belonged to Razor. The private lives of the Savage family were sacrosanct.

Bayou and Leslie had discussed death before. Each predicted they would be the first to meet the reaper. "Guess she won the bet." Bayou's sardonic thought brought more grief than he intended.

"Death leaves a heartache no one can heal; love leaves a memory no one can steal." He whispered to a deaf ear. He'd heard the verse at a funeral once upon a long time ago, and it stayed with him over the years. Not the kind of thing Razor would ever say.

Bayou always felt like the tallest pygmy around Leslie and Razor. Their raw talents were more powerful than his. They were his anchors, and now they were gone.

A fierce and foreign pain tore through him, doubling him over. He fought the exhaustion and imminent loss of consciousness.

The pain grew deeper and thicker. Agonizing stabs shot through him as hundreds of demons scratched and clawed at his body and memories. Bayou lost the battle to flashbacks of ghosts and demons torturing him and Quirk. He became more twisted with every convulsive intrusion.

Mist surfaced through his pain-racked mind as a tool to keep a failing grip on his dimming awareness. He couldn't let the damned Magi get to his daughter. She was all he had left in this world, and his mission was to protect her.

Mist, the newly conscripted owner of the Bloodstone, stood four feet away, her eyes darting between Leslie and Bayou. The Bloodstone chose her when Leslie died. The battle had been her baptism, first communion, and confirmation all rolled into one...and she wasn't even Catholic.

Mist rolled over, returning to remnants of the horrors she's seen. She sat up, scared shitless, as she watched her father writhing from the invisible agonies attacking his soul. She'd seen her father battle the demons and trolls from hell many times before, but nothing like this. He was bloodied and crazed, desperately seeking shelter inside the guitar's aura.

The guitars lit up and levitated towards him.

Mist knew what ghosts could do. Her recently healed broken arms and ribs lent unmitigated testimony to the facts. She raised the Bloodstone high above her head and allowed the pulsating red fog to engulf what was left of the room. A feral scream bellowed from a place in her she'd never been, in a voice she'd never heard.

Quirk jerked free from his near coma in an instant. The Bloodstone's aura renewed his strength and energy as he moved toward Mist.

Bayou could feel the demons' assault. He could no longer distinguish between the realities he'd lived through. He'd lost count of the battles and dimensional realities. Bayou felt the stifling evil smother him just as the Bloodstone began to work for him.

Bayou focused on Razor's abandoned Fender and the recently acquired Telecaster. The Bloodstone permeated through the cloak of evil and Bayou reached out. The guitars continued toward him, floating urgently off the ground. White, then electric blue energies, connected the guitars. His hands co-mingled with the fretboards.

Mist and Quirk watched in stunned silence; the guitars turned towards Bayou and fired. Bayou's beaten frame absorbed the supernatural lightning bolts, and he lifted off the floor as the glowing guitars circled him, connecting with him through the red and blue-white charges emanating from the neck. His body floated like a crucified puppet.

His head came up, chin slowly tilting. Bayou howled an amplified, blood-curling wail. The last remaining wall of the structure disintegrated from the force of the roar and reverberated through the Battery. The agonizing cry was heard as far away as the Old Customs House.

The guitars continued streaming bright blue and red beams through Bayou's torso. He focused on the healing white-blue-beamed energy from the Esquire. He needed to clear the cobwebs fast.

The dark rusty-red energy of the Telecaster flashed into his body. Bayou felt the differences in the energies. The Telecaster had belonged to Hendrix Buchanan. Bayou claimed the prize after defeating the Hendrix ghost even as Buchanan tried to persuade Bayou to join the Magi's hordes. Perhaps the Magi had tainted the guitar as he had Buchanan. Bayou didn't care. He wanted to heal, and kept pulling the energy into his body.

Mist was terrified. "Something's wrong! The Telecaster's energy is wrong, it feels evil!"

Mist intensified the Bloodstone's powers to gain more control over the turbulence surrounding her father.

Quirk had never seen any ghost fighter, including Razor, work the magic of two guitars in concert.

From his experience, he knew that when agents tried to incorporate good and evil energies simultaneously, the demons printed a one-way ticket to an early grave. The red and white-blue bolts coursing from the guitars increased as Bayou floated higher, absorbing the energy. The destroyed house sizzled with paranormal energies. The guitars danced around Bayou, fueling energy into his drifting frame.

Quirk and Mist recognized the evidence simultaneously; Bayou was becoming more powerful by the moment. The room pulsated with crackling rumbles as energies kept flowing into the increasingly crazed ghost killer.

Bayou regained a little bit of his senses. Something was wrong. The guitars' energies began to compete, creating an energy vortex. Matter and antimatter swirled around and through Bayou. His willpower was all that separated the two. His mind and body shredded as the guitars battled to control the ghost fighter. Another ear-splitting howl exploded from Bayou's lungs with the force of a CAT-5 hurricane.

Mist felt the Bloodstone glow brighter as Bayou's wail intensified.

Bayou took control of the Bloodstone. Mist let go, desperately seeking out her mentor. Using her clairaudience ability, she foraged through dimensions, seeking Leslie's spirit. Leslie remained silent.

The Bloodstone shot from Mist's hand like a high-velocity, fifty-caliber round. She watched the energy triangulate around Bayou's head. The Bloodstone joined the two guitars, slowly circling the crucified Bayou. The talismans alternated their colorful piercings. The Bloodstone inserted its mystical photoelectric spectra analysis, gathering control over the line and absorption emissions from the guitars. The light show synchronized with the hard rock chords Bayou pulled from the guitars. Bayou glowed in concert with the talismans' different colors now. The music pounded in waves of heavy metal subwoofer bass, corkscrewing ears within a four-mile radius.

Mist felt Bayou stabilizing the music and energies using the Bloodstone's control. She and Quirk relaxed...just a little. According to theory and science, what Bayou was doing couldn't be done. She glanced at Quirk. They were mesmerized as Bayou healed himself; the colors of his flesh returned to normal. When he was finished, he floated back to the floor. The three talismans slowed their circle around him and came to rest, awaiting their captain's next command.

The glow dissipated. The three warriors stood in silence. Bayou looked into the eyes of his daughter and the eyes of his good friend, Quirk. Sanity mercifully returned to the guitar ghost fighter.

Bayou spoke. "Nice to be back. Y'all need to know these energies are volatile, so this is a temporary fix at best. The Telecaster has an evil presence within it, and I have just a few minutes to return to the Institute. The fretboard on the Esquire is a key to all of this, and we've got to decipher the code to understand our next steps. If I get lost again, look to the writings of John the Baptist and the prophet Daniel. They left us clues to defeat all the Magi and every son of a bitch he brings with him."

Bayou's eyes took on an eerie glow never seen from or by any ghost fighter before. Quirk thought he'd seen it all. Mist was still pretty much a rookie. Experience and exuberance melded into confusion.

Bayou's eyes rolled up into his head; he turned pale. Quirk caught him just before he hit the floor. The Esquire assumed "protect mode" and hovered next to Quirk. The Telecaster assumed a similar attitude giving the guitars the appearance of watchdogs guarding their master.

Mist activated the Bloodstone and relieved Bayou from Quirk's cradled arms. Leslie's body gravitated to the Bloodstone's new proprietor, and the tattered bodies of the ghost fighters floated on either side of Mist, as if on stretchers. The guitars rested easy as Quirk strapped one to each shoulder. A portal opened, and the battered ghost fighters were mercifully transported to the Institute.

Chapter 3

Quirk was the first to appear in the infirmary. The Bloodstone sensed the urgency of the required repairs to Bayou, Mist, and Quirk, and brought the group exactly where they needed to be in the shortest time possible.

Mist followed through the tunnel's shimmering entrance, flanked on either side by the floating remnants of Bayou and Leslie.

Doctor Jupiter Marcella Diego scrambled through the hospital. The blaring alarm claxons bounced through the canyons of hallways as her lithe and athletic strides carried her closer to her destination.

J.D. reached the infirmary just as the crimson tunnel disappeared behind Mist.

She quickly assessed the situation in her inimitable style and began barking orders to the staff of nurses and doctors who stood slack-jawed by the unusual entrance of the ghost fighters.

"You'd think they'd get used to these comings and goings," she thought.

"Judy! Get Quirk into Exam Room One, put Mist in Two and Bayou in Room Three, and do it STAT! Get that child covered and make her presentable!"

"Johnny! Get three doses of the elixir ready, and I want it done in less than a minute! Move, Doctor!"

Judy Sawyer gathered her team, moving mobile stretchers into place; they gently laid the bodies down and rolled the gurneys into their assigned examination rooms.

Leslie's body was covered from head to toe by a pristine white sheet. An orderly slowly rolled her through the halls towards the autopsy room.

Doctor John Kohlbeck rushed to the meds refrigerator, opened the biometric lock, and withdrew three vials of Quirk's famous "blue elixir". He grabbed three syringes and placed a vial and a syringe in each room in less than sixty seconds. He felt like a rodeo champ, happy to beat J.D.'s time requirement. Every man J.D. ever knew was eager to keep her happy. Poor bastards never stood a chance, but by God, they sure tried.

J.D. went to Bayou first, seeing his condition and recognizing the symptoms of a life force quickly fading. Bayou lay still in the bed as the nurses swabbed his wounds with soothing antiseptic sponges and wrapped the bad ones with sterile gauze. J.D. swiftly loaded a syringe with the blue juice, found an unscathed vein in Bayou's arm, and carefully injected the miracle cure into the bloodied ghost fighter.

"Judy, give him a sedative. I want him down for twelve hours. These people need a break, and I will ensure they get one this time."

"Yes, Ma'am...." That was the only answer Doctor Diego wanted to hear.

Johnny Kohlbeck was about to give Quirk his shot when J.D. entered the exam room. "Thanks, Johnny. Please go help Judy tend to Mist. I'm going to take care of this big lunk myself."

Quirk was still basking in the glow of the Bloodstone and couldn't feel the cuts, scrapes, and bruises covering his body. He felt good enough to offer a salacious grin to the good doctor and winked. "Thanks, J.D. I don't feel all that bad, all things considered. How's about you and me take in a little dinner after your shift?"

J.D. worked hard on the "can't touch this" attitude but failed miserably. She couldn't remember the last time she was this happy to see a man. The woman melted into Quirk's arms and heaved a sigh of relief.

"Damn you, Quirk! I told you to be careful! Look at you. You look like hell! Wait until the Bloodstone wears off, and you'll think about something other than gettin' into my pants!"

Quirk grinned. "Yeah, Babe. But not right now. So how about dinner?" He stood up to give the Doc a lusty hug. He damn near cracked his head on the bed frame as he tumbled backward, landing mostly in the sack, completely passed out.

J.D. let a small gasp escape as she watched the big man fall. As strong as she was, the voluptuous doctor just barely prevented a fractured skull; grabbing his muscular wrists and slowing the toppling tree, she fell with his weight and landed on top of him. Quirk was out. She brushed her lips across his cheek, as much with relief as passion. "Later, Big Guy...later."

J.D. adjusted the Director of the Ghost Defense Institute on the narrow bed and covered the man with sheets and blankets.

She injected Quirk with the elixir and a sedative, turned out the lights, and moved to Room Two.

Doctor Diego was determined the three warriors would survive, awaken, healed and well rested. Rumor had it, they were going to be busy very soon.

Oswalt entered the infirmary as the last injection was administered to the fallen warriors. He saw the shroud-covered body on the gurney and feared the worst for Razor.

When a strand of Leslie's red hair slipped from under the blood-soaked sheet, he vomited to the nearest receptacle. He couldn't even try to make it into a restroom. Oswalt was devastated. He headed for the refuge of his office and the bottle of eighteen-year-old Scotch he kept in the file cabinet.

Chapter 4

Quirk woke in those early hours when the sun and moon argued over which would light the day. The mountain air slipped through the window, and he took in a deep breath of the freshness. His head was clear as a bell; his body refreshed and, for the first time in over two hundred years, satisfied.

He was home, in his oversized king bed, six hundred thread count Egyptian cotton sheets swathed his healed body. The down comforter was just the right weight against the early morning chill.

The silky raven hair of Doctor Jupiter Marcella Diego cascaded over his left shoulder into the middle of his chest.

J.D. grinned lustily, wrapped her arms around his neck, and pulled him closer. They moved together in a rhythm reserved for long time lovers, closing on the moment in harmony.

In the afterglow, they lay in silence, nearly exhausted, watching the sun win out over the moon, rising over the eastern mountaintop.

"Not bad for a two-hundred-year-old warrior," said the good doctor.

"You had to remind me, didn't you? I guess there's more to the blue juice than we thought."

They laughed and spooned, waiting for the automatic coffee maker to brew this morning's wake-up call.

Quirk came to the hospital, six hours ahead of J.D.'s scheduled time out, and quietly used his com unit to call for a car and driver. He slipped out a side door, hopped into the long black limo, and bid the driver maximum speed. In less than an hour, he returned to the infirmary, clean-shaven, in a starched white oxford shirt, blue jeans, a blue blazer, and freshly shined Rockports. He smelled of soap...no foo-foo cologne for the legendary Director. As usual, he commanded the attention of everyone within eyesight.

"I believe we had a dinner date, Doc, and your shift is over."

Bayou and Mist were still out cold.

J.D. was awed by the speedy and remarkable recovery she watched swagger through the infirmary doors. Her cheeks turned crimson, and the staff stood in disbelief during the shift change. None of them could ever remember Doctor Diego blushing at the sight or sound of any man.

Quirk put his arm around her waist and walked her towards the door.

"Your chariot awaits, Mademoiselle."

J.D. dropped her smock at the front desk, slipped her version of the blue blazer over her crisp white blouse, and was promptly swept off her feet by the man of her dreams.

They sipped vintage Mumm Cordon Rouge on the way to a gourmand's delight Quirk discovered during his reconnaissance for this evening. They feasted on raw oysters and steamed artichokes, Caesar salad, medium rare filet mignon, asparagus slathered in Béarnaise sauce and then finished the meal with

Bananas Foster chased with Louis XIV brandy in crystal snifters. A perfect beginning to a perfect night.

The driver left them at the door of Quirk's retreat in the mountains.

As the sun added warmth to the light of day, J.D. purred, "I could get used to this."

Quirk reluctantly slid out of bed. "Time to get back to work, Darlin'. Next time, I'll cook up some Eggs Benedict, and the best damned Bloody Mary you've ever had. I've got to see about the Institute."

As he moved to the kitchen and the aroma of freshly brewed coffee, he glanced through the kitchen bay window at the crimson sunrise.

"Damn," he muttered. "Red skies in the morning..."

Chapter 5

At exactly six in the morning, Oswalt woke to the blaring alarm and the annoying ringtone of his com unit. Coming to life from the depths of REM sleep, he struggled with the coordination of mind and body. His hand missed the com unit on the first pass.

"Whaatttt?" He tried to say. The suede sweaters on his teeth and tongue made it hard to articulate his foggy thoughts.

Waking up by the second, he hollered to anyone who could hear him, "Are the ghosts attacking?"

He couldn't think of anything else to say as he began to focus on the security indicators glowing on his wall.

"Sir," the perimeter guard spoke excitedly. "Something or someone just walked right through the front gate. Whatever it is, it's headed straight for your office. Every agent we've sent to investigate has failed to report back."

Oswalt watched the sequence of alarms on the board, confirming the guard's assessment whatever or whoever was headed straight for him and around, through, or over every sentry post between him and the front gate.

He screamed into his headset, "Security, where in the hell are the camera feeds?"

The first alarm at the entrance to the administrative wing sounded. Oswalt's awakening came more swiftly, quickly approaching panic.

When the alarms woke him up, he'd been dreaming of Leslie, still trying to process her death.

Some force was walking straight through the Institute's security as if they were no more than wet Kleenex. Alarms were going off all over the facility.

He yelled into the headset, "Is it a ghost? Do you think it might be Leslie coming back?" Oswalt was ever hopeful.

"We don't know, sir. We're not getting ghost readings, but something just scrambled every monitor. Every agent on premises has failed to communicate. Regardless, Director, you need to get to cover. I figure you've got about ten seconds left."

Oswalt jumped up. The sensor on his office door indicated it was about to open. The door was wired to open only with his optic-scan or from within. Oswalt could only stare in amazement as the two-feet-thick steel door swung into his office. The temperature in the Oswalt sanctuary dropped ten degrees.

Oswalt imagined the archangel of death as the six-foot-four, two hundred-and thirty-five-pound hulk darkened the doorway.

The lighting in the room shadowed the man's face, making for an even more mysterious and imposing entrance. He walked with the confidence of an accomplished athlete. He wore a long black duster over the garb of a Catholic priest: black slacks, clergy vest, and jacket accented by a bright red collar. The black pointed-toe cowboy boots added an extra couple of inches to his already substantial height. The nearly white-blond hair was closely cropped, his chin square, and those infernal eyes matched the crimson collar peeking between the tabs of the black clerical vest. He looked like Special Ops...a member of the Jesuit Order, perhaps, the Vatican's Gestapo.

He slid from the shadows, locked eyes with Oswalt, and asked, "Are you the Director?"

For the first time in his career, Oswalt wished he didn't carry that title, and hoped there might be someone further up the chain of command. Of course, there wasn't. This set of circumstances was all on him, "Yes," Oswalt moaned, feeling completely exhausted, worn out, weary, and cornered.

The stranger gazed through him, and barked, "Where is Leslie? I need to see her!"

Oswalt became as curious as he was frantic; this had to be a nightmare. The dark stranger with eerie eyes violated his sanctuary. He was alone, cornered, and unaccustomed to either feeling. Oswalt struggled to regain control.

The tall, mysterious stranger never let his penetrating stare wander. "Look, if the human race has any chance of surviving, I have to see her. Tracking through the death dimension is a topographical bitch. Take me to her. I've seen her about to die. The Magi has chosen her as the sacrifice to his power."

Oswalt thought he detected an upper Midwest accent in the stranger's brief speech. A bit of relief sprouted as Oswalt realized the stranger was, after all, just a man. Mysterious, most certainly, but still...just a man.

Oswalt stood up quickly. "Who the hell are you?"

The stranger responded in a clipped and curt cadence. "That's a reasonable question. My name is Cornelius. Hurry up. We're running out of time." Oswalt cleared his throat, regaining composure and confidence.

"Excuse me, 'Cornelius,' is it? Forgive my ignorance, but how in the unholy hell did you get in here? *What* and *who* are you to so easily crash the best defenses in the world? How did you get through our security systems?"

Oswalt noticed a glistening on Cornelius' face and hands.

Cornelius recognized the need to address Oswalt's observation, "I sweat when I use my powers."

"Powers", thought Oswalt. "Shit. More fucking powers. Guitars, Bloodstones, magic, telepathy, and now this freak. I *really* miss a good ol' M-16!"

"Hold on, Cornelius. I need to soothe the troops." He reached over and took the time to respond to an anxious security squad.

He spoke hurriedly into the com unit, "Situation under control, code four-thirteen-niner."

The predetermined code gave the security squad notice that everything truly was under control and Oswalt wasn't just making noise.

"Get Steve, Jade, and Jed Harris in here now! Everything is OK. Turn off the alarms." He wanted to call the other ghost fighters but knew they were a few hours from functional.

"Sir, are you sure you're OK?" One of the guards insisted on asking.

"Yep...I'm fine, guys. Now get on it." Oswalt kept his eyes on Cornelius.

Cornelius sat down, and Oswalt got a whiff of the glistening. At least the weird-lookin' dude had to work up a sweat to cut through their security.

Cornelius hung his head and spoke in a low, tired voice. "I've only used my powers on this scale once before. The Magi's bitch tricked me into annihilating a village in the Dakotas. I'm honor bound to make that right with the son of a bitch."

Oswalt caught an inkling of how tired the dark man in front of him really was. He no longer represented a threat. Finally awake, Oswalt realized this was *the* Cornelius Leslie spoke of before she left for her fateful rendezvous in Charleston. He was the asset that would help the ghost fighters defend the Institute.

Oswalt processed the information, still focused on his initial question. He was surprised the young man was unaware of the current circumstances. Oswalt posted his query again.

"Why is it so crucial that you see Leslie?"

Cornelius answered with an undertone of exhausted impatience.

"The answer is simple, Director. I penetrated Leslie's defenses a year ago and linked them with her dimensional travels. I need to find her and assess our mutual strengths. I believe we will help each other in battle with the Magi. We share a common gift."

Cornelius had confirmed he was unaware of Leslie's demise. Oswalt decided to keep that information private for a moment longer.

The disconcerting color of the big man's eyes nearly matched the crimson collar in his vestments. Oswalt wondered if Cornelius dressed for effect. If he did, it worked; he was scarier than anyone Oswalt had ever met. Cornelius continued with a subtle conciliatory change in attitude and tone.

"She is truly gifted. I've detected her energy many times over the years when she ported from one dimension to the next. I know she's here." He hesitated. "Her signature was different during this last port; I got here as fast as possible. She's somehow hidden herself from me. I've known the approximate location of this place and that she was close by. I felt her flow through a different dimension and lost track of her. My whole life, I believed I was the only person on the planet who could do that. The Magi does it, but I knew of no other with the capacity for inter-dimensional travel. I thought we should make contact if she were a survivalist like me. Leslie is multifaceted, and I want to assess our similarities. If she works for the Magi, I will have to kill her."

His voice was matter-of-fact and callous. The man made no empty threats. Cornelius carried the look of a killer.

"I know she's here, and I've read the news about you and what used to be this clandestine group. You and your ghost fighters are trying to wipe out the Magi. I'm here to help. None of your ghost fighters has any *real* powers. Your guitar players are barely adequate. She is the only warrior with a discernible measure of power. Without her, you and this Institute have no advantage in fighting the Magi. She is the real power. Now, for the last time...where the hell is she?"

He stood up, "I'm not here to harm you or your team. That's not my purpose. Call her and tell her to come here if it that'll make you feel any better."

Oswalt kept quiet and tried to put on a genial face. He couldn't. The strain was too much. He thought of beautiful Leslie and the last time he saw her on his sofa.

He dropped his head down and allowed his eyes to drift into those of the stranger, squinting through tears. "Yes, you've tracked her here. And I agree she had incredible gifts. When she arrived at our Institute, she opened my mind to what true power was. Her powers, her 'sleight of mind' dimensional travels were remarkable, and I'm glad she maintained a residency here, if even for a short while."

He continued. "Cornelius, you need to know. Leslie is dead. We still haven't figured out what happened in Charleston. We know the Magi killed her and Mist transported her body back here."

Oswalt wanted to stop, but he couldn't help passing on a bit of the pain. He shoved the guilt as far down Cornelius' throat as he could.

"You should have made your presence known before the Charleston battle. Maybe you could have saved her. She needed more power. They all needed more power. They were too damn tired for another battle so soon, but there was no one else I could send. *Hear me?!* They were bone tired. They needed you. I had to let them go because there was no one else. What the hell took you so long to show up?"

He relived the nightmare, trying to make sense of it, obsessing over his need to put order to everything. That was his gift, wasn't it? Oswalt's anger kept boiling to the surface. The next statement spewed like venom, "Good timing, asshole, if you're so damned powerful, why didn't you know they needed your help? Your clock's off just a bit. Maybe you're afraid of the Magi. Whatever you thought, you really missed the Charleston battle, and that's what ended her. You're late. And the rest of us are fucked."

Oswalt's face was as red as Cornelius' eyes. He was surprised with his rant in the face of the crimson-eyed Hulk.

"Now, welcome to Armageddon with the rest of us. You have the good fortune to grab a damned good seat for the next performance because Leslie predicted everyone here would have a front-row seat to the battle that will destroy the human race in three days. Which, by the way, have now become two."

Cornelius kept his powers in check...to Oswalt's benefit. The red-eyed giant was full of rage, shock, dismay, and disbelief. He began a deep breathing exercise he'd learned early on to control his powers. He slowed his mind and racing heart, absorbing the information from Oswalt. He withdrew a few feet, putting distance between him and the Director, as he reviewed the verbal assault. Never taking his blazing eyes from Oswalt, Cornelius was adapting his algorithm to this new information.

Oswalt glared back at him. He needed time to think.

Cornelius seemed lost. He appeared to be going through a mental exorcism, walking around the spacious office in small, asymmetric circles, incanting something that Oswalt couldn't make out.

Oswalt needed J.D. to handle this on-the-edge situation. Now that he was thinking again, he remembered that she sedated all three ghost fighters, and they were not to be bothered until she released them.

He slowly reached over and picked up the com unit. Cornelius didn't seem to care. "Please get Steve, Jade and Jed to me STAT."

They could help him sort out this new development until the ghost fighters woke up.

Fifteen minutes had passed since Cornelius walked into Oswalt's office. Oswalt was positive he'd missed lunch.

Chapter 6

Three security guards walked slowly into the room, guns at the ready, cautious in their approach.

Cornelius kept his head down, exhausted, and chuckled. He spoke to the guards as much as to Oswalt. "Conventional weapons won't stop the Magi!" He chortled again, guttural and seemingly on the verge of hysteria.

The door opened. Steve and Jade Johnson, disheveled and alarmed, came to an abrupt halt. They both looked, as they should, rudely awakened from much-needed sleep and curious about the scene confronting them. Jed Harris followed directly behind, still in his pajamas and a pair of silly-looking Bullwinkle slippers. The slippers *almost* provided Oswalt with much-needed comic relief as Jed came up just short of stumbling into Jade.

They listened as Oswalt brought them up to speed and gawked at the towering Cornelius and his blood-red pupils. They were impressed that this unknown intruder had bypassed the Institute's premier security system.

Cornelius looked around and said, "OK, I'm rested, let's get to her body. I know it's here, but I can't find it; it took me too long to get here."

None of them could believe what he just said. What the hell was he talking about? He must be as crazy as the eyes made him look.

Cornelius began to move toward the door. The guard closest to him put a hand on his shoulder. The other guards sensed a threat from the big man and began to close in.

Cornelius looked each one in the eyes and grinned—the sockets of his eyes filled with the fiery red of his irises. Crimson beams shot from his hands. The beams hit the three guards square in their chests. They never had time to react. Each staggered back a step, tasered with fifty thousand volts, and tumbled in a forward free fall, smacking the floor hard and face first ...broken noses all around. Cornelius looked like a demon come to life.

Oswalt and the three insiders watched in shock as the big man's irises returned to their dangerous crimson hue and the whites once again surrounded the mirror to his soul. The moment was a surreal and bizarre display of power that took all of two seconds from start to finish.

"He would have been a hell of an asset if he'd shown up in time," Oswalt thought bitterly.

Oswalt glared into the otherworldly eyes of the yet-to-be-determined friend or foe. His voice cut with the same bitterness as before. He was still pissed that Cornelius came to the party a day late. "How did you do that?"

Cornelius cooled, "Easily....and I can do more when I am pissed."

Steve and Jed, the ever-ready scientists, were curious.

"Damn good", Jed said looking at the knocked-out guards. "Let me guess, your powers are way beyond hypnosis?"

They were both struggling to control their need for understanding and calling for measuring instruments. Steve knew this person was dangerous and he had to tread softly. As scientists, interest in the phenomena standing before them was genuine.

Jade jumped in, "We haven't seen true extra-sensory powers in over two hundred years, except the ghost fighters. Where did you come from? Are you from their period? How did you get your powers?" These were shared questions in the minds of those present.

Oswalt felt relieved; the support he sought had arrived.

Cornelius looked down at the guards. "We don't have much time; my story is quite simple. First, I need to see Leslie's body. I have to get there fast. I've been as patient as I can be. Let us go...now."

The emphatic urgency wasn't lost on the audience. Oswalt abdicated to the authority of the red-eyed stranger.

"All right. We'll wait to hear your story. Let's get to the storage area, and you can see Leslie's remains." The words caught in his throat, and Steve, Jade, and Jed were still trying to wrap their minds around the word "remains" as they exited Oswalt's vault.

Chapter 7

Quirk brought J.D. a cup of coffee and hit the shower. He called for a car to run her back to her place, to prepare for the continued revival of Bayou and Mist.

Quirk put on a pair of jeans, boots, and a fresh polo shirt. He threw on a light leather jacket, pecked J.D. on the cheek, and headed out the door.

"I'll see you in about an hour, Doc. Things should start jumping pretty quick once Bayou and Mist are up. If Leslie's right, we've only got a couple of days to get the Institute ready for the next wave."

"Watch your ass, Quirk. I want some more of it."

"Damn, she's as sexy as she looks," he thought. Quirk couldn't remember the last time he enjoyed a woman's company as much as that of Doctor Jupiter Marcella Diego. He threw her a kiss and stepped out to the attached garage.

Quirk decided to ride his Harley back to the Institute. He wanted a full twenty minutes of fresh mountain air in his face and twisted, two-lane roads to clear his head before charging the day and getting the troops to prepare for Leslie's prediction. There weren't that many left after the last three battles, but they were the toughest of the bunch. Hell, they'd survived two bad-ass Magi characters and as far as Quirk was concerned, 'still standing' was a badge of honor, in its own right. Quirk tore through the mountain back roads, leaning low through the turns and enjoying the adrenaline rush.

A scowl grew on his face as he approached the empty guard house at the entrance to the GDI. The scowl grew to concern as he passed post after post of empty security stations. He arrived at the doors to the infirmary before he saw the first sentry.

"Good morning, Director Quirk," the sentry snapped to attention.

"Good morning, my ass. Where the hell is everybody?" Quirk was not nearly as jovial as he had been twenty minutes earlier, and he knew J.D. was at least a half hour behind him.

"All due respect, sir, I'd appreciate you hearing the news from Director Oswalt."

Quirk's mood darkened before the man finished his sentence. "Fine. And where am I able to find Oswalt?"

"I believe you'll find them in the infirmary, sir."

"Them?" Quirk was beyond pissed at that point. He didn't care for surprises at all. The automatic doors opened as he half jogged into the reception area. It was six-thirty and the shift change put more people in front of him than he's seen in the last eighteen hours. "At least there are people in *here*," he mused.

Quirk rounded the corner down the hallway where he knew Bayou and Mist would be quartered, probably rising from the J.D.-induced coma by now. He was about to tap on Bayou's door when he spotted the back of Oswalt's head, the white hair of a big man in a long black coat, and the easily recognized entourage (for which he was unprepared at this hour of the morning).

The length and breadth of the long black duster was disconcerting and stood the old warrior's neck hairs on end. He continued down the hall past Bayou's room and approached the crowd with practiced stealth. He was just a yard away from Jade when Cornelius spun around with unconscious speed and fixed the fiendish orbs on a much-surprised Director Quirk.

The empty sentry posts suddenly made a lot of sense. Quirk stood tall and met the priest's eyes with zero trepidation. Cornelius was impressed with the fearless legend standing his ground, empty handed.

"Who's our new friend, Oswalt? And what's up with those eyes?" Quirk tuned in to the cooler air which seemed to surround Cornelius.

Cornelius let loose a roar of laughter. "I've been told you've got the tact of a three-pound sledge, Quirk. Nice to meet you."

Cornelius stepped forward with an outstretched hand. The two met halfway and the test was on. Quirk grabbed the big man's hand knowing equal pressure would be required to eliminate any advantage the red eyed stranger carried with his size. The frosty flesh betrayed the fiery eyes in the white-haired behemoth. Their eyes swapped daggers for a good thirty seconds, Cornelius careful not to unleash his weapons on the unsuspecting Director.

"We've got work to do, young man. Let's continue this contest at a later date." Quirk was determined to keep the upper hand. They released their grips and turned to the gawkers at the door leading into Autopsy.

Quirk swung open the door to the refrigerated arena and stepped through to be greeted by Doctor John Kohlbeck.

"We've come to see Leslie," Oswalt declared. He couldn't yet wrap his mind around the "remains" word. But he was acting more in charge than confused. The pecking order seemed restored.

Kohlbeck moved to the eight by ten wall of nine refrigeration units, the last way station for field agents bested by their opponents. He opened a two by three door, revealing the telescoping tray where Leslie's body had been placed the day before. Steve, Jade and Jed stood on the left, Oswalt and Quirk on the right and Cornelius at the top of the tray. The tray whispered out of the steel sarcophagus on silent rollers.

The blood-soaked sheet laid crumpled on the stainless-steel tray...the *empty* stainless steel tray.

"Holy shit!" Oswalt roared. "Where's her body?"

Chapter 8

J.D. walked through the doors of her domain at the very moment Oswalt and his group made their unnerving discovery. She was far enough away from Autopsy to miss the anguished howl.

J.D. checked with the resident, a few of her nurses and flipped through various charts and reports with particular focus on Bayou and Mist.

"Where's Doctor Kohlbeck?" She asked the R.N. tending the sign-in desk.

"Last time I saw him he was headed to Autopsy."

"Okay...any noises from our favorite patients down the hall?"

"No Ma'am. They've been quiet all night long...no surprises there."

"Yeah, you're right about that. Well, it's time for reveille. Let's get 'em up and check their vitals." J.D. checked her watch. It was almost seven and they'd had close to eighteen hours of well-deserved deep sleep. J.D. called for Judy Sawyer to meet her in Bayou's room and headed down the hall.

J.D. saw Judy just as she got to Bayou's private room. They were almost through the door when Oswalt came running out of Autopsy, shouting commands. J.D. watched Oswalt, the hysterical scientists and the wide-eyed historian scramble up the hallway. A towering and oddly dressed young man followed behind. Quirk was between the white-haired giant and the rest of the team. His poise spoke of the quiet confidence she had grown to expect from her man. "My man," she thought. "Boy, it's been too damned long."

"What's all the fuss?" J.D. managed, as Oswalt approached.

"Leslie's body is gone!" He shouted. "***Gone***, for God's sake! What in the hell is going on around here?"

Oswalt was uncharacteristically frantic. He rushed past J.D. towards his office and the comfort of his command center. He knew he could bring order to the situation if he could just get a grip on the highly unusual circumstances. The chaos was unnerving to his typically organized mind.

Steve Johnson and Jed Harris moved in the direction of the lab, to gather measuring instruments and examine security videos of the autopsy area. They were certain a rational explanation could be found with the proper tools.

Jade followed her husband for no particular purpose other than the solace she found in his company. She had nothing but her own confusion to offer.

Cornelius and Quirk were deep in thought as they neared the doctor and nurse who were about to wake Bayou. Quirk was close enough to J.D. as he spoke. "J.D., I'm not sure what the hell is happening, but the security of this facility has been severely compromised. You and your staff should be on guard. I'll get more security guys to the infirmary. This is Cornelius, and I'll have to save further explanations until after we sort this out."

Cornelius offered his hand and J.D. took it, unable to wrestle her eyes away from the stranger's rusty-red pupils. She was taken aback by the cool flesh of his firm handshake.

"Pleased to meet you, Doctor."

"Likewise,...I think."

Quirk continued, "We're gonna need all hands on deck as soon as you wake Bayou and Mist. Please do what you can to get them fully alert as quickly as possible...and thanks...for everything." He managed a quick, undetected wink.

"Sure, Quirk. I'll see to it immediately. I'll have 'em up and in Oswalt's office inside of thirty minutes. What else can I do to help?"

"If you come up with any theories about Leslie's disappearance, I'd be happy to hear what you've got to say. Right now, I'm gonna go see what I can do to settle Oswalt down and brainstorm ideas with him. Cornelius here will undoubtedly have some ideas of his own. I think we've found a new ally. I'll talk to you later. Join us when you can."

"Later," she said. "Remember what I told you this morning."

The big men hurried off to the admin wing and Oswalt's base of operations.

"You two got a thing goin', huh, Quirk."

"You don't know me that well, Cornelius and this is no social event. I'll thank you to keep any irrelevant bullshit to yourself."

Cornelius kept quiet, stayed in step and smirked...just a little.

Chapter 9

J.D. opened the door to Bayou's dimly lit room. Bayou lay motionless in the hospital bed. Judy stepped to the side of the bed and let the guard rail down. The creaking mechanism startled Bayou and he bolted up-right, reaching for the talisman guitar. His arm flailed in empty space.

"Easy, Bayou. It's just us," J.D. spoke softly.

"Wow, Doc...how long have I been out?" He was coming around.

"Y'all ported here yesterday in the early afternoon. You were pretty beat up and in desperate need of rest."

"I know you're right about that, but there's a war comin' and we've got to get ready." The urgency in Bayou's voice was obvious. He'd not forgotten Leslie's premonition. "What time is it?"

"Just after seven. I'm going to turn up the lights and get you fed, showered, and dressed. We've got a new turn of events and Quirk needs you and Mist upstairs, pronto."

Nurse Judy raised the dimmer switch to brighten the room and walked to the window. She drew back the curtains, filling the room with clear Carolina blue sky and the rising sun.

"Bayou, this is going to clear your head a little faster and put you on full alert." J.D. drew a syringe and poked a vein in Bayou's right arm.

"There's a fresh set of clothes in the closet. Towel, wash cloth and all the toiletries you'll need are in the bathroom. You best hurry up. Quirk's waiting. I'll have breakfast here by the time you're out of the shower."

"Thanks, Doc. I'm not sure what you just shot me with, but you can skip the coffee. I don't believe I'll be needin' any of it." He flashed the infamous Bayou grin and for the first time, Judy noticed his crystal blue eyes. Bayou didn't miss the look. He hadn't experienced a special "moment" in a long damned time.

There are, in the lives of mortals, precious moments when a certain glance is held for an extra split second in time. Man and woman connect on a remarkable plane known only to each other. In cases of good fortune, opportunities present to explore the depth of that moment. Neither Judy nor Bayou missed the connection. They each stored the mutual curiosity for future consideration.

Judy and J.D. crossed the hall to Mist's room and repeated this morning's duties.

Inside of twenty-five minutes a freshly showered, dressed and well-fed Bayou Savage stepped into the hallway just as Mist opened the door to her room. The father-daughter bond superseded that of the ghost fighters. Bayou and Mist embraced with the fierce love and intensity only a close-knit family can know.

J.D. stepped in close to the pair and spoke softly. "I don't want to break this little reunion up but Quirk and Oswalt are anxious to see you two about ten minutes ago.

Bayou and Mist hustled arm in arm, happy to be alive, off to see the wizard.

As they rounded the bend in the hallway, Bayou and Mist bounced smack into Razor.

Chapter 10

"Holy crap, Grandpa!"

Razor staggered back from the impact.

"Geeez, Dad, you look like death eatin' a cracker."

Razor didn't look a whole lot different than he did yesterday when he stumbled out of the war zone headed for the local tavern. Torn clothes, a little more stubble on his face and what looked like fresh scrapes on his knuckles.

"Yeah, well you should see the other guy." The stench of stale Jack Daniels nearly knocked them both over.

"You drunk, Pop?"

"Maybe a little...still. I might be blowin' about a point one five. Don't matter. I figure y'all need some help. I'm real sorry 'bout Leslie, son. Apologies to you, too, Mist. I think I drank all the Jack in Charleston between yesterday afternoon and this mornin' tryin' to forget what I did. Found an after-hours joint off the Battery. Them boys know how to party." Razor did a little two step, trying to maintain balance and composure. He wasn't quite himself, as they say.

J.D. stepped around the corner, on her way back to her office.

Razor bellowed, "You're a damn fine lookin' woman, Doctor. How the hell are ya?"

"Bayou, what's goin' on?"

Bayou quickly explained the situation and J.D. swung into action. She got Kohlbeck on the com, quickly ordered up food and meds with a change of clothes to fit Razor.

J.D. turned to Razor. "I'm just fine Mr. Savage, and I hope you are," she said in her most matter of fact, professional voice. "Why don't we step in here for a minute and let's have a look at you."

"Ah, hell, Doc. These ain't nothin'." Razor...the cavalier jester, flirting in the process of passing out.

J.D. grabbed Razor by the elbow, rather forcefully, and steered him into an empty observation room. Judy and Bayou followed them in. Mist elected to wait in the hall.

Bayou walked Razor into the shower and turned the cold water on him. The effect was by design and instant. Razor howled against the icy water and pretty much came to, both at the same time. He stripped off the tattered rags, lathered up and poured plenty of shampoo onto his greasy mop. He turned on the hot water and took the safety razor from the hand Bayou stretched through the curtain. Razor shaved as the hot water pounded out some of the kinks in his battered body.

As soon as he stepped out of the shower, J.D. poked him in the ass with a needle full of the magic blue juice and helped the oldest warrior stretch out on the bed. Judy began swabbing the wounds with antiseptics and stitched the few which required more serious attention.

An orderly brought a tray of biscuits, gravy, eggs, bacon and a pot of steaming black coffee...and a gym bag full of clothes. "These oughta fit him."

Judy rolled the hospital table with the tray of food over the top of the bed and began feeding Razor. After the sixth bite, Quirk's magic concoction kicked in and Razor came fully about. He looked a bit dazed and confused as he took the fork from Judy's hand.

"Thank you, darlin', but I think I can handle this feeding from here."

The blue elixir had worked its magic and Razor's wounds were disappearing quickly. The glint in the pale grey eyes was clear and bright. Razor was back. Razor scarfed the breakfast down like a convict headed out for work detail.

The transformation took a little over an hour, from start to finish. Bayou and Mist were going to be late, but man...did they have a surprise for Quirk. Razor shoved the last bit of biscuit into his face, chased it down with coffee and looked around for something to wear.

J.D. performed a final exam on her wayward patient, declared him fit for duty, even if he did need some sleep, and tossed him the gym bag full of clothes they'd rounded up. Razor caught the bag in mid-air. Nothin' fancy, which suited Razor just fine. Boxer briefs, thick white cotton socks, jeans, a heavy black cotton tee-shirt, Carhart work boots and a leather Carolina Panthers warm up jacket, old and worn, well preserved from a by-gone era, just like Razor. He jumped into the clothes and bounced out the door. The garb looked Saville Row custom fitted. He was set. The blue juice coursed through him like a runaway freight train.

Mist threw her arms around the two favorite men in her life as they stepped into the hall and Razor gave the family hug a new definition.

"Where's the Esquire?" Razor was definitely ready.

"Both guitars and the Bloodstone are up in Oswalt's office," Bayou informed his father.

Three generations of ghost fighters walked to Oswalt's office to spring the surprise.

Chapter 11

Bayou pushed the buzzer to Oswalt's office, and the door swung open with the "swoosh" of an air lock. Oswalt, Quirk and Cornelius were looking down at the chart table, examining the perimeter and lay-out of the Ghost Defense Institute.

Quirk was the first to look up and see his three friends. "Razor! You old bastard! Damn it's good to see you." He went to his oldest friend and wrapped him in a bear hug. Razor reciprocated.

"You didn't think I'd let you have all the fun, did you, Quirk?"

Oswalt walked over and shook Razor's hand. "Thanks for coming back, Razor. We're going to need all the help we can get."

Cornelius backed into a darker corner of the room, unimpressed with the new arrivals or the camaraderie. He'd made his disdain for the guitar ghost fighters known to Oswalt. Oswalt wasn't about to stir any dissension within the ranks. He wasn't yet completely at ease with Cornelius, but he was pretty sure the ghost fighters would want him to join the ranks. His jury was still out on the value Cornelius would bring to the game.

"Excuse me for asking, but why are y'all looking at these maps and plans? The damned demons don't come through any fences or doors. They come through anywhere they feel like." Razor was the first to articulate the obvious.

Quirk responded, "Of course, you're right, Razor. We're trying to figure a location where they might make their first move. We've spent some time evaluating the last battles and the Magi's moves."

"Well, we've killed two of the sons of bitches and a bunch of his buddies. How many more do you think there might be?"

Cornelius stepped from the shadows. "Actually, I believe the last and most deadly Magi will be the next foe we face. He will be the shape shifter, second only to the first fallen angel. I've met one of his friends. And, to give you all a little piece of mind, I had success in delaying the impending attack. I know Leslie gave you three days' notice. I was able to extend our timetable by four days. We have six left to prepare."

There was a collective, if skeptical, sigh of relief from the scientists. The ghost fighters were a bit more reserved. This crimson eyed, sudden comrade required more certification before he became "one of them."

"Sorry, son. I don't believe we've met." Razor trying to be cordial sounded like fingernails scraping a blackboard. He stuck out his hand and stared into the fiery orbs of the tall man without even thinking of backing down. The big man's icy hand caught Razor by surprise.

The Esquire began a slow ascent with a minimal glow; the Telecaster didn't seem to care all that much for Cornelius or his attitude, either. The tendons in Bayou's neck and back stretched taut and Mist stood a bit taller with a firm grip on the Bloodstone.

Quirk watched the scene unfold with educated curiosity. He wondered on which side of the fence the Savage family would find Cornelius. The tension in the room answered most of his questions.

"OK, boys and girls. Let's settle down. We're all in the same sandbox and we need to play nice." Oswalt had a way with words.

Tension and body language eased, and some semblance of a truce coalesced in the Director's office.

"Cornelius, I think it's time we heard your story, if you'd care to share with us. You ***are*** the new and unknown kid on the block." Quirk took command of the uneasy situation. "We're all hoping you might shed some light on Leslie's disappearance."

Quirk's last sentence caught Razor, Bayou and Mist completely off guard.

Cornelius looked around. "It's a long story..."

Chapter 12

And so begins the story of Cornelius and how he came to be. In 2186, details of the Religious Wars of 2012 and the subsequent radical reduction of the earth's population were faded memories. In the following hundred and seventy-four years, the world had passed through tumultuous sequences of evolving social order.

After savagery, barbarism and finally a renaissance, a semblance of civilization was restored. During the period of restoration, the various controlling entities saved enough science, agriculture, technology, adaptation and innovation to rekindle the human spirit.

Survival of the fittest was the easily recognized absolute. The planet had been cleansed and life began anew, albeit with a head start.

First and second generations of ravaged survivors passed their interpretation of history to the third generation mostly by word of mouth. Factual history commingled with myth and legend created a reality the third generation could not begin to substantiate.

At the end of "The Last Great War", The Americas remained the strongest economy in the world. The number of fortunate few roaming the vast expanse of countryside plummeted from over three hundred million souls to less than two and a half million in less than a year.

The rest of the planet suffered a culling which reduced populations from eight billion people to less than a meager two billion. The housing shortage disappeared along with the population. The neutron bombs devastated the people of earth and left the architecture intact. "Empty nest" became a vulgar term.

By 2186, those who even bothered to discuss the world-altering clash were labeled "elders". They became the scholars in the fledgling beginnings of institutes for higher learning. These men and women retrieved digital history from resurrected hard drives, rummaged through libraries of former universities, rediscovering literature, studies, research projects and historical information. The philosophers and artisans even renewed some appreciation for the arts.

Chapter 13

2147 was the here and now for Jacob, the seventh son of a seventh son. Jacob was named after a biblical character favored by his mother. He and his wife, Leah, lived in the lands formerly and currently recognized as The Dakotas.

In the instant he met Leah, he knew she was ***the one***. Leah blessed him and calmed his lust for the wilder side of life. Jacob gladly settled down. Leah was a strong woman. She was a good, solid, down to earth, and practical companion who loved to laugh. She didn't care what chair Jacob occupied at his family's table. They made their home together and as long as he put out the trash, worked hard, and gave her the respect she rightly deserved, the household ran like a well-oiled machine...sturdy and quiet.

If you didn't respect her views, she would wrestle with you until you did...or on the off chance, change her mind.

He loved her with all his heart and knew she was his one and only. She was the consummate 'soul mate'. Hell, she put up with all his shit, and kept the boys in line. He freely admitted that he needed her and loved her unconditionally.

Jacob stood on the front porch of their home on the prairie, gazing past the far away horizon, reviewing his life and the most recent incredible months of unusual events.

Leah – the love of his life – had given birth to six boys. The sixth son proved to be an excruciating delivery. Leah's doctors informed them the boy would be her last child. Complications during the caesarean delivery prevented any more children. The risk to her life was too great. Because Jacob had been a seventh son, he and Leah often fantasized about their own seventh son. They both wanted a seventh son, if only to prove the prophecies wrong.

As it turned out, they discovered raising six boys was enough excitement. Jacob and Leah soon forgot about their not-so-private inside joke about the seventh son of the seventh son.

In the three years since Levi's birth, they adjusted, and life was good. The fantasy of a seventh son fell deeper into the filing cabinet of forgotten hopes and dreams.

Then all hell, or heaven, depending on your point of view, broke loose.

In early May, in the middle of the kitchen, on an otherwise un-noteworthy day, Leah cramped and doubled up in debilitating pain. Jacob rushed her to the hospital, certain she'd ruptured an organ. Her stomach swelled rapidly on the way to the E.R. Spasms and contractions racked her tiny frame.

The "emergency" took four hours to resolve, and Jacob was told Leah had nearly been lost to him.

The doctors claimed it was a miracle.

Jacob thought that if the practitioners didn't want their collective asses sued into the dirt, they were certainly obliged to declare this pregnancy a "miracle".

The news leaked to the press within hours.... doctor-patient confidentiality lost somewhere in distant archives.

It didn't take long for the media to pick up the story. Jacob and Leah were inundated with requests for interviews.

Every variety of pastor, priest, evangelist, self-anointed preacher, and quack cult leader throughout the federation cried out for him to clarify, qualify, or simply explain Leah and her condition.

The cult leaders were the worst. God spoke exclusively to them and directed their every move. Each had specific instructions on how to construe and resolve the situation. This was ***their*** story, to be sure.

Most of these nuts, from laymen to professed clerics, weren't even versed in the Bible. *Everything* in the world suddenly had *everything* to do with Revelations. Far too many people had read *those* passages in the Good Book. Too many people believed Jacob and Leah were about to unleash the Antichrist into the barely resurrected world!

There didn't seem to be a person alive who believed what happened to him and Leah. Or worse, they *did* believe the outrageous possibility, and super-imposed their own subjective interpretations to the event. Leah carried the harbinger of the Apocalypse, or the Messiah...take your pick.

Jacob continued the stroll through the archives of his memory, seeking perspective for the dilemma at hand. As the sunset bloodied the Midwestern horizon, his mind careened through the possibilities. Of course, Jacob believed Leah. She had no explanation other than Jacob must be the father. Really. Where do you find time to fool around with six boys running around the house?

He kept processing the "blessed event". The bottom line was that his practical, funny, and unquestionably faithful wife went to bed barren and woke up the next morning three months pregnant.

Jacob gripped the Mason jar and slugged down the fiery liquid, freeing him, for a moment. He felt like a batter at the plate, blindfolded, unable to see the sphere hurling towards him, yet knowing the ball is on its way at frightening speed.

The pungent juice burned his gullet...fires of hell, he imagined. He waited, anticipating the kick from the high-octane alcohol to lash out. It did, and he appreciated the nearly instant buzz. He wanted the drink. No...he *needed* the drink.

The effects from the white liquor continued to grow as thoughts tumbled through his head. Maybe the book of Revelations was right, after all. Scraps of arguments twisting in the hurricane of his mind spawned a brutal headache. Jacob self-medicated and took another pull from the jar.

Here it was, twenty-one hundred years since John educated the chosen, and Jacob's senses were being stretched to limits he never imagined he could withstand.

He was all too familiar with the legend of the seventh son of the seventh son and its powerful impact on the superstitious. The story was his birthright. He seriously underestimated how many people believed the fable and how many idiotic interpretations surrounded the story.

Preachers and priests served up endless sermons about the seventh son being the Antichrist and the thousand-year reign of evil that would follow him. Jacob lumped them all into one big pile of voodoo dung, along with the snake handlers, refusing to give in to their rants.

The twisted religious zealots were not the only problem. Script writers from a reviving film industry decided their input was needed. Ancient pre-war movies were resurrected and studied to provide fodder to the burgeoning cannons.

He definitely needed some "perspective" at the moment. Hell, he'd need a full-time shrink, if this shit kept up. The constant microscopic inspection from the media was beginning to fray his nerves. He gripped the Mason jar as a child might hang tightly to a nana blanket.

He contemplated his previously happy and well-adjusted life.

Those had been the good times. The "blessed" event had taken place and completely wrecked his life. He hated it. He hated the media and hated the attention-starved morons, especially those long-lost relatives climbing up, down and around the limbs of the family tree. He knew they'd been bought, cashing in on their genealogical or marital relationship to the harried couple.

These were the same parasites that never showed up at the family weddings, reunions or funerals.

He thought, "This must be what lottery winners went through after they hit the 'big one'." Jacob took another long pull from the Mason jar. He was beginning to enjoy the temporary respite from the storm.

And the storm ***had*** been damn weird. Jacob had more or less, come to grips with the reality of the situation and no matter which way he turned the Rubic's cube over, it simply didn't add up. Cold chills ran down his spine as he processed. The swelling buzz from the white liquor only buffered the brunt of the impact.

His practical, factual and let's not forget, non-menstruating wife swore to him she went to bed with no chance of another child and woke up three months pregnant. The ultrasound tests had clearly indicated the embryo was a boy.

A boy. Previously, an expected and anticipated eventuality for Jacob and Leah. The family's genetics slanted seriously towards the recombination of gender bias.

The thought that this child was to be his seventh son careened through the caverns of his mind. Maybe the damned prophecies were true. They couldn't be, could they? The odds that he and Leah were bringing the Antichrist into the world were longer than for winning the lottery.

Leah's mystery pregnancy had to be a coincidence.

Jacob had an itch working in the back of his head he couldn't quite scratch. The itch was working its way up to a gnawing aggravation. The 'boys' night out' designed to give Leah much needed and well-deserved quiet time lingered and wandered through his head. They were only gone the time it took for a quick trip to the library and to stuff some ice cream into the six sons...not quite an hour, or was it more? She was napping on the couch when they got back. That night was ***exactly*** the night before Jacob was forced into the white-knuckle drive to the emergency room. He pulled another mouthful from the mason jar and eased into the wooden rocker placed on the front deck for peaceful gazing as the sun slid into the prairie sand.

Chapter 14

Six months later, the "blessed" boy was born with the right number of fingers and toes, weighing in at a healthy six pounds, six ounces, in the evening of June 6, 2186, at six o'clock, straight up.

Leah groaned, moaned and ultimately shrieked through the mercifully final push, bringing the child into the chaos that was this new world. Attending physicians and nurses suddenly felt an unnatural chill in the air. The room's ambient temperature dropped ten degrees and didn't creep back up to comfortable until the child was removed to the nursery.

The day became more bizarre as the hands of the clock made their slow journey around the face of the ancient timekeeper. The nurses on each shift felt the peculiar chill when they approached the new baby, even though the thermostats never registered a drop in the nursery's climaticaliy controlled environment.

The small man-child's eyes were perfectly rounded, full of knowledge...and red as molten lava. His powerful angry glare spoke volumes. He definitely didn't want to be in this place, in this time.

The freaky circumstances surrounding the birth of the cold and angry little man fueled the press hounds into a frenzy.

Already maniacal over the bizarre and supernatural occurrence, the poor little tyke became the "story of the fleeting moment". Andy Warhol's 'famous 15 minutes' prediction held true, centuries later. The eyes cinched the deal.

The frightening red irises sent the reporters and the nut jobs off the reservation. He wasn't an albino and the doctors could not explain the eyes....fuel to the fire.

Jacob and Leah named him Cornelius, after her grandfather.

Chapter 15

Jacob hoped Cornelius would make it to adulthood. The frail little man with the angry eyes struggled through the first thirteen years of life on the prairie. The seventh son was constantly hammered by bullies and whacko fringe groups at school.

The whackos split into two categories. In one camp, Cornelius was the savior, returned to redeem. These kids were "kinda friends", but only because they were awed by the possibility.

On the other side of the playground, he was the Antichrist, destined to bring a thousand-year reign of fire and terror. The Antichrist schizos outnumbered the savior group.

The bullies were simply hateful little bastards, preying on the weak. Some things never change.

School officials and teachers did little to discourage the bullies. Cornelius was a disruption to the natural order, and they mostly wished he'd disappear into the world of the homeschooled.

Cornelius was raised to believe in Christ. He knew he wasn't the Antichrist. He believed Christ had existed in the flesh. He believed in Christ and prayed constantly for growth and strength, if for no other reason than to kick the bullies' asses. He tried to fight. The results were monotonous. His tiny young ass took a whippin' on a regular basis. Cornelius stayed pretty well bruised up through the eighth grade.

The older brothers didn't help much. They wanted Cornelius to toughen up and "grow a pair," as they often teased. Their mocking laughter wounded little brother. The brothers weren't mean spirited. They believed in the law of the jungle and wanted the seventh to survive. Their methods were dubious, couched in good intentions.

Six brothers looked at him the way the rest of the world did... he was a freak of nature with weird red eyes and a bizarre chill that followed him everywhere.

Early in his freshman year, Cornelius began to fill bigger shoes, longer pants and wider shirts. The six brothers became increasingly aware of subtle changes in the seventh.

Cornelius had secrets and began showing off a bit. He demonstrated powers not exactly obvious to the bullies, whackos or even the teachers. These powers were growing stronger every day. Cornelius was afraid...sort of...not nearly as much as the repentant brothers. They developed a newfound respect for the seventh, and a sudden interest in his well-being.

The second day of school in his freshman year the walk home turned ugly. Not for Cornelius. On ***this*** day. Johnny Cosseto, the biggest, most aggressive bully in young Cornelius' history, decided it was time to set the tone for the coming year. He knocked about the hundredth pair of sunglasses off the face of suddenly sprouting Cornelius and threw a punch at what the punk always called the "demon eyes".

Cornelius had been through enough of the Antichrist moniker, the broken sunglasses, keeping cool with what Leah called "non-threatening tonalities", and most of all the bruises and ass kickin's. It was over.

He leaned to the right and jerked Cosseto into him, grabbed his right arm as he twisted around and tossed the punk over his right shoulder, slamming him on his back into the dirt. Keeping the bully's wrist in his left hand as Johnny floated over Cornelius' shoulder, four members of the Antichrist movement listened to Cosseto's elbow snap, and the shoulder separate with sickening "pops".

Cosseto's running buddies stared in disbelief. Bobby Astarita started towards Cornelius when he realized the kid's red eyes were much darker than normal...bloodier, he thought. The air surrounding their formerly easy prey was colder than normal... a lot fuckin' colder. Everything about this situation was not nearly as normal as the last eight grades had been. Apparently, Cornelius wasn't all that easy anymore. Astarita may not have been the sharpest knife in the drawer, but he wasn't completely stupid. He turned on his heels and ran like hell in the other direction, leaving Cosseto whimpering on the hard packed sand with a broken elbow and a dislocated shoulder. Cornelius turned to face the remaining three and all he saw was their backsides headed in opposite directions.

In that instant and forever after, life as Cornelius knew it changed.

There was nobody around to notice the dark cloud pass across the sun, smothering daylight, casting an ominous shadow over Cornelius and exaggerating the depth of his ruby red eyes.

Cornelius reared back his head and howled...the lone wolf awakened...and *she* was watching.

Jacob and Leah didn't ignore the six brothers' whispers. They simply filed them under newfound hormones and sibling rivalry. They explained puberty to Cornelius and closed that chapter in the book of growing up.

Cornelius looked up the unfamiliar word. He was pretty damned sure this wasn't any sort of puberty he could find in a dictionary. Puberty didn't roll visions or prophecies of death and mayhem through your head. Puberty didn't give a teenager these God-awful headaches.

Then came the voices.

Chapter 16

Cornelius would barely hear the peculiar whisper when he was alone. No one else ever heard the voice but him. He wasn't superstitious but he knew something was very different about this voice. Cornelius didn't believe the voice had its origins in this dimension.

There were other realities he could tap into, and the voice was definitely not of this world.

Cornelius quickly came to grips with the radical variance in his genetic makeup...he was even okay with it. He got better at figuring the wide spectrum of weirdness and their derivatives. His loneliness was replaced with many mysteries.

He used what he called 'logical judo'. He would write out a problem as a short story, collect and examine the facts, then search the solution in this dimension. If answers didn't come in this dimension, he discovered and opened doors to other dimensions. There he put out "feelers" to uncover answers he hadn't thought of.

His limited education and experience often allowed this rather inept sleuthing to follow him into his already troubled sleep. "Nightmare" doesn't begin to describe the horrors in slumber claimed by the scarlet- eyed teen.

The investigation process was fueled by vague intuitions, but he knew one day he would be powerful enough to tap far deeper into the dimensions he used as his private university.

He could already see into some of the other dimensions. They appeared as lime green doors floating to and around him. He controlled the temporal displacement and was comfortable playing dimensional run and gun.

Cornelius knew he was not like his mother and father or his brothers and damn sure nothing like the little shits he went to school with. He often wondered how many there might be like him and where they lived. He probed other dimensions in search of others like him...with no success. Only *her* voice kept him from total isolation. There had to be others, if not exactly like him, at least with some talents in common. The voice validated his theory.

Cornelius had a developing telepathy which permitted an elementary sort of mind reading. He had a "feeling" around the kids at school and some of the adults. He could be inside their heads, unobserved, and know their next steps. He discovered he could produce pheromones and dopamine to influence people's reactions to a minor degree. This gave him a big boost in confidence.

His parents rightfully instructed their youngest son to keep these secret tricks from doctors or any authority figure whose path he might cross.

Cornelius had yet to gain control over what he called the "violent testosterone" reaction. Johnny Cosseto had been the first victim of that unleashed fury.

So far, his system worked pretty well. He was a straight "A" honors student with a four-point eight GPA. He aced all his classes. He could find the answer to any question in another dimension. He couldn't see through the doors, but he could get the answer. He didn't know how, but he could.

He developed an athletic prowess, and all the coaches were happy to have him in any sport which he chose to participate. He was growing bigger and worked hard on the farm. Jacob kept him busier than his other brothers, probably to keep him out of trouble. High School became a playground for the "chilly one", as he was nicknamed by teammates.

He took advantage of the turnaround his life had taken, and *she* kept track.

He still couldn't find the source of the voice. There were too many combinations to determine where the voice originated. The voice was a psychic vampire, intruding on his thoughts, always unwelcome.

The vampire voice was egocentric, vile, angry, even despicable and most of all...isolated. Every soul- sucking encounter violated the cardinal-eyed wonder called Cornelius.

The voice knew Cornelius was on the hunt. Cornelius could *feel* the voice and he knew the voice knew Cornelius was seeking its source, tracking dimensions, determined to identify and confront the demon. Or perhaps, the voice was only playing him. Some twisted version of Marco Polo, and Cornelius wore the blindfold.

He finally tried to make contact. To ensure as much isolation as possible, Cornelius walked deep into the cornfield, and stampeded the dimensions, exploring all open avenues, reaching for the source. He flamed out from exposure to the overwhelming flood of images that careened through his young mind.

Cornelius didn't know it at the time but everyone within a seven-mile radius immediately contracted a migraine headache of biblical proportions. He never found out. At that point, he didn't know the full scope of his developing powers. His brother, Levi, found him passed out in the middle of the field covered with corn husks and nearly half dead...and *she* watched with glee.

Many times, Cornelius didn't understand all the images flooding his mind. These intruding thoughts generated pictures of pyramids from some ancient lands. There were lots of thoughts like those. Sometimes he could see what appeared to be human forms pointing at stones suspended in midair, floating into place from their direction onto the pyramids.

These creatures were unusually tall, and clothed in long black flowing robes, much like the nomads in the ancient Middle East. There was always a feeling of evil with the stones and pyramids. Some of the thoughts were so intense he had no choice but to let them go. He cut those visions off as fast as he could. Cornelius recognized a connection between the harsh images and the peculiar whisper.

He knew the headaches were from dimensional overload. He perfectly understood and accepted this after a while.

Somewhere around his fifteenth birthday, connected and complementary voices joined the mind game playing in Cornelius' head.

Certain thoughts weren't evil at all. He had visions of a red-headed woman, with a white streak in her hair, trying to reach him. Then a blond-haired girl appeared holding a glowing crimson stone in her hand. Why were they calling him? They scared him. Not as much as the stones, pyramids and the whisperer, but nonetheless...why did they keep surfacing? He was sure he had never met either of the two women.

He never gave up though. He kept trolling for the source of the mysterious voice.

There was yet another feminine voice in his head...darker, but soothing. *She* explained his birth wasn't as mysterious as they claimed. The voice whispered many things to him, sometimes comforting, soothing thoughts. Other times suggesting Cornelius perform wicked deeds on unsuspecting victims. He refused the dark suggestions.

The quiet voice whispered a sneering chuckle every time Cornelius tried to fight back or turn the voice off.

Where did the voice come from?

Cornelius stared at the nineteen-year-old in the mirror. He stood six foot four and packed two hundred and twenty-five pounds of kick ass into a sculpted frame. He stood ram rod straight and the only thing narrow about him was a thirty-three-inch waist.

He settled into the wrestling program because he was allowed to put his brawn to use and dish out more pain than in any other sport. Football was no longer violent enough to suit his temperament. The rules of engagement had been "pussified" in the early twenty-first century and serious contact had essentially been eliminated for fear of irrevocable injury. Cornelius watched some of the old vids of famous "Super Bowl" contests. He decided those pansies had just as well taken up knitting.

He punished wrestling opponents with a vengeance nurtured by years of abuse. Cornelius was attracted to the sport in high school and made the varsity squad his first year at the university. With his telepathic abilities, he became a harsh antagonist.

He didn't drink or smoke. He toyed with and annihilated adversaries two weight classes heavier. His personality was eccentric, but brilliant. Cornelius discovered an unexpected revenue stream in underground cage fighting. University wrestling made the rare bruises and cuts easier to explain.

Quite by accident, the "chilly one" was invited to one of these fights, more of a dare than an invitation. Once inside the underground cavern on the outskirts of town, Cornelius was hooked. This was gladiator heaven.

The hole in the ground had been carved out with what must've been huge machines. The ceiling was at least a hundred feet high. Were it not for the huge LED stadium lights, the bookends of the bleachers would have been cloaked in darkness. There had to be a thousand spectators in the cavern, ringing the cage in three-hundred-and-sixty-degree symmetry. He read the thoughts of all fighters in the arena...simultaneously flooding his consciousness...and the gamblers! Good God, the gamblers! Cornelius was awed by the amounts of money wagered in silver and gold coins. No paper trails here, he thought.

And *she* spoke to him. "This is where you belong right now, Cornelius. This is your moment in the darkness. Show yourself!" And he did. In a matter of months, "The Chilly One" became the headliner for every event held in what the gamblers called "The

Hole". An undefeated monster that covered his head in a mask. No eyelets...no slit for his mouth. An opaque sack of cloth never to be removed.

His parents were proud. The seventh son of the seventh son was just a bullshit myth. Or at least their son, even with the red eyes and some weird habits, was mostly normal. Life on the farm became increasingly comfortable. Twice a month gold and silver coins appeared on the front porch with no explanation. The older brothers rode the wrestler's coat tails of the seventh for as long as they could. By the time Levi graduated from the university, Cornelius had won all the legitimate scholastic championships in the country. He was the number one ranked wrestler in the entire federation...and the undefeated champion in "The Hole". And *she* watched him become a man.

The family kept his powers secret.

His syncopation was always ahead of the competitor. On the mats and in the cage, it appeared he could read his rival's mind. Jacob tried not to think too deeply about it. He was in nirvana that one of his sons was getting national recognition. When the Olympic Games were resurrected, Jacob was certain his seventh son would be first choice in the coaches' draft.

There was no offense or defense he couldn't master. He harnessed incredible physical power and was unstoppable.

Cornelius moved as if everyone was in slow-motion but him. His quick energy and numbing pins became legendary. His vicious attacks in "The Hole" brought new definition to "no holds barred" mixed martial arts. His lucky opponents left the arena on stretchers. The less fortunate, who had somehow angered the big man, left with an I.V. bag suspended above the gurney which wheeled them into a waiting makeshift ambulance.

Cornelius smiled. He loved the battle, the grappling, the holds, the opponent's struggle and the final merciless pin to the mat. The team had just won another great match. In the stands, he noticed a woman paying extraordinary attention to his glistening torso, barely covered by the skimpy singlet. She was dark, he could tell. The gymnasium was not so well lit as to warrant the big framed, black sunglasses. Her coal black hair was mostly covered with an even darker scarf.

She kept the black raincoat wrapped tightly around the fullness of her body, shapely calves a teasing appetizer pouting beneath the hem of her cover. Her fire engine red lips and creamy calves offered the only contrasts to the shadow she cast across the gym. Cornelius couldn't read her. That was as unusual as it was disconcerting to the seventh. He was, of course, intrigued. Lust for a new conquest was never a second guess for the crimson eyed warrior.

After his victory, the woman lingered long enough for Cornelius to approach.

"I'm quite sure we've never met before," he said in his most casual voice. "Surely, I would have remembered such grace and mystery."

"Well then," replied the shapely enigma, "how did you know my name is Shirley?"

Cornelius bellowed laughter and the shadow woman allowed her own chuckle. She extended a calf- skin gloved hand and drew him close enough to savor her fragrance. In a low and sultry voice, she whispered, "Daciana. Pleased to meet you, Cornelius.

I've waited a long time for this." The familiarity of her voice almost gave him away. Cornelius kept calm.

"Dinner, then?" Cornelius hadn't been shy since his last year in high school.

"Why, of course," came the simple and expected reply.

He finished showering, dressed for the occasion and headed through the double doors of the locker room to his motorcycle.

They agreed to "The Dark Night Out" cuisine. This peculiar and special restaurant served 6 course meals in total darkness. The wait staff wore night-vision goggles. Cornelius found the setting more conducive to his intended finale if a woman couldn't actually see him eat on a first date. His powers required significant quantities of calories. His appetite usually shocked people—especially first dates— and he was starving.

He couldn't have known Daciana's diet required no known nutrition...only one of the reasons she was so quick to agree to the dining adventure with which she was completely familiar. The staff knew Daciana. Each one looked forward to sharing her extravagant selections from the menu in between their duties to actual hungry customers...all in the dark...the staff ate well when Daciana came to dine.

She stood next to the Norton Black Shadow, a restored relic from pre-war America. Cornelius walked toward his dinner companion. She threw open the black trench coat and left nothing to the wandering imagination which had filled the young warrior's mind. She was stunning in the paleness of her nudity. Her breasts were full and superb, nipples hard, tight and small, just the way Cornelius liked 'em...he guessed a perfect 36 D. Her sculpted waist melted into flawless hips, thighs and down to the teasing calves. She tossed the coat and pulled a pair of black leather pants, short sleeve sweater and black riding jacket from a bag at her feet. The thick framed black sunglasses never moved from her face. The trench coat went into the bag, and she slid into knee high boots with six inch stiletto heels. The appetizing calves became dessert in the seventh's mind.

"I've always wanted to ride one." He couldn't see her eyes, but he was sure they were dancing with desire, mocking his thirst. Sultry, lusty, and beautiful. Cornelius made great efforts to keep his hands quiet and to subdue the raging desire in his jeans. He was ready to throw the magnificent creature to the ground and have her then. But...anticipation is often rewarded through patience. This was a lesson learned in many facets of the life Cornelius had come to live. He slipped his leather jacket on, straddled the Norton, and pulled his new companion onto the back. She wrapped her arms around his waist, pressed her firm and ample breasts against his muscled back and the Norton exploded into the night.

Chapter 17

After the sumptuous dinner at "The Dark Night Out", Daciana was in a playful mood. "Let's take a ride out west of town, Cornelius. I want to show you something."

"How far do you want to go?" he asked.

"Well, all the way, of course. I want all of you tonight." She removed the sunglasses for the first time. Cornelius had never been more surprised in his life. Daciana's eyes were on fire! The crimson lust burned deep into his heart. Cornelius had only guessed at what was in store for him this night. She flew into his arms, reaching her arms up around his neck, pulling his face to her lips and opening her sensuous mouth to accept his lusty reaction. Cornelius had never experienced such passion...or felt such heat...ever.

"We have to get out of here before we burn this place down," he laughed. She pulled away, reluctantly, he could tell.

"OK. Let's ride. I want you horizontal in a hurry."

They headed west on the Norton. Daciana's hands slid from his waist to his groin and began a gentle massage. Cornelius had a hard time keeping the big bike on the winding two lane road. When they were far enough out into the country and he couldn't stand it anymore, Cornelius pulled the bike under the cover of a cluster of massive oak trees. They were on the edge of a small town and the night was pitch black with nothing but stars to light the sky. Cornelius rolled out the extra-large sleeping bag he kept in the saddle bags of the bike. They tore at each other's clothes, rolling around in the grass like the animals they were.

Just enough light from the full Dakota moon drifted through the leafy canopy as Cornelius anticipated her sensual lips. A quick and bright gleam from her teeth was as sudden as his reaction.

With astounding speed, in a much-practiced move, he swung his right fist into the left side of her head. Before her head could move, the left fist closed the other half of the vise, and her head exploded from the impact. The crimson orbs which had filled her eye sockets popped like kettle corn. The last sound Daciana made shook the trees under which she lay.

"Well, shit!" Cornelius was disappointed. "I didn't think you were a fuckin' vampire!" Daciana didn't speak. Her fangs dangled from the lifeless mouth Cornelius had been certain was destined to please him. The crushed skull barely hanging on to the creamy white sculpted body created an incongruous image, even in the twisted mind of "the chilly one." To be sure that this little fling was definitely over, he jerked the smashed skull from the last dangling vertebrae and heaved it into the darkness. "That's the last head you'll ever give." His roar filled the quiet night. Any living creature within earshot kept the silence as if their lives depended on it.

Chapter 18

The old dude's lips didn't move.

Cornelius caught a glimpse of the vagrant looking mess from the corner of his eye. The threat that only he could sense put his body on full alert. The old man was unarmed, Cornelius detected no weapons. *Something* very wrong was headed his way with evil forethought and malice. He prepared himself for the old man. He spun around, crimson eyes glowering.

Nothing. Not a soul in sight. He walked past his motorcycle to the clearing past the stand of Oaks.

The 'chilly one' knew the stranger was following him. If he had to use his powers, this place was as isolated as he could hope for. The old man stepped from the shadows into the light of the moon.

"Good evenin', Cornelius, good match tonight." His tone was amicable enough, even melodic. Cornelius wasn't fooled.

He knew for damn sure this had nothing to do with wrestling and wondered how much of the recent mismatch he'd witnessed.

The old man smiled, acting like this was an everyday encounter with an old friend. His voice was close to hypnotic. "Your work is a pleasure to watch, inside ***and*** outside. I was certain my old friend Daciana would seduce you. Your reflexes are stupendous."

The old man answered the question Cornelius was most interested in. He took three strides and was close enough to eliminate any damning testimony. The old man didn't flinch.

"Cornelius, spare an old man some time, if you please. I've watched and waited for this moment. This ***proper*** moment to solve a riddle which has befuddled me since the day you were born. A clarification, if you will, for an old man who has anticipated your opinion over the years about a certain passage I've often pondered."

"Go ahead." Cornelius spoke, scanning the area with his personal radar, guaranteeing privacy.

"What do you think of these verses in the Bible?"

Cornelius sensed the verse, page and numbers the old man would quote, and he grinned at the prospect. Good choice he thought, in light of the most current events. Cornelius was happy the old man had approached, and he relaxed a bit.

"The New Testament, Second Thessalonians chapter 2.1 through 12." These were some of his favorites. Mysterious and compelling.

Cornelius had memorized the passage and they recited in unison. The two men glared into each other's eyes as the verses filled the silence of the woods. The night became increasingly bizarre.

He sensed the old man shared the same passion as they nearly sang the verses. The stranger had a pleasant voice and a natural gift for the telling of stories. Their voices were nearly harmonious.

"Let no one deceive you in any way; for that day will not come unless the rebellion comes first and the lawless one is revealed, the one destined for destruction.

He opposes and exalts himself above every so-called god or object of worship, so that he takes his seat in the temple of God, declaring himself to be God.

Do you not remember that I told you these things when I was still with you?

And you know what is now restraining him, so that he may be revealed when his time comes.

For the mystery of lawlessness is already at work, but only until the one who now restrains it is removed.

And then the lawless one will be revealed, whom the Lord Jesus will destroy with the breath of his mouth, annihilating him by the manifestation of his coming.

The coming of the lawless one is apparent in the working of Satan, who uses all power, signs, lying wonders, and every kind of wicked deception for those who are perishing, because they refused to love the truth and so be saved.

For this reason, God sends them a powerful delusion, leading them to believe what is false, so that all who have not believed the truth but took pleasure in unrighteousness will be condemned."

When they finished the old man dropped his eyes to the ground, for a thoughtful moment.

"So", he asked, "are you the person the scriptures describe?"

Cornelius raked his power over the old man and went still. There was much more to this old bum than could be seen or even sensed.

The emotional radar Cornelius had so long relied on was blank. He felt a strong surge of power...like a lightning bolt, ready to explode. Concentrated energy crackled around the old man. His aura was visible.

Cornelius felt the hair stand up on the back of his neck.

The old man kept smiling, "What's wrong son, cat got your tongue?"

Cornelius heard the old man laugh, watched as he stepped closer... watched as the stranger grabbed his black leather jacket. Watched as if he were a bystander to the scene. He felt himself moving towards the bike, but he didn't feel his feet on the ground.

Cornelius was powerless as the old man guided him over to the Norton Shadow.

The next thing he knew, they were cruising down the highway at warp speed. Cornelius knew the voice. The voice he'd been trying to find for years. Now the voice had found him. He listened, turning right, and then left when the voice directed him.

Cornelius heard the old man's thoughts through the wind rushing past them. "I am ***not*** your enemy. You really don't want me to ***become*** your enemy!"

Cornelius fought to regain control of his powers. The motorcycle was stopped. The old man stood directly in front of the town and snickered as he began to morph into a larger being.

The old man grew to immense and weird proportions.

To Cornelius the beggar had taken the image of a huge genie escaping the bottle, coming to life, after thousands of years in captivity.

In a voice that shook the surrounding dirt, the genie bellowed, "I am the Magi! Let's see how powerful you have become! Did you like me controlling you? See if you can stop me now! Unleash your power! Or are you still that candy assed, little red-eyed sissy? Yeah, I know your past. I've known you from the time you were conceived and everything you've done or said since!

You think kickin' little Cosseto's ass was a big deal? Punishing those pussies in high school and college and mangling those dumb asses in the cage fights was bullshit! You think tearing the head off one of my favorite generals gets me excited? You ain't seen nothin'....you're a punk. C'mon and show me somethin', punk...let me see what you've been holding back!" The Magi taunted Cornelius.

Cornelius could feel the evil emanating from the Magi; a vile brackish odor tainted the back of his throat with every breath he took. The stench was overwhelming, and he struggled to retain his composure....and his power. He recognized the stink. Some folks called it brimstone.

He heard the clamoring of demons, howling and gibbering. Languages and dialects from three-four-and five dimensional warps pierced his eardrums and bounced around the inside of his head like bowling balls in a box car. His body was being torn apart.

The Magi yelled at him in some unintelligible language as orange pyramids circled his body, mystically appearing from his hands.

Cornelius knew the best defense could find a weak spot. It was always there. He couldn't afford the time to practice his standard M.O. of patience and waiting for the right shot were off the menu. His mind was melting from the brutal psychic assault.

He had to make a move and make it now, he knew that for damn sure. His subconscious was screaming to attack!

Cornelius focused his power. He felt a slight release, as if the Magi had let go of the leash. The Magi continued to taunt him.

Taunts didn't bother Cornelius...hell, taunts were a way of life for most of his short time on this earth. On the other hand, being controlled against his will scared the shit out of him. He kept pulling in his power, building the strength he thought he'd need. Green energy bolts had recently and somehow become part of his psychic arsenal. The seventh had long ago stopped questioning how or why these powers came to him. He'd learned to throw the bolts with great precision.

He focused on center mass and let loose a volley of the newfound weapon. The Magi guffawed as they fell to his feet like poorly thrown darts...and he kept taunting.

"If you ***are*** the antichrist, the legend writers must've been dead drunk when they imagined your great power. You're a gnat! Is that all you got? What a puny excuse you are for the privileged owner of so much power. Maybe I should take control again and make you my piss-ant errand boy. You will clean and cook for me, until I put an end to your pathetic life."

The bite and sting of the all too familiar bully finally burned Cornelius to the core. He was starting to shake, fear feeding the thought of being the errand boy. He knew the Magi could make it happen. For the first time in a long time, Cornelius felt fear penetrating holes in the defensive dyke he'd spent nineteen years building.

He took a deep breath and focused on the style he'd spent the last few years training. He knew what he was about to do would bring on the mother of all headaches and it would last for days, if he survived. "Fuck a headache, that's personal collateral damage. I need to be shed of this bastard right now."

He heard the Magi mocking, laughing, the scorn hanging in the air like a thick fog. He saw the energy bolts leaving his fingers turning bluish orange. "Those are new," he thought. He'd never seen those colors before. He dug down deep, pulling on any reserves he could find. He thought about Johnny Cosseto and the years of pain and humiliation. Cornelius summoned all his strength and unleashed the gathered power into one massive beam of energy.

Silence. He looked around. He was on his knees. Immobilized, unable to stand.

He rolled onto his back. It hurt to smile. But he did it anyway. He was amused by those new colors. He had beaten the old man, or genie or whatever a Magi was. He won. That was something he had become used to. He still took pride in every victory. The Magi was nowhere to be found.

He laid there for an hour until he saw headlights approaching. From a life of hiding, he forced his wasted body to get up and pulled himself and the motorcycle deeper into the trees.

He saw the first police cruiser drive slowly past his hideaway as it rolled down the main drag into the town.

He saw their lights flash onto the town sign. Cobbsville, North Dakota, Population 666. Cornelius remembered a history lesson about this town. After the wars, some idiot named Cobb claimed all the property in the town of Leith and converted a once quiet place on earth into a haven for white supremacists. Cornelius wondered if any descendants of Cobb had survived the wars and what their take on white supremacy might be tonight.

Then he heard the laugh from a place other than the here and now and he knew he hadn't killed the bastard. He recognized the tone.

He heard voices coming from the cruiser stopped halfway into town. He scanned the crackling message and heard the cop screaming into the mic, "Dead people all over town, some kind of massacre. Bring weapons, dogs, shit, call the militia. I need backup immediately and bring plenty of body bags. Better call the Feds! This might be some bio-weapon!"

That couldn't be, what in the hell could have killed a whole town and not affected him? Cornelius left the bike in a thicket and walked the perimeter of the town, staying out of sight. He pressed against the back wall of a building then opened a door leading into what looked like a church rectory.

The old door opened on squeaky hinges. The approaching sirens and emergency vehicles drowned out any minimal noises he made.

What was going on here? He was exhausted, his thought processes were constipated.

Four bodies were splayed in front of him. Blood oozed from their eyes and ears. Pain and torture etched their faces and Cornelius was certain the end had not been quiet for these citizens. He went further into the church and discovered a priest lying on his side, dead, beside the altar. His features mirrored those of the four found in the rectory. He and the priest were the about the same size. Odd...he thought. And the laugh from far away startled the big man.

The priest's sharp white collar was stained dark red...blood red, to be exact.

He didn't know the full "how", but he knew the "who". The damned vagrant...Magi...asshole genie...whoever he was, had tricked him into using his powers on these innocents. The Magi orchestrated and choreographed the entire movie and now this town gave a whole new definition to "Ghost Town." Cornelius had been played like a cheap fiddle and killed all these people. He'd forgotten a primary rule of the hunt...always know what's behind your target.

Without thinking, he bent and stripped the priest down to his underwear. Methodically, he removed his own clothes, he dropped his wallet and anything else that claimed his identity. The seventh put the priest in his wardrobe of the previous evening and dressed himself in the blood drenched uniform worn by the man of God. He reached down and grabbed the only memory he would carry from what had just become his past life. He put the old worn sunglasses over his crimson, glowing eyes and walked.

As he passed the four bodies in the rectory, he spotted a box of crisp white collars on the desk and stuffed them into the suit coat pockets.

Cornelius stumbled from the back of the church, working hard to maintain his balance. He was depleted and barely made it to the thicket and his motorcycle. He stretched face down along the length of the Norton for a good long while, his face on the cool metal of the gas tank, feet on the ground and arms draped over the handlebars. He listened to the chatter and groans from the men and women who had arrived and begun the gruesome task of cleaning Cobbsville. Each unanswered knock on a door meant more death waited on the other side.

He slept, or passed out...when he jumped awake, the moon was falling into the grey light of morning. Cornelius pushed the bike out of the thicket onto the pavement. He pressed the bike forward to about a mile down the road and kick started the big engine to life, certain he wouldn't be heard from this distance. He glanced at the fuel gauge and put Cobbsville and everything to do with The Dakotas in his rearview mirrors.

Cobbsville was a short seventy-five miles from Jacob and Leah's farmhouse. Electricity had been restored to the federation in the late twenty-first century, so news traveled fast. Bad news traveled faster. Some things never change.

When word reached the farm about the massacre in Cobbsville, Jacob's heart sank. Cornelius had not come home the night before. His clothes and wallet were found in the church.

Ten months later...Jacob's thoughts wandered less frequently to the disappearance of his son and the slaughter down the road. He, Leah, and the boys had been questioned twenty times apiece by every cop, private investigator, lawyer, medical examiner, and Federation authority within a thousand miles. None of them had any answers and their curiosity was only overshadowed by their anguish. Each one missed the seventh in their own way.

In his heart of hearts, Jacob knew something evil happened that night. He also knew the powers Cornelius had grown to accept. His intuition led him to convict Cornelius of killing those town people. He also knew someone, or something must have...***had*** to have provoked his son to that lethal level. Cornelius was raised to be a good son, good brother, and a good man. He learned and exercised judicious control over his formidable strengths. Jacob never once thought the devastation wreaked in Cobbsville could have been an accident. But as for the what or why, he had no clue. His son was nobody's fool and one of the most powerful forces to ever walk the planet. If someone or something took Cornelius down, then what hope was there for the rest of them?

Jacob sometimes still wondered if he would ever see or hear from his son again. He hoped his seventh son was still alive and still free. If he was, and someone or some force had attacked him, Jacob had at least one certainty to hang his hat on. Retribution would be vicious and bloody.

Chapter 19

Cornelius was accustomed to a certain type of moment, when he was first found out.

"Please allow me a quick history lesson." He spoke to his captive audience, tuning to their curiosity. At least they appeared to have the brainpower and patience to listen and comprehend what he was about to explain.

Jade, ever the historian, was all ears. She slid the recorder from her pocket, a reflex from years of interviews. There had been no reference to Cornelius from any of the ghost fighters. He didn't exist in any of their stories or anecdotes. And Jade knew them all by heart...word for word.

Leslie had only briefly mentioned Cornelius on her way to Charleston. The man was a mystery.

Could he have come from 2006? She was incapable of being distracted, at the moment, by anything but his story. There were no recorded instances of powers or an entity such as presented by Cornelius.

"During the years before the Great Religious War of 2012, technology took a giant leap. Nanotechnology was used to develop computerized vegetation that would change colors when certain chemicals were detected. The technology was incorporated into military strategies to facilitate the detection of mines in the ground.

The electromagnetic pulse, or EMP, impacted the frequency of these nano-bots. Cornelius paused.

Steve responded, “Yes, the electromagnetic pulse weapon was used in conjunction with the Neutron bombs in that war. Cornelius, we know what it is.”

Jed moved in closer to Cornelius, looking directly into the ruby orbs; assuring him he wasn’t the only scientist in the room familiar with the technology.

Cornelius continued, “Then you’re aware the EMP weapons were thrown into the mix with Neutron Bombs during the war of 2012. The military strategy was implemented to destroy all communication before the first strike would be launched.

Evidently, the nano-bot's frequency was somehow altered during the combination of EMP and Neutron bombs. The effect was catastrophic for mutants like me with suppressed and frightful powers. No one caught it. No one cared.

The nano-bots were programmed to a certain frequency known only to the armies allied with the Federation.

“Unfortunately...” sorrow clouded his crimson eyes. “The nano-bots’ new and accidental frequency was a precise parallel to the frequency which we psychic humans possessed. If I’d been alive during that disastrous war, the frequency alteration would have killed me along with the rest of my kind.

The tale Cornelius unraveled had a distressing effect on the big man. “For the first three months of 2012, the enemy used many frequency destroyers. They inadvertently showered all of civilization with their global broadcasts.

No one was prompted, at any level, to take defensive repellent measures. No one could have known the effect on the many people with my abilities."

Cornelius wrinkled his brow. "It killed all the gifted people with any form of extra-sensory perception. That is the truth!"

"The broadcasts put a genetic killer inside the brain of every active true paranormal mutant. The mutant population, which had been inbred, kept secret from the whole population, was destroyed. Then the bastards kept running the frequency destroyer for years afterwards as a precautionary measure."

Cornelius red eyes seemed to be spinning, alternating between a scarlet and crimson spirited animation.

Jade got it then. All the pieces were coming together.

He resumed with a small smile, "All psychic agencies experienced many unexplained mass deaths in that time period. They knew it was unnatural, but they were looking for ghosts. They were searching in the wrong direction.

He saw the looks of shock.

"The veil of time covered its tracks well. One of the worst genocides in history went unnoticed because no one knew what, how or why someone would want to kill these people. It killed great agents on both sides of the battle and each side blamed the other side for the unnatural pre-deaths.

"The war distracted any cause-and-effect analysis of the events. On a global scale it was a small number of deaths. All in all, it was just a small historical miscarriage.

Cornelius actually laughed.

"Those in that time period hid their abilities in efforts to maintain their identities and secret powers."

"Yeah," Cornelius continued, "I also cracked the Institute's files; I know that most of your data was lost, destroyed by the electro-magnetic spikes like everybody else's. I also know the Institute blames it on the celebrated Razor Savage/Magi battle, but what you don't know is that there were active agents until 2012. All Razor unconsciously did was use Leslie's and his own powers to kill the first Magi. He closed the portal to ghosts for two hundred years eliminating any access to this dimension, which by the way was an incredible act. I have studied that and tried to replicate it. Even Leslie didn't know how he did it."

This was news to Steve. His melded Bayou imprint felt a surge of proud recognition. He knew that when Razor was pissed, he would do anything in his power to end the pissed-off state. Razor had more unconscious power than anyone suspected, and his brain fought with automatic fire power. Steve had recorded Bayou and Razor both in the heat of battle putting out seven hertz when they started playing guitar. Seven hertz could potentially kill a person.

At the height of their battles, he recorded 12 to 15 hertz output. Twelve is the supposed bowel-loosening "poop frequency" long pursued by twentieth-first century rock musicians.

Cornelius kept on, "I thought I was hallucinating. The Magi tricked me in the past with illusions and set me up with me killing innocents.

"I....," he hesitated for a moment, "I knew he was becoming more powerful and I thought this was another Magi trick. I had 'seen' her trying to duplicate the portal closing before she died; she couldn't do it by herself and didn't trust me enough to invite me to help. I sensed her, but I couldn't tell where she was located."

He reached for words, trying to complete the horrible memory. "I felt what she was doing, and I lost her, the connection suddenly broke. I didn't know, I thought she was still alive."

Cornelius began a deep breathing exercise which lasted a full minute.

He let out the last breath and turned to look at them again, back in control. His disconcerting red eyes were scanning the room, lost.

"Bottom line, Razor and Leslie did ***not*** wipe out the extra sensory perception," he murmured in a trailing, distant voice.

"With all the records lost, they seemed to be the logical candidates to blame. The ghosts did disappear which led to a diminished need for special powers. No others who could access that frequency were born... until me. As far as I know, I'm the only one who has unlocked the inhibiting governor. I think before the war of 2012, certain people who had psychic powers had a certain type of energy signature that had been the focus of scientific experiments."

Steve jumped in, "You're correct. I read that during the early twenty-first century doctors used a medical device/process called an MRI scan which generated an electrical field of one-kilohertz pulse rate which matched the natural firing of brain cells."

Steve finished the thought, "You know Jed, other neuroscientists suggested this imbalance in the two hemispheres allows certain psychic individuals to see things others would not...i.e., other dimensions, corporal spirits, energies that move through dimensions. I remember reading through all that junk when I first got to the Institute to see if it would help resurrect Bayou.

Steve continued, "Due to the war all scientific labor was pushed into defense of the country. The Great Religious War of 2012 halted all research and because of the EMP and Neutron Bombs used, all data was lost during the war.

Cornelius nervously entered back into the conversation. "My brain is a cyber neuron-gateway. I can use my brain to motivate your muscles through electrical stimulation. With my natural ability, when I can manage the stress, I see the natural energy patterns of the universe. Yet growing up I could only see the energy patterns of the life forms of this current dimension....sometimes when I was alone and could focus a little harder, I caught glimpses of other dimensions.

I use signals from my motor cortex — an area of my brain that controls stimuli, and coordinates my electrical brain activity. I can intuitively 'feel' your body electrical functions. I then use an intuitive mathematical data analysis algorithm to know what buttons to push to neutralize my opponents. I can also feel ghosts in the same way."

A hush descended when he mentioned he could manipulate the same offensive function to ghosts.

He tried to explain, "I can see the source and destination of how the demon energy patterns move."

He grinned suddenly; "Let me give you an analogy that you scientists will appreciate.

The way that I see and track ghosts is very much like how the scientists of old tracked comets that traveled through multiple star systems... I can see how energy moves and direct the path it takes to its destination. To put it in ancient terms, I am much like switchmen on the old railroads...when a train needed to move to different tracks, they threw a switch to move the moving locomotive to a new track but never stopped the train."

Cornelius continued "When I engage, I try to be non-invasive during the access time of that person's brain," he said.

He looked at the fallen guards he had downed, "By the way, your guards are fine."

"Time is running out and I can also track energies. The major difference between Leslie and me is I have an additional sense that she didn't possess. I know exactly what and where the death dimension is. I can see the vortex. She's in there and needs us now! The Magi is trying to turn her. She is trapped and soon will need our help."

Steve rubbed his forehead in a nervous gesture and glanced at the others. No one had ever been able to see the "death dimension". Yet this young man seemed legit, odd as that sounded, Steve started to speak but was interrupted by Cornelius who wanted to stave off any bad news Steve might have to offer.

"I am a raw Magi in this dimension!" he exclaimed in exasperation. "I have their powers on this side, but I'm not sure how to use them. Leslie was going to train me!"

Jade had slowly worked her way behind the newcomer. She pulled the trigger on the tranq gun and caught Cornelius in the back of the neck. His body seemed to slow to the speed of cold molasses as he turned to Jade, his dimming crimson eyes in complete and pained disbelief.

Jade hated the look he gave her. He kept his eyes fixed on her as he toppled to the floor, immobilized from the jolt. The look he gave her was that of the betrayed. He was as stunned from the dart as he was from the betrayal... Jade was *almost* ashamed as she watched Cornelius fold into the carpeted floor.

The ghost fighters needed this time to regroup and investigate the stranger. His story, after all, was pretty hard to believe.

Two hundred years, no ghosts, no powers and now one super powerful, crimson-eyed Mastodon surfaces. Not only claiming powers stronger than Leslie's but a Magi himself.

Chapter 20

At the same time on the other side of the Institute, Oswalt had his hands full. Cornelius was still knocked out. The best-trained agents from all the best black operations from around the country were streaming into the Institute to pay their respects. Leslie's funeral service was in five minutes. The sudden and unexpected appearance of Cornelius had taken precedence over the inevitable and completely skewed the time clock.

Oswalt looked around. It was time to get going. He tried to remember the last funeral he had been to and what the funeral director had said. He was drawing a blank. All of the dead agents' funerals he had been to lately had been choreographed with the Institute's PR department. This was different.

He glanced at Razor looking at his watch impatiently and couldn't help but smile. Razor had that in-your-face look with the yellow Fender Esquire strapped across his chest, right hand at the ready, with the neck and tuning pegs pointed towards the floor, much like soldiers in by-gone eras kept their AK's on alert. He looked just as formidable as his reputation. The gathered stared and hushed comments encircled the room.

Razor had said many times the funeral is for the living, the dead could care less and that if he died, keep any ceremony under fifteen minutes or his ghost would come back and choke the shit out of all of them.

Oswalt quickly took in the room, looking each member of his trusted confidants in the eyes and, with proper tone and confidence, took charge. “Folks, we have to go downstairs and pull off the charade of Leslie’s funeral. Each of you knows the part you play and I’m counting on you to be, as you have been, expert in your duties. We will resume here after the game is played and go get Leslie.” The assembly followed Oswalt, Director Quirk and Razor to the gathering place.

Oswalt stood shoulder to shoulder with Quirk, Razor, Bayou and Mist in the center of the rotunda, preparing to begin the funeral services. All eyes were focused on the hovering casket, bookended by the two guitars and the Bloodstone casting the reddish hue from above. Oswalt, then Quirk, then Razor, then Bayou and finally, Mist, each gave heart wrenching eulogies to their fallen comrade. Each had their own version of the lovely and extra-talented young woman who had accomplished so much and saved so many in her short tenure with the Institute.

Oswalt walked up to the platform and silence filled the room.

He started, “This is a memorial service for one of our most cherished agents, who died in the line of fire, Leslie Quinn,” and he hesitated; then decided to add in a hushed reverence, “Savage”. “She died protecting mankind. She died serving her country and she was a friend of mine. To be honest with you it is hard to believe she is gone. I knew her well, and believe me I can tell you, there was no agent who gave as much and went beyond the call of duty than her. She personally saved mankind’s ass three times with her actions that I know of.”

Oswalt felt himself choking up and said, "Well I promised to just say a few words, Bayou....., Bayou Savage is going to conduct her eulogy."

Many agents gasped as Bayou Savage came around the corner. The blue magic elixir had been wearing off. The pain was in control, but his body looked as it had post battle. He stood at his full six feet and solid one hundred eighty-five pounds. His crystal blue eyes smoked. He was black and blue, but he had his head held high.

Instead of the Hollywood manicured version, they saw a musician soldier, the genesis figure behind the legend.

He had a psychedelic guitar that was shooting off mini-sparks, strapped across his back. He wore black creased pants with a starched white shirt. The black guitar strap made it appear the guitar was floating upside down behind him like a gun ready to be pulled. He truly looked like a ghost-fighting legend. His father, the famous Razor, turned and smiled. Razor was proud of Bayou. Mist, his daughter, looked proudly at her father and saw his beaten condition but the determined look on his face and knew her father was ready.

He walked slowly and gave Quirk a brotherly nod. You could have heard a pin drop.

The President looking on in the oval office put his coffee down and said to the Joint Chiefs of Staff, "My God, look at him!"

Bayou was black and blue with exposed stitches everywhere skin escaped the confines of his clothes. Only Razor, out of everyone, wasn't shocked. Razor was pissed. He was pissed that his only son had suffered such a beating from the legions commanded by the Magi. Revenge, bloody and harsh, swelled in his guts. The Esquire began to shoot fiery darts from the tuning pegs, preparing to match Razor's fury.

Bayou looked out over the room and started talking. He was a natural talker. He started in with no fanfare.

He smiled, looked directly at the audience and started. "What we have here is what in quality is called an existential risk. Leslie understood that. An existential risk is one where an adverse outcome would either annihilate all human life or permanently and drastically curtail its potential.

An existential risk is one where humankind as a whole is imperiled. Existential disasters have major adverse consequences for the course of human civilization for all time to come." Bayou had the gift of making an audience reach. His voice wasn't preachy, but the sincerity and natural system approach he took to everything made his words carry even more weight.

"Y'all, Leslie Quinn Savage died fighting the dark side to give mankind another chance." He paused to let that sink in.

"I just found out from Mist, my daughter, that the Bloodstone showed Leslie what would happen if she went to Charleston. She saw her fate here at the Institute after the San Diego battle. She knew the risk of coming to Charleston and knew for damn sure that she would die. She went to Charleston knowing that she was on a suicide mission. According to Mist, there was no hesitation on her part."

He paused, his bruised face adding heaviness to the speech. "Leslie looked destiny in the face and fought till she took her last breath." He looked down to the marble casket.

"I was there when she took her last breath. I was there when she died; all the ghost fighters were there. I saw her take the blast from the ghost that killed her. We took out the ghost, a powerful ghost called the Magi, the damn ghost that killed her, but we were a second too late to stop him from killing her. If she hadn't shown up, Quirk and I would not be here. We were almost dead when she showed. Fellow agents, she died saving another agent's life at the expense of her own. Please remember one thing, these ghosts are cunning and out for our extinction. Leslie made a choice and sacrificed her own life to save the rest of us. She could have walked away, but she didn't."

His face showed a sad, immutable look of loss and regret. After all, she had been his lost sister. He stopped, surveying his audience, wondering if they had a clue how important her sacrifice had been. "Most of you didn't know her. I have known her for over two hundred years and wouldn't be here today if not for her. She was cute, funny, and smart and loved music. She could be innocent and fun-loving, making you forget your problems with her humor and great listening skills. The sands run out in the time allotted in Earth's hourglass for all of us. Her gift was that she knew her future, and she chose that moment in Charleston as her time."

He canvassed the room till he found Oswalt. "She appreciated the resources that you provided her, especially when you found her that old Fleetwood Mac recording. It was her most prized possession. She burnt those tracks out. If she were here, she would wink at you and say, 'Keep cool and keep doing your organizational thang.' Oswalt, she always called you the 'Shield' behind your back because of the way you protected and fought for us. She appreciated you, dude."

Oswalt gleamed and Brown was pissed, knowing the President was looking at this total waste of Institute time.

Bayou gave the group a hard stare, something he had inherited from Razor. "She died knowing that it was her time to die, all the chips had been played. This battle was all or nothing according to her prophecy, with the big battle three days away. She would say if she were here, to trust your heart, have no second doubts. She didn't have any second doubts and followed through at the cost of her own life.

People, she knew going to Charleston would kill her, but she went. Her last prediction was that the Institute had three days before the final ghost battle would happen here."

Bayou slowly turned at and looked at Quirk. Everyone could see how much pain the body movement cost him. He winced at every quick move. He stared straight at Quirk.

Bayou continued, "If she were here right now, she would say, "Quirk, handle the assholes that throw bureaucracy bullshit at Oswalt and the Institute!" and he laughed. "She would also say in her hokey way, 'Keep the faith!' You and Razor always grounded her as to what the realities were."

He smiled again at Quirk, the beat-up Quirk whose blue elixir had also worn off. Quirk who had killed the Magi who had killed Leslie. "If she were here bro, she would tell you she appreciated all that you did for her. You were a great mentor to her; I know we talked about it a lot. Even at your pessimistic worst you treated her with respect and never doubted her power even when she doubted herself."

Bayou glanced at his father, Razor, who was listening.

Razor didn't turn from the stare but gave his son the patience he didn't afford many people.

"Razor, Dad, if Leslie were here, she would tell you to pick up that guitar of yours and kill as many ghosts as you can. That it is opening day of ghost-hunting season and with no kill limit. Bag as many as you can."

He glanced over next to Razor at Mist. She was holding the Bloodstone cradled in her right hand. He smiled thinking about what she had tried to do before the service.

Before the service had started, she and Steve Johnson had caught him. "Dad, let me use the Bloodstone to heal you."

"No, I want to feel the pain, and I want to show the other agents that this is not a video game. Thanks sweetheart, but I am doing this for Leslie."

Steve Johnson had the reprocessed elixir. "Bayou..." he held out the potion.

"No, Steve," and Razor explained again that he wanted to experience the pain for a while longer.

Steve walked away shaking his head. He muttered something what if the ghost attacked during the service, and the risk of not being able to fight at full capacity, but he kept walking away. He knew not to push.

"Mist, Leslie would say the gig is now yours. Use the Bloodstone to find and detonate the ghost portal. She would say trust your instinct. She was proud of you and what you did at Woosley Heights. She said you earned a purple heart on your first outing, which should make you a legend by yourself. She used to tell me that you're probably the most intelligent of all of us dumb Savages." All the ghost fighters laughed at the putdown.

The watching crowd shared the intended laugh. Some agents swear it was the only time they ever saw Mist Savage blush.

"She told me that you did great at the Whaley House, and she was proud of your gaining confidence. I think she went into Charleston knowing that if she did die that she had a successor that could she be proud of. She had a niece, a ghost fighter ready to take up her mantle and that would make her proud."

Mist started crying. Her face looked tired and strained. Standing bravely as people and cameras looked at her; the tears exposed her vulnerability and the big shoes she knew that she was now going to have to fill.

"Steve, Jade and Jed, you guys provided with her a solid friendship. She loved the get together we had at your house. She loved the cookouts and workouts." Finally, he sighed, "I think the time of Revelations chapter twelve, verse 12 is upon us. We have a short time left before the big battle. But before we fight, let us send Leslie off in southern style."

Bayou looked down as a strong sunlight beam shone through the skylight and lit up the white marble coffin. The whole scene looked surreal and holy.

Bayou walked over to where he had stationed the guitars which were beside Leslie's coffin. The agents and audience starred in clouded curiosity at what he was up to. Bayou bent over and picked up the Hendrix Buchanan Fender Telecaster. The movement caused him to grimace with pain.

He motioned to Quirk who walked up and picked up his 1966 Martin D-45, followed by Razor who picked a 1953 Fender Esquire.

Bayou captured Steve Johnson's attention and motioned for him to come up also. The only other instrument left was an original 1953 Fender Esquire Steve had purchased from an antique dealer to match the look of Razor's guitar.

Steve had played it before and had been embarrassed because he had thought maybe he could ignite a secret power it harnessed and fight in battle if needed. He hadn't been able to activate the awesome power. That was when Mist had first displayed her powers and made the guitar part of her fighting arsenal. Steve would never forget the uncomfortable memory. All that coursed through his mind as he walked and straddled the guitar across his shoulders.

Bayou looked out with eyes slightly tearing, "We are going to play a goodbye song for Leslie. It was customary in our time period to play a goodbye song for fellow companions. This is a song that came from our time." Steve looked over at Bayou hesitantly. What song was Bayou talking about?

Bayou smiled and started the opening licks to "Free Bird," an old southern anthem packed away in Steve's fractured brain in his Bayou imprint memories. Steve remembered it was a sad song with a volcanic fast past ending with screaming guitars. To his surprise he realized that he and Bayou would be playing the dual screaming leads together. He let the memory of the song start to float to his conscious mind. His finger memory was starting to activate. He let them go into the famous G, E minor, F, C, and D chord progression.

Steve kept his eyes closed and started to play the familiar, but not familiar, rhythm echoing in his memory banks. The old guitar felt natural in his hands. The old worn-out frets played smooth and gentle as he fingered the fretboard.

The agents looked eagerly on as Bayou went into the opening lead; He slurred his finger on the b string and slid up to the familiar G note up on the neck.

Quirk started singing with his natural powerful voice. It sounded good to all, and J.D. held her breath. Quirk demonstrated a natural flair for giving words a life of their own. They all listened and embraced the sad song. None of them, agents or guests, had ever heard the ghost fighters play together and this was an incredible awe-inspiring event.

Razor kept the foundation and timing with his rhythm guitar. He looked like an ancient god with the guitar in his hands.

The chorus came and Bayou and Quirk belted out perfectly matching harmonies. The heartrending-bruising song had a haunting melody of breaking, ringing guitar notes. It produced a sharing of poignant feelings for the listeners.

The song slowed and then started to its overdriving fast climatic finale. None of the ghost fighters opened their eyes. Razor sped up his tapping foot, and Quirk commenced strumming hard matching Razor's bass rhythm avalanche. Steve and Bayou started screaming matching dual leads on their guitars.

Then Steve dropped into the matching rhythms of Razor and Quirk, leaving Bayou to play a solo lead.

Bayou was making the guitar cry and scream by striking the notes, bending them unmercifully and making the sound swell like a thousand guitars. His guitar set off a glow as he screamed, and he started floating off the ground going in a clockwise motion.

An unexpected cold breeze suddenly exploded across the room. The smell of brimstone followed a second later.

Leslie's coffin appeared to be putting off a light, and the air above her coffin appeared to be gathered in a swirling vortex.

Razor felt it too. Some ghost bastard was trying to do something to Leslie's coffin.

Mist unconsciously surrounded the guitar players with a red force field and fed them the Bloodstone energy. All their streams of energy focused back to Bayou. The Bloodstone also froze everyone in the room in a stasis field.

Agents wanted to join the fight, but all movement was stolen by the Bloodstone. The agents' thoughts were eaten up by the unfolding events. All were watching with their very eyes as the most incredible event of their lives unfolded.

The damn legends were true; the Ghost Fighters were really real, with real damn legendary powers. You had to see it to believe it, and they were seeing a full blown ghost fighting hurricane.

With his eyes closed, his fingers manipulating the frets like a madman, Bayou blazed and bribed the Telecaster into ghost-killing force mode. Bayou was playing Free Bird faster than any guitar player in history. He played the song as though he wrote it, and his fingers were getting faster.

He poured all his pent-up emotion into the guitar. His anger feelings fostered and poured out through his fingers on the fretboard. To the agents it looked like spontaneous combustion was erupting from his fight fist.

He thought of Leslie dying, Jon and Bob dying, his mother dying of breast cancer. He fed all his rage at not being able to stop any of it into the guitar. Red tears came out of both sides of his eyes as he continued to play, floating ten feet off the ground with his guitar firing out searing white and blue energy blasts at something no one could see above the coffin.

The wind was blowing around him at gale forces, yet he kept playing. He kept bending the strings, screaming the g lead notes, forcing the strings until they could bend no further.

The guitar found what it was looking for. He was playing faster and faster, while moving closer to the malediction inside the portal. A stream of charged particles from the guitar, transmitting energy into the portal, was unraveling the complex processes behind the larger-scale particle portal accelerations.

Through the center of the domed rotunda, a searing yellow spike of fire pierced the domed ceiling of the rotunda and the Bloodstone's protective umbrella, which suddenly became nothing but warm butter. As the spear sunk to the base of the hovering casket, the flash blinded everyone in the sprawling room...for a split second and as quickly as it struck, the bolt reversed course up and through the casket, the red hue of the Bloodstone and the glass dome, leaving no evidence of its arrival or departure.

A small portal was opening, pulsating, above Leslie's coffin, made visible only by the blazing blue fire from Bayou's guitar.

Mist floated up halfway between Bayou and the other fighters. She gathered all her remaining strength and pushed the

Bloodstone to boost Bayou's guitar playing. The newly acquired streak of white hair swirled in the howling wind horizontal to her body.

The guitars, with no assistance from Razor or Bayou, floated up and above the casket as the Bloodstone broadened its protective hue to encompass all those attending the celebration of Leslie's life and her formidable contribution to the warriors of the Ghost Defense Institute. Razor's guitar assumed the autopilot attack formation close to Bayou, firing the electric light show so many of the Institute's personnel had grown to appreciate.

The guitars focused their simultaneous attack on the developing presence that was centered over Leslie's hovering casket. A barely visible portal was forming, pulsating and growing as the guitars generated a more forceful and destructive aggression to the apparent evil emanating from within the menacing portal.

Mist floated up halfway between Bayou and the other fighters. She gathered all her remaining strength and pushed the Bloodstone to boost Bayou's guitar playing. Her new pronounced white streak was blowing with the rest of her hair horizontal to her body.

Bayou felt the energy feeding in. He opened his eyes and saw the portal. He felt the evil trying to come through. He turned the Fender directly into the portal and floated to it. His fingers were now unrestricted with the Bloodstone feed. He could feel the guitar energy violating the effigy trying to come out of the portal.

As quickly as the portal had appeared, it spread into a shape as large as the entrance to a split road highway tunnel and imploded. It sent a shock wave through the room, knocking all down except the ghost fighters.

Bayou and Mist were still floating.

One and all couldn't believe their eyes. Their ears were ringing too.

Bayou and Mist floated down.

As they touched the floor, a beam of sunlight showed directly on Leslie's coffin.

Bayou, beat up and tired, looked up at the incoming beam and smiled. He looked at the agents now getting back on their feet.

He smiled, "That's Leslie saying, "Thank you Bayou... and get your ass, and every other you can find, prepared for the oncoming attack." He continued to smile, thanked them for coming, acting like the battle was no big deal. He walked off the makeshift platform followed by the other ghost fighters. No one said a word and the room was completely silent as they strode tiredly out.

With a limp Bayou walked down the hallway to his room, incubating an anger to kill. Leslie would be avenged. The Magi was going to be a free bird himself soon.

Within minutes of returning to Director Oswalt's office, the group was surprised by an unwelcomed visitor. Surrounded by four agents, Brown, the Institute's twisted CFO, snake and alleged playboy, strutted directly towards Oswalt. To Oswalt, Brown looked like a despicable venomous snake crawling out of a wet muddy pit in the holler, looking for somebody whose day he could ruin.

Brown looked at Oswalt and smirked. He'd heard the rumors about the "amazing" Cornelius. This was his moment. Behind Oswalt's back, Brown had worked his malignant persuasion on the President. The President finally caved to the mealy-mouthed bureaucrat, if only just to shut him up. Brown wrangled a position of authority over all Institute operations, exclusive of the ghost fighting unit and extended members of the tactical team. Brown believed he had arrived at a time to put Oswalt in his place. This delusion had persisted and became long overdue...at least in his twisted little mind.

Brown smiled to himself. Everybody he wanted was here for the special occasion. One of those dumbass ghost fighters had finally gotten what he predicted would happen. Exactly what they deserved. The young one, Leslie, had showed an insubordinate streak when he asked her about her expense reports.

Now was the time to oust Oswalt, take over and cancel this fiasco and waste of Institute time and money. He'd have to maneuver a way around the President's order to exempt the ghost fighters from his control. "All in due time," he muttered to no one listening.

Quirk surfaced from the shadows, with only a slightly exaggerated stride, placing his sizable boot in Brown's path. Brown took a free fall into the office floor. The move kind of hurt the former director more than a little. The big man was still nursing wounds from his last ass-kicking received in Charleston. The hurt was far less than immediate gratification. Quirk's pals in the Oval Office had already given him the heads up that Brown badgered the President into a successful power grab. The sniveling little prick was on his way with a mindset designed to embarrass Oswalt in front of as many ghost fighters as were assembled.

Quirk thought about the relativity of consequences. Kicking Brown's ass shouldn't take too long. Just a little warm up to defensive strategies against the prophesized onslaught. He needed a bit of stretching anyway. He figured two days was about all they had left before the thorny lingering dead came after the Institute.

His immediate objective was to assess this Cornelius character and put the minds of the inside team to rest, one way or the other. The jury needed to be called in and decisions made. No more time out.

Brown, after his short trip to the floor, moved his pudgy frame to an upright status, flushed with inevitable embarrassment and a slightly swollen nose. The room became very still and quiet. Only Brown's bodyguards moved, pulling weapons, pointed at Quirk. They were surprised by the cold stare of the big man covered in cuts, bruises and open wounds. Intimidation was one of the smaller arrows in Quirk's quiver.

Quirk glared at Brown, "C'mon, take a shot, ain't nothin' but air between us. Come on, little man. Aren't you the one who says you don't understand the Neanderthal brains of us southerners? Here's your chance! Talk or fight. Either way you're going down!"

Quirk leaned his chin out, daring Brown to do something. "You want the truth Brown? Truth is you can't handle being a Director. Not here, and damn sure not now. You're nothing but a half-ass bureaucrat about to get a whole bunch of good people killed with your bullshit politics and back room deals trying to bring this Institute down."

He spoke his piece just loud enough for the agents to catch the disgust in his voice. Brown's boys kept their weapons trained on the old warrior, as a tad of trepidation began to creep into their minds over their allegiance to Brown.

Quirk treated Brown to one of his more menacing smiles. "In my day, men would settle this sort of tripe mano a mano. You get my drift, weasel?"

Brown started to squirm like a worm on a hook. "Arrest this man immediately," he squealed. Two agents took tentative steps to grab Quirk.

Quirk summoned the last of his reserve and ingrained muscle memory and brought both agents to their knees. The remaining two agents were quickly reinforced with three agents from the hallway. The first two went down with one-two roundhouses. First the left, then the right. Another of Brown's poorly trained boys closed in. Quirk dropped to a half crouch, grabbed the agent's gun hand, relieved him of the weapon and pulled the man into him, using the agent's own momentum to throw him over his shoulder into the pile of guys already on the floor. The third member of "the cavalry" stepped back to the sanctuary of the hallway.

One of the leveled fellas managed to get a hand on his weapon and got a shot off at Quirk. Quirk heard the round leave the barrel. In slow motion, the round ejected and another slid into the receiver.

Having barely seen the move in his peripheral vision, he rolled left and ducked the shot. The idiot who fired the shot let loose a string of profanity. Quirk turned and leveled a menacing stare at the poor bastard. "Look, man, this was supposed to be easy. Brown's boy was pleading. "Give up and we will take it easy on you." Quirk grinned.

He aimed the confiscated pistol and fired. The alleged bodyguard squealed at the sudden fire in his calf. Before anyone could move, Quirk stepped behind Brown and jammed the gun under Brown's chin, jerking his head back, with a tight grip on the pudgy punk's hair. He savagely twisted Brown's body in front of him, facing the stunned Brownies. With Brown's body shielding most of the old warrior, the untrained became reluctant actors in the unfolding misfortunes of war.

Quirk took a deep breath; he was getting too old for this shit. Damn Brown and damn his old slowed down reflexes but thank God they still worked. He mentally weighed his options. In the end there was only one option. It was simple economy of motion, time, and energy.

He pasted Brown again, knocking him out. He glared at the bodyguards, and they slunk out the door and disappeared. Quirk smiled. One less pain in the ass.

Chapter 21

Somebody, somehow, penetrated the superior security of the GDI. The press got wind of the story and media idiots were dumb enough to leak highly classified information to the easily manipulated public. The press bought into whatever they were being fed, regardless of the source. Growing ranks of reporters were assembling at the guard gate of the institute.

Oswalt suspected Brown. He didn't know how, when or where, but the irrefutable fact that the press was here meant the breach could only have come from the inside. One of the ***more*** disturbing disclosures was Leslie's very private funeral service. The bogus rumor mill alleged that Leslie had been trained by the inept and completely unqualified Brown.

Oswalt had to laugh even though the bullshit lent credence to the theory that the corrupted son of a bitch had somehow scammed the media into his corner. Brown craved influence and power. This time his deceit crossed the line. Oswalt engaged the IT gurus to get on it and find any holes in the Institute's IT security. The objective was to trace Brown's phone calls and emails in order to discover if the leak came from the weasel's office. Oswalt claimed the "innocent until proven guilty" mantra of the former United States, but his body language was broadcasting the opposite. The IT dept was hoping for guilt, since nobody liked Brown.

Oswalt still had to deal with Cornelius. At least he had some backup now. Only a minor relief after witnessing the man's capacities...if he even ***was*** a man.

The red eyed curiosity was still unconscious...out cold. An impromptu and cursory investigation substantiated his occupation as a postmodern artist. Cornelius' cover provided a resume which included work at the local Bruce Yates Studio in Asheville.

The big man was evidently well respected for his talents within the art form dubbed 'electroclash'...whatever the hell ***that*** was. Oswalt knew the Bruce Yates studio was a legitimate and well- respected high-end music and art studio. Further research proved Cornelius was a legal citizen with no arrest record.

His academic accomplishments were more than impressive and caused increased scrutiny during the "deep dive" investigation. According to his file, Cornelius had the power to divide prime numbers to the sixtieth decimal point, calculate fifth roots, and raise numbers to the ninth power in his head.

Steve ran the DNA "gene ware" program on the unconscious subject and found some unusual genetic properties.

When Cornelius woke, the shit would hit the fan due to his unique and overwhelming powers. The inevitable awakening was approaching fast. If Cornelius could penetrate the dimensions, then he could tell the team when and where the ghosts were going to attack. "Think about it later," Oswalt told himself.

The phone rang. Not now, Oswalt thought. He looked and groaned. The President, ***dammit!!*** He recognized the caller ID.

"Oswalt. What the hell is going on over there?" The President's speech was clipped and quick. "Brown called and said that you had captured an infiltrator; Brown said this infiltrator was loaded up with some kind of weaponry that allowed him to breeze through your defenses. Is that true?"

Oswalt felt his face flush as he struggled for the right words without lying.

"Sir, Brown is a finance guy and has a voracious gift for embellishment and, if I may speak freely, he's as full of shit as a Christmas turkey."

"Did someone penetrate your defenses and end up in your room early this morning, yes or no?"

"Yes," Oswalt grunted through gritted teeth.

"Look I don't give a shit about you or Brown and your pissing contest down there, what I do care about is defending this country. How did he do it? Do you know? Again, just answer yes or no, I don't have time for bullshit or excuses."

Oswalt was grateful the President spoke his mind in simple, politically incorrect language.

"Yes, sir, he came through the perimeter without destroying any of the structure. Our scientists think he has an unfamiliar genetic makeup that allows him to absorb and dissipate energy on a level we can't comprehend...but we're working on it, Sir. He can control any system's energy, bio or synthetic."

The President asked if they could use Cornelius as a weapon.

Oswalt said, "We knocked him out, he is being held in an energy dampening field in the new lab right now. We will ascertain his capabilities as soon as he wakes up. By the way, we recorded Leslie's funeral ceremony and we've forwarded the video to your office. The Institute is now live, and feeds go straight to you and your analysts. If we fall like the Alamo, at least you can see what worked and what didn't. We figure we have two days left at best."

The President thanked Oswalt for the recording and signed off with requests to be kept in the loop.

Chapter 22

Bayou had been an urban legend for the last two hundred years. His suspected suicide and the many movies about him had made him an icon with cult status. He even had a term named after him in the Institute, "Bayou-dize", which meant carpe past. When someone had a pleasant older memory, the term was used.

Reports various agents read about him were almost beyond belief. The public didn't have a clue as to what was really going on. Only the senior level officials of this formally covert war could access and read Bayou's profile. The reports appeared to be somewhere between "no fuckin' way" and "well, maybe." Especially accounts of the last few battles. Bayou, Quirk, Razor, Mist. Steve, Jade, and Leslie fought and won ***every*** battle, with no casualties on the good guys' side. Until Charleston. That battle cost Leslie her life. The winning streak stopped there.

Bayou looked up from his dark reverie and grimly thought, "Time to wake up Cornelius!"

Chapter 23

Cornelius came to just a little more than pissed. SHE knocked him down and out with one damned dart. ***NOBODY*** had been able to put him down since puberty. He began to lift himself off the gurney and was just as amused as he was surprised to find 4-inch black nylon straps binding his wrists and ankles to the gurney. Still coming out of the haze from Jade's dart, Cornelius put extra and required effort into snapping the useless tethers.

The minimal effort drained him a bit and he realized whatever drug he caught was more powerful than anything he'd encountered...EVER and that's sayin' a lot. The memory of the beauty who shot him lingered in his curiosity. Why had she done that? To what end? To what purpose!? Cornelius had a few questions for his possible teammates. First get rid of the drugs in his body. He closed his mind and began cleansing his body of the drug.

J.D, Steve Johnson, Jade and Jed watched his recovery from the presumed safety of the leaded glass shield between them and Cornelius. In theory, they could see him, but he couldn't see them.

Cornelius returned to his natural senses. As he wrestled with the "why" of recent events, trying to make sense of the sequence, he felt a sudden spark. An immediate urgency to expose the prophecy. The visions which permeated and tormented his entire life were of a prophecy, a prediction, which he'd been tasked to complete. All the omens, each more intense than the last, indicated he was running out of time. He leapt from the gurney and charged the viewing glass.

"The prophecy, don't you understand? How long have you idiots kept me out? We're running out of time!!!"

At the same time as the assembly of voyeurs walked out from behind the shield and into the confinement cell, Razor, Quirk and Bayou slipped into the room, behind the viewing shield. Cornelius felt their presence and chose to ignore the warriors.

Jade kept the shock gun pointed at his gut. He saw "the look" and settled slowly into a relaxed glare, at the weapon, the three men and one gorgeous woman in a doctor's smock standing with her.

Steve started, speaking as if he was the only witness to what each of them had seen. "What Cornelius did was formerly deemed impossible. Using only his mind, those high-density nylon straps snapped like cheap kite string. This kid cleaned the entirety of drugs from his system in less than a minute."

J.D. and Steve were the most amazed at the sight of skin color flushing as they watched his face and neck change color. As his mind commanded his body, his arms changed color. No one had ever seen this kind of power before. Hell, no one had even ***heard*** of this before.

Jed stepped closer, oblivious to any danger. He was simply being the curious scientist that he was. "Cornelius, how did you do that?"

Cornelius took a few steps toward Jed. Jade kept her aim steady on his torso. He glared at her "toy" and the weapon flew out of her hand into the wall and shattered into tiny pieces. Time stopped for a moment and the group took a hesitant step back. The collective curiosity had suddenly turned to an unraveled red flag.

Except Jed. Unfazed, he continued his amiable conversation with the red eyed fellow and exclaimed, "Now that was cool! Pure PSI energy at 100 megawatts, I have hoped for a day I would see ***somebody*** kick some psychic energy besides the Savages."

Cornelius was direct and to the point. "I will only say this once. I could take each of you out with the blink of an eye. Actually," he chuckled, "that's exactly how it could happen. But, as your good fortune would have it, I need your help to bring Leslie back."

Their eyes were riveted to this modern miracle. But each kept a wary distance.

Cornelius returned Jed's inquisitive stare and couldn't help but smile. Jed had that innocence which made him an obvious and harmless curiosity. That personality trait alone, made him immediately likable and approachable.

While Cornelius talked Steve took a closer look at their newfound question mark. The big man scanned and measured six foot four and weighed two hundred and twenty-five pounds. Genetically, he was from the Midwest with a German/Nordic ancestry. In a nutshell, the extent of all acquired knowledge regarding the crimson eyed stranger.

"My brain has acquired a certain level of performance concerning paranormal activity and its connections with the physical realm. Human experience is brain based. Understanding the neurobiological basis for encounters with spiritual realities occurred early in my life.

AHHH, BULLSHIT! Now is not the time for this! I'll explain after we save the planet!" The red flag began to twitch again. "You guys should come on in and let's get this shitshow started!! We need to focus on the target! Yesterday morning, Leslie sent a crystal-clear mind fuck that knocked me conscious and out of the rack. She transmitted the exact measures, tools and weapons required to fight the Magi. As the movie played out in my head, I was terrified when she described what had to happen in order to protect her father, Razor.

Her telepathic transmittal included everything I had to do. Leslie pulled the strings on the Bloodstone to reveal my instructions.

I tracked her using the abilities of the Bloodstone she gifted me that morning. But I couldn't open the damned portal fast enough." He slammed his hand down on the counter. A subtle drop fell from his eye. "Through her eyes, I saw her port into Charleston, I watched the portal open, I heard her saying goodbye to Bayou, Razor and Quirk. I was in her mind. I felt her die and I damn near died with her.

Son of a bitch, I failed, for all my damn power I couldn't get there fast enough. I, I… got scared seeing the Magi, I felt his evil and I froze. When she needed my power the most, I fucking froze.

I was too late to save her, but I will protect her ghost. She's waiting for me, for **US.** I need your help!" Cornelius pleading was an anomaly. "I must be near her body and use the

Bloodstone. She said Mist would have to augment my powers with the Savages. The mega-shit is about to hit the fan."

He hesitated and gave them their first ray of hope in the upcoming battle. "I can feel the evil son-of-a bitch and with her help on the inside I think we can bushwhack him when he comes through the portal. She told me to tell you, it is a long shot, but she thinks she can help us from the other side.

He looked down, "I will use all my powers to make up for my cowardness, my screw-up or I will die. Either way I am in this fight."

He looked determined. "Either work with me and follow my orders or get the hell out of my way. Either way the Magi is dead, I promise. Leslie will be avenged." The ghost fighters were impressed with his commitment. Bayou remembered his solemn pledge. Cornelius just echoed the exact words.

Jade looked at Cornelius with a new perception. She wondered if he was a lost descendant of the Savages. The man sure sounded like one.

The explosion refocused all attention.

Chapter 24

The attack came from the Hendersonville Road side. A bomb blasted with enough force to blow a four-foot hole in the outer perimeter wall. Oswalt ran into his office. The funeral was forgotten. Then he not only heard but he felt the second blast. The impact made him think the ghosts were initiating their version of "end of times".

The Institute's head of security, Beth Jones, dismissed her usual friendly tone. With greatly higher decibels and certainly higher urgency, the frantic woman hollered into the system's microphone. "Humans, not ghosts, are attacking the eastern perimeter. There appear to be several incoming armed personnel!"

Razor, Bayou, Quirk, and now Cornelius, found the nearest video monitor between the blasts. The bird's- eye view of the situation took little time to evaluate. Quirk grabbed the closest head and mic set and began barking orders.

Special ops teams poured out of the Institute under Quirk's commands. They flanked the breach in the wall and pummeled the fucking idiots with tear gas, smoke and flash grenades. Each one was wondering, who in their right mind would be pro-ghost?

There were about thirty-five militants attacking. They dressed in some sort of comical black ninja garb firing small arms through Institute windows unsure of targets or effect. They were somewhat organized. Quirk and his teams had a minimal window to organize, but they were seasoned professionals. Training and organization had been bred into these people long ago. Still...the scene was chaotic. Quirk's subconscious flashed the nightmare of Brown gleefully recounting the early onslaught to the President.

Quirk, after hearing live fire from the opposition, increased his resistance with the order to subdue with concussion grenades. Those had the desired effect and the ninjas stopped to rethink their alleged strategy. Quirk sent two teams in a full-frontal confrontation. He sent another team on recon around the perimeter. They found another unexploded bomb on the back side. A munitions expert easily disarmed the improvised explosive.

It was then a fat ghost with a Chef outfit showed up. With both hands he shot blue donuts straight into the forces, killing them. He kept it up and walked straight into their line of fire. One militant armed and shot a flame thrower straight into Pierre's spectral form.

He laughed and the flames went through him with no noticeable effect.

"You bastards, trying to kill these good epicureans, especially my friend Razor. Take this!" he shouted and shot a blue acrid-smelling donut that surrounded the holder of the flame thrower. It appeared like a blue acid ring of death descending onto the helpless attacker. He screamed as it made contact and screamed louder as it started to constrict.

Everyone watched what happened next in slow motion. "Let this be a lesson to you all!" and with that he constricted the donut, cutting the man and flamethrower in half. Blood blasted out in a dark red shower everywhere and the two human halves fell to earth, split in half.

He then grabbed the last five assailants who charged in. He grabbed all five with the same donuts.

Some of the agents stared in disbelief.

Before anyone could react, Pierre yelled, "For you, Razor!" and dissected all five in a single blast of greenish death from his right hand.

The combined forces under Quirk signaled each other so as not to be killed in friendly fire.

They approached and mopped up the bodies that Pierre hadn't killed.

Quirk radioed to Oswalt. "Oswalt, Beth did film this correctly, right? We had cameras stationed and recording this?"

"Yes," Oswalt responded, not quite understanding Quirk's point.

"Review and edit it immediately and release it to the press. Spin it revealing the Institute was attacked by a renegade ghost at the same time the pro-ghost militants attacked. Say the Institute was lucky. Release information the ghost which mysteriously surfaced did not know one human from another and wiped out all the stupid pro-ghost forces and we, given enough time, dispatched the rogue and all is well within the walls of the GDI."

Oswalt roared with laughter. The real Quirk was living up to an incredible legendary past. They both heard Beth Jones who was listening in through the security dispatcher also laugh. "Brilliant, Quirk!" Her words summarized the entire event, and they all laughed again, thinking of the effect on the pro-ghost forces.

Using the press to your advantage was Quirk's first rule of thumb.

Chapter 25

Beth Jones' voice came through Oswalt's and Quirk's earpieces. "Boys, it was a planned attack. There is a note next to the blast scene taped to a wall. They wrote it in big letters, probably for the press cameras. Check out what it says."

She zoomed the cameras where Oswalt and Quirk could see the writing on the note.

The note said, "Quit killing ghosts or face the consequences!" It was signed "The Pro-Paranormal Militants".

Since San Diego they had been in the news and were becoming a major pro-ghost Institute countermovement. Now the shit was a double blind. The Institute could not only be attacked by ghosts but idiot humans who considered themselves friends of the ghosts. The resurrected fighters were astounded that the "cancel culture" had survived through the years. Each believed the hypocrisy of that movement would have been exposed and canceled through its own ridiculous premise.

Oswalt shook his head, didn't the morons remember San Diego when the United Nations sent their peace representative? The demons ripped him to shreds.

So much for sanity in what the press was calling the "eschatological pantheistic time, or the end of the world times!"

"Amateurs," was what the bomb expert said.

Quirk called for all top brass, including ghost fighters to meet. It was now 11:30.

Everyone was there, the leaders of Alpha (CIA best), Bravo (FBI best) Charlie (DEA) and Delta (Army Rangers) and Echo (Green Berets), Foxtrot (Seals). Steve, Jade and Jed were there to represent the scientists.

Bayou and Razor carried their guitars, slung across their backs. Mist held the legendary Bloodstone close.

Oswalt directed the meeting. Brown sat at the "children's table", unobtrusive and strictly restricted to the role of silent observer. "Silent" being the operative word.

Everyone stared at the newcomer glowing ever so slightly with a reddish aura not too far separated from the hue of the Bloodstone.

Steve introduced Cornelius to everyone. He shook hands with Bayou, Razor, Quirk, and Mist. When he touched Mist, he did not release her hand. He stared straight into her eyes trying to find memories of Leslie. He quit probing and looked around the room; he especially stared at the beat-up condition of Quirk and the even worse Bayou. He knew what Leslie would want him to do.

Cornelius shocked everyone with his next move.

"Mist," he said, "please trust me on what I am about to do." He sounded almost scared. "We are running out of time, and Leslie told me from the other side what I was to do."

Everyone within earshot looked shocked but Mist. Her life had grown so strange lately her expectations of surprises had dwindled to a trickle. With no hesitation she matched his stare.

After all, **she** was the mistress of the Bloodstone and the guitars. "OK, what did she say to do?"

"This... Please raise the Bloodstone above your head and activate the healing power. I'll assist, if you don't mind."

Her obvious body language spoke more than the proverbial thousand words. "What the hell, why not."

Mist raised the Bloodstone and immediately felt Cornelius' application increasing the power of the stone. It was as if Leslie was standing next to her again. A stream of pure mind energy expanded her powers. The rush lit her up like a Roman candle. She suddenly felt juiced with the energy, stamina and endurance of an Olympian athlete.

The gathered group looked to Quirk for guidance.

Quirk had been in enough situations to allow this one to play out. Mist, the Bloodstone and the tall stranger would need all the power they could muster. If Cornelius could help, let it roll. Better now, than right before the battle. Practice, after all, still makes perfection...welllll, most of the time.

Razor glanced at his guitar and saw no start up glow and figured the situation was weird but okay. Let it ride, trust his granddaughter. He would only interfere if the guitar lit up.

The Bloodstone rechanneled to a darker red. The intensity of color forced all in attendance to turn away or shut their eyes.

Two beams shot into and through Quirk and Bayou. Their bodies lifted from the floor a decent 5 feet, just short of the 15-foot ceiling and merged into one. Both were sort of surprised but neither fought. This time was overdue anyway, and the healing began immediately.

As the agents regained their abilities to experience the display of Bloodstone power, they watched, a bit dumbfounded, as the red lightning strikes pierced the two men who, only very recently, seemingly merged into one...were currently suspended, back-to-back. The red, translucent cocoon wrapped their bodies from head to toe. Heads held high, backs straight, eyes closed as the warmth of ancient mystic power flowed through them.

Bayou's guitar executed a 180 degree turn and was now strapped to his chest in stasis with him.

Quirk and Bayou felt the healing from the Bloodstone. In full view of everyone, bruises and stitches began disappearing. Even the grief from Leslie's death seemed to surrender to the stone. Bayou and Quirk felt an amazing relief which had been nonexistent since the events in Charleston. They were returning to former prime and excellent fighting condition as the Bloodstone worked therapeutic cures, still unheard of in western medicine practices.

In the corners, Air Ion and EMF detectors sounded alarms manifested by the unusually enormous energy. Levels off the normal scale went largely ignored, given current circumstances. To call the attendees mesmerized would be a colossal understatement.

Neither ghost fighter fought the energy. Each soaked in the resurgence of vitalities lost in the recent and less than victorious battles. Most agents were slack jawed from the experiences just witnessed. Nothing in their background could've ever prepared them for ***any*** true psychic experience. Bayou and Quirk still floated, invisibly perched five feet from the floor, 10 feet from the ceiling of the old manufacturing plant. Small deep red sparks danced away from their beat-up bodies as they were gently returned to Terra Firma. The healing was done, and they stood, once again, steady on the original concrete slab of the Institute.

Under the direction of Mist's newly acquired contributions, Mist and Cornelius worked in concert, as the red eyed stranger's impact boosted the power of the stone. She felt the welcome feeling of Leslie tapping into his power. Cornelius was learning the healing process, amazed at how quickly Mist had absorbed the adept abilities held by Leslie. He had tried to heal before with limited success. He instantly recognized the missed steps. Leslie had taught the young Ms. Savage well.

They worked as if they had known each other for years. She could feel how he monitored her every move, mimicked her every move. Had she been like this with Leslie? She no longer remembered. His power felt like Leslie's, but raw where Leslie's strategies were proven and polished. Both ghost fighters were now healed, inside and outside.

It was then she felt it, it came without warning and scared the shit out of her. Mist felt Cornelius taking over the Bloodstone. His raw Magi power overrode most of her controls; Mist barely maintained her grip on the Bloodstone. The universe was experiencing power it had not felt since Leslie was alive. The walls vibrated violently, easy prey to the Bloodstone's energy ricochets.

She screamed and struggled to fight him. All the agents froze not knowing what the hell was going on. Mist still maintained a small part of the Bloodstone power. Bayou quickly spun into fight mode and watched for the target.

Cornelius shot a small morsel of the Bloodstone's power directly into him as another trail of the crimson tendril floated through the wall.

"Betrayed" was all Mist could think. The son of a bitch was a traitor and probably working with the idiot pro-ghost forces and possibly even the Magi and his newfound band of Dullahans. Interesting bunch, those Dullahans. Irish mythology claimed they only appear in the face of approaching death....an increasingly likely outcome.

Bayou was passed out on the floor. Mist sought out the guitar's energy and jerked the talisman into radical fight mode, directing the blue-white electrical charges into Cornelius with extreme prejudice.

He extended his right arm, using the hand as a makeshift shield. The blue-white bolts deflected off the mini-force field he'd created.

The agents all drew their weapons, not sure what to do.

Mist stared at Cornelius who carried the determined stare of a bullfighter ready to bring down the final blow to his bovine nemesis. She was confused. He was killing Bayou ***AND*** Quirk, the GDI's best tactician, and she hadn't seen it coming. Mist was pissed at herself. She depleted her wilting remaining power.

They stared at each other, the guitar firing into his force field and his left hand directing the energy of the Bloodstone into Quirk.

An explosion rocked the gathered fighters. The crash of equipment and doors slamming echoed through the halls of the institute.

Then it was over. She had been too late, even with all of her incredible power.

She would always try to remember the next sequence of events. Each was a source of consternation for years. Cornelius stopped directing the Bloodstone energies into Quirk. The unintended and mysterious tendrils ceased their travels through walls to points unknown. Cornelius released the force field and looked right at her. Those red glowing eyes of his looked pale from the effort. She almost hesitated.

But, she didn't hesitate and fired another full blast into him. The son-of-a bitch had killed Quirk. A bewildered gaze made its way from Cornelius into Mist's fiery eyes. "Why attack me? Don't you trust me?"

Cornelius watched the blue-white stripe cross the room in slow motion. He felt helpless knowing he didn't have the energy to fight. He looked her straight in the eyes as the full blast knocked the Bloodstone out of his sturdy hand. The blast impaled him and he hit the wall trying to roll with the hit. For a split second, he traveled back to the football field. The Bloodstone skidded across the floor into Mist's waiting hands.

Mist heard a crack and he fell face forward and crumpled into a heap. His right arm broke instantly on impact and three ribs cracked. He passed out immediately even before he made floor contact. The psychic quake ended quietly.

The Bloodstone floated over to her, and she let the guitar float back over Bayou's inert body.

She ran over to Quirk who was looking straight up into the ceiling. He had a big shit eating smile on his face. Mist thought

Cornelius had attacked and probably burnt out Quirk's brain. No one smiled liked that when normal.

"Welllllllll," he spoke and slowly sat up, "Let's see if that son of a bitch was telling the truth. He said Leslie formulated a damn good strategy and told him to do this; Cornelius beamed it to me as he replenished me." Quirk still smiling said out loud, "What a damn good plan, I would never have thought of it."

Mist stared at the old ghost fighter and looked deep into his eyes. He seemed to be perfectly alright, but the words were not making any sense.

"What do you mean?" she asked, not having a clue as to what the hell he was talking about.

Quirk slowly stood up and moved over to help the now awakened Bayou stand up. Razor closed the distance and helped both now recovered ghost fighters stand.

Bayou and Razor felt it at the same time and were shocked. Before anyone else they knew what was coming. Up to that point there had been only four people in history that could produce that feeling and one was now dead.

Quirk extended his hand and from around a corner his old friend, the over two-hundred year old, 1966, Martin D-45, glided into his hand.

Razor was the first to move and understand out of everyone there. He looked at Quirk and grinned, "So the boy detoxed the bullshit out of you!" and Razor laughed. "Now hopefully you got some power and a decent damn guitar weapon. Good ax, that Martin, now put on some silver strings and let's set up a strategy! We got a war to win, so get with it.

Quirk slowly set up, feeling unusual. He felt younger and more vibrant. He grabbed the guitar with a newfound significance. He now had a weapon to replace the cumbersome spook-splitter. He strummed the guitar feeling its power. He was standing on top of Mount Everest, only a mountain climber, or poor musician would understand.

The power was always there, lying dormant, but now it was boosted a thousand-fold. The musical connection from person to instrument was deep and personal with multiple memories. It was like before he had been playing mired in a vat full of molasses. He fingers felt quicker, he could fight and kill faster.

Quirk was now a legitimate certified and newest guitar ghost fighter. Razor, Bayou, Mist, and Hendrix, who was now dead, were the only previous guitar ghost fighters who had ever lived.

He could feel the guitar. It was a new, yet familiar feeling.

He had an affinity for his ax, his mistress for years. He had caressed the neck and knew the feel the guitar from long years of mutual wear and tear on each other.

The only difference now was that he knew that if a bad ghost surfaced, he could kill it by strumming the right licks. He could turn music emotion into energy. After two hundred and fifty years it was about damn time. He smiled, he was the only Director in history to have this power, and then he frowned. It might not be enough. The shit was about to hit the fan. He glanced at the Martin and decided that he and the guitar shared enough history to go down together. It was a hell of a lot better instrument of destruction than the spook splitter.

He stretched feeling healed and replenished. Now, where the hell was J.D. when he needed her? Certain thoughts and actions would have to wait; he didn't have time, dammit.

Chapter 26

Mist raised the Bloodstone over Cornelius and made the contact to fix his broken bones. The Bloodstone choreographed a deep red light crisscrossing over Cornelius's body.

He awoke instantly and knocked her across the room with a pure reactive instinctive mode. His power was beyond belief.

The Bloodstone, though, reacted and created a cushion and she intuitively made all three guitars focus their destructive energy on Cornelius. She was the only person alive who could harness the energy of the Bloodstone and the now three guitars.

He froze, she froze, and all ghost fighters froze. Cornelius saw the three guitars facing him and backed down.

He looked at Mist and apologized. "I'm sorry, please heal me."

Mist, looking petite, feminine, with her understanding hazel eyes stared back at him. She raised her hands and started the process. Cornelius joined in. She realized that he was the heir successor to the Bloodstone if anything happened to her. Together, working with him, they healed his broken arm and cracked ribs.

The whole interaction took only about one minute.

Cornelius stood up and looked around to the faces of the ghost fighters and squad leaders of the best fighting forces on the planet.

He walked over to Quirk's Martin and waved his hand, an emerald-green light sprung from his fingers and the strings turned pure silver.

Quirk smiled, "Nice trick, kid."

Razor smiled also, taking it all in. "While you are at it, Cornelius, redo these strings in case we get in a battle. We don't need any broken strings today." Cornelius looked at Razor. Razor stared back with gun metal gray eyes of the wolf. Razor brought new meaning to the old "if looks could kill" with his "don't ever fuck with me" expression. He held up his guitar unflinching at Cornelius's stare. It would take more than a mean stare to back him up. Razor suffered no bullshit from anyone and that included a raw Magi.

Bayou walked over joining his dad with his spunky psychedelic guitar held up too. Razor's thinking was logical to everyone present. If Cornelius had powers, it wouldn't hurt to do a little preventive maintenance on the guitars before battle. Cornelius looked preoccupied but fulfilled the request. His red eyes started to glow with simmering intensity. With both hands raised to shoulder height, a ruby red bolt sprung from his hands, streaking towards the guitars. Cornelius provided the guitars with renewed energy and superior power. His left hand focused on Razor's ax and his right on Bayou's. Each guitar manifested their individual signatures. Razor's Esquire radiated a deep pearl blue and Bayou's glistened with an intense white heat.

Finished, Cornelius tired red eyes looked at Oswalt who had joined the ghost fighters.

He whispered quietly and controlled.

"Please, if there are no more requests, take me to where Leslie's body is; I need to contact it to do what I have to do.

No one moved or said anything except Razor. "I don't know what kind of bizarre mental landscape you got going on in that head of yours, but I do have a question."

Everyone paused. Razor walked right up to Cornelius, "Did Leslie tell you to do that?"

Cornelius met the stare. Razor reminded him of one of his best coaches. He almost said, "Yes, Coach!"

"Yes," Cornelius said, "I can hear her at times from the other side."

Razor spoke without hesitation, "Then let's get him there quickly, he has already given us another weapon in the battle by enabling Quirk to use his guitar. If he can help my dead daughter, then let's get going."

Quirk, with the guitar strapped to his back, looked now exactly like the pose Razor and Bayou normally wore.

Armed with their guitars, Quirk surveyed the situation, "Cornelius, Mist, Razor, and Bayou, go to Leslie's body. I will stay here for the moment with Oswalt and direct our security forces for any more incoming pro-ghost attacks."

Beth's voice came over Quirks and Oswalt's tele- connection.

"Bad news, we had a report that more pro-ghost forces are going to attack at midnight tonight."

Oswalt spoke first, "Did you leak the Pierre video to the press?"

"Yes," she said, "I am hoping that that will prevent future attacks, but it sounds like this one was already prepared in case the first one failed. From what the President's information sources tell us, the Forces are going to launch rockets, mortars and then invade. Numbers are predicted to be three hundred."

"Any good news?" Quirk asked, sounding irritated.

"Yes, they think they have a fix on where they are holing up and plan on a raid at dusk. That's all the information we have."

Everyone had been standing close enough to hear the conversation.

Razor said, "Let Pierre do sentry duty, promise him for every bastard he kills I will share one of my secret recipes."

Before anyone could do anything, Pierre materialized right in front of them.

Cornelius almost fainted. The others were used to ghosts and used to Pierre.

Pierre hugged Razor before Cornelius could use his ghost destroying powers. He couldn't afford to take a shot at Pierre without hitting the old ghost fighter. It didn't matter anyway. In total amazement he watched the interaction in shock.

"You meant it, you really meant it!" Pierre had the biggest grin a ghost had ever been recorded showing.

Razor looked at him with a competency look. "Now look Pierre, you must kill the bastards first, and to get my best recipes you have to kill them slow and gory right in front of the other stupid bastards. Do you understand?"

"Sure," Pierre laughed, "just repeat what I did earlier but make the anti-cooking bastards know how much we hate them."

"That's right; the son-of-bitches will probably go after the kitchen first!"

"Oh," Pierre gasped and turned mean orange. "I swear to you Razor I will slow cook and roast the bastards that are trying to stop our cooking. I will go on Perimeter search right now," and he looked mischievous, "if I do a real good job I want the corn bread recipe first, you sly old devil. You know that, and your banana pudding I lust after."

With that he faded away.

Everyone spoke at the same time. Razor shut them all up, including Cornelius.

All who knew him knew exactly what he was going to say but might as well get it out into the open, especially in front of Cornelius who didn't understand Razor's value system.

"Look," he said facing Oswalt and Quirk. "Pierre doesn't need sleep. If he thinks they are breaking in here to destroy our kitchen, so be it. He and I will work it out later. Just be thankful that the son-of-a bitch is on our side. With these pro-ghost morons, it's either be killed or kill them. We don't have time for frigging around here. Let's kill all the bastards, period. Subject closed."

Bayou laughed at the look on Cornelius's face. "It's okay, we use whatever we have available. I have been thinking of getting some really bad guitar players and loud drummers and sending them to torture the ghosts. Maybe they could play a shitty rendition of 'Ghost Riders in the Sky' and make the ghosts embarrassed to come into this dimension." Everyone laughed at the same time.

Quirk added his two cents, "Maybe we could send some white lightning over to their dimension and get them ripped. Like the Trojan horse, we could put a keg in every graveyard and invite them to have a drink. Ha!" Again, they all laughed.

Mist threw in her two cents, "How about giving them all a case of diarrhea. Did you know that was the number one cause of death in the Civil War?" She laughed, "If we could somehow introduce a spirit infectious diarrhea that would put them in a shitty mood to fight."

It felt good for a mini-tension relief moment for the ghost fighters.

With that Razor grabbed Cornelius and said "Leslie is buried this way, let's get going. If you are bullshitting me kid, I am going to ram this guitar up your ass, understand."

Cornelius had never been talked to like this. Bayou could see this truth and grinned. Being raised by the old bastard you grew to love him and his black and white way of dealing with reality. He usually was right, but blunt. He never asked anything, he gave ultimatums.

There was no doubt in anyone's mind that if Cornelius was lying about the Leslie connection, he would need a proctologist to help remove the guitar out of his ass. Razor didn't bullshit, didn't make requests, ultimatums were his style; and Cornelius was at the epicenter of one of the biggest threats Razor had ever made.

Bayou and Mist quickly ran after Razor who was holding Cornelius by his elbow walking fast towards Leslie dead body.

Chapter 27

Oswalt directed Steve, Jade, and Jed back to research and see what the best of all possible weapons would be.

It was immediately decided that the spook-splitter and the mini-quantum disrupters they had used in San Diego were the best bets.

The scientists went into overdrive making the devices and Jade set up a print area with instructions and found a suitable test area for the devices.

Quirk came down and called a mini conference with the appointed squad leaders. All squad leaders were given weapons according to size. The bigger ones got replicates of the spook splitter and "regular" size agents as Quirk called them got the quantum disrupters.

The leader of Alpha (CIA best) was given the tasks of monitoring international events in case the ghosts attacked someplace besides the Institute. If they survived, they might have to port immediately someplace else. The leader of Bravo (FBI best) was given domestic jurisdiction and worked closely with the President so that in case the ghosts would try to take out the White House, they could port into there.

The leader of Charlie (DEA and FDA) was given the task of tracking and monitoring any leads on the upcoming attack in coordination with the leaders of Alpha and Bravo. The leader of Delta (Army Rangers) was given full outside security. They were told to work with Quirk and Pierre. The leader of Echo (Green Berets) was given full time inside perimeter security, The leader of Foxtrot (Secret Service and the Seals) was given ghost fighter security. The Secret Service was perfect for this after protecting the President. They also knew what was at stake.

Quirk masterfully put the different plans in action and settled down to hear from Bravo and Charlie leaders any information about the upcoming attack.

Head count now at the Institute was at seven hundred bodies. The strategy for curtailing friendly fire was a nightmare within itself.

Quirk proposed and listened to the best defensive brains on the planet formulate a plan. He put the full countenance on defense.

As he told them, "Our defense might be like picking up water with a pitchfork, but we are all that is left. Let's defend mankind."

Quirk noticed that Brown was actually scared by realizing for the first-time what Quirk had been afraid of for over two hundred years. The ghosts were getting tired of playing around and were into taking over this dimension.

The leaders of Delta and Echo asked about offense.

Quirk looked maliciously over to Brown, "Wellllllll, Brown, what do you think?"

Brown actually surprised him and said the only intelligent thing anyone could say.

"We have to trust the ghost fighters; it will be a question of power, not tactics." Quirk noticed Brown's hands were shaking and his voice was quaking slightly. He looked pale and scared.

Quirk smiled at him. Brown was an asshole, no doubt, but he was right about that. It would be a question of power and Cornelius was the key. He intuitively knew it, and he hoped like all hell the kid knew what he was doing.

Quirk looked at the leaders of the best fighting forces in North American history and wished them luck. They had at best a few hours before the attack tonight and then the biggest battle in mankind's entire history tomorrow.

He smiled at all of them, because he had read that Davy Crockett had smiled at the troops in the Alamo before taking on Santa Ana. It was a glorious smile. He knew that he couldn't bullshit these people, but they understood and smiled back. Leadership is taking on the task that no one else wants and make sure to go down smiling with the ship.

It was one big smile fest that would be contagious. Quirk felt the best he had felt in over two hundred years. This was his destiny; this was his fate. He grabbed the Martin and walked out to see if Razor had killed the young upstart yet.

Chapter 28

The ghost fighters walked into the rotunda where Leslie was entombed in the white marble casket rising off the floor. Agents were scurrying around, not paying them much attention. Jade set up a video camera to record the event.

"Yes," Cornelius said. He looked at Razor as if asking "do you need an explanation of what I am about to do?" Obviously, he didn't know Razor, who either totally trusted you or didn't trust you at all.

Razor said, "Damn get on with it, son, we are losing valuable time." This time Cornelius almost smiled. Razor's attitude was just what he needed. No more shock guns or questions, just get on with it. He raised his hands and emerald-green fire ripped the white marble coffin in two. Shreds went everywhere.

Mist had the Bloodstone lit up like a red sun, but she didn't know what to do. The force of the explosion had made Bayou and Razor cock their guitars into fighting stance automatically. They all poised and watched as the cloud of dust settled. They all stared in shock and disbelief. Suspended in mid-air was Leslie's body.

The agents who had been in the room were professionally trained and had their guns out. Like the ghost fighters they were stunned and not sure who to fire on. All guns, Bloodstone and guitars were focused on Cornelius. One wrong move and he was dead. End of story.

He seemed unaware of anyone but Leslie. He floated her body over and had it come to rest right beside him at waist level.

Leslie's face looked composed, and the big hole in her side where the Magi had killed her brought tears to all ghost fighters. Except Razor, who got a pissed off look on his face.

"Hurry up, I don't like to see my daughter like this in front of a bunch of strangers." Cornelius nodded.

With no hesitation, he put both hands on her suspended head and asked Mist to feed him the power of the Bloodstone.

He then asked Bayou and Razor to add their guitar energy to the Bloodstone and focus on him. A wind kicked in and mystical forces were being brought into play. They all felt it. Cornelius was going to try to go through the lost death dimensions to contact Leslie. His green light kept dancing on her head making her head looked like it was full of caged green lighting.

The wind was now at full gale force, yet Cornelius kept it up. He screamed as the united energies of the ghost fighters channeled through him. They all trusted him, he knew, but this was harder than he thought. He contacted the dimension, but now he was looking for Leslie.

He found her fighting the Magi, surrounded by six figures, as the death squad resonated through his brain. Her spirit was almost totally destroyed, yet she was still fighting. He realized that this was a different Magi than the one that had killed her. They must have been successful in killing the one in Charleston.

"Leslie!" he yelled, and through her eyes gave her all the energy he had pent up. They made contact. All the ghost fighters saw what Cornelius was seeing. Leslie was fighting with her natural strength. Cornelius comprehended instantly that she had been more powerful than he had realized. The Bloodstone had just been a talisman, she was a raw Magi herself, to be able to fight this long.

Leslie took on the red, green, blue energies flowing into her. She shot them straight into the orange- black death flames the Magi was pointing at her. She swelled and shot her best shot. The Magi reeled and Leslie yelled "Watch out, I am coming through!"

Like a bullet train she shot through the portal and entered the room knocking everyone over. Six dark figures chased her from the other side of the portal. The portal closed behind her and the implosion knocked everyone into the closest wall. With relief Jade realized that the six figures hadn't made it through. Her brain went into overdrive. She thought she could identify the six figures, the Magi death squad. If her insights were correct, the Magi had pulled the worst evil figures in history as his henchmen.

All was silent. An eerie quiet filled the room. Quirk, from the other room, heard the explosion and ran as fast as he could. His guitar lit up strung across his back and automatic energy reaction brought his body up to fight, a cursory reflex from too many battles. He listened intently as he ran, listening for a trap. He entered the room and saw a memory he would never forget. Guitars, Bloodstone, and four passed out breathing bodies, plus one see-through body with the back turned towards him with what appeared to be a big hole in its side. Quirk had seen too many ghosts and their wounds to give it any significance. Kneeling over one of the bodies was a ghost. The ghost appeared to be a female ghost.

Quirk unconsciously threw his guitar to the front and positioned his guitar to kill it. He focused and nothing happened. The female ghost turned around with tears in her eyes, leaving the dead body to face him. "Hi Quirk, long time, no see, did you miss me?"

Quirk stared in disbelief. The same dress, the same impish smile, the same look of respect and disrespect at the same time. Leslie stood up and opened her arms, "Come pain or shine, I'm back!" She grinned and started floating towards him.

Quirk looked at the actual dead body with the big hole and then looked at the ghost. The hole was still there. His saw white spots in front of his eyes and his knees felt weak. She stopped two inches from his face. The whole room went dizzy, and he knew that something was really wrong with this picture. It couldn't be, he had seen her die, he had brought back her body. For the first time in his life, Quirk passed out from pure shock.

Chapter 29

J.D. looked around. Damn, she thought. Somehow, though, she wasn't shocked, it was like this was normal. Passed out bodies and floating ghosts were now becoming a "normal" part of her reality. J.D. looked at Leslie floating over Quirk's body. Even though he had passed out, he was already stirring. Those old fighting instincts resurfaced.

J.D. rushed over to him with smelling salts that she pulled out of her emergency bag.

"Come on baby," she cooed, "time to wake up."

Quirk took a whiff and shot straight up. "Shit, he stammered, how about a kiss on old Terra Quirk" and pointed to his lips. "I'll need an infusion of J.D. Cajun magic lip mojo. Hell, if you kiss me, I'll even play you my favorite song, it's called 'Tulips on my' .... he stopped, looking at Leslie's floating ghost.

She smiled, not taking her eyes off of his, "Don't have time sweetie, the world is ending in about 30 hours. Once you save the world, I might think about it! If you manage not to get yourself killed."

"Wellllllll, if I save the damn planet, I sure as hell better earn a kiss," he laughed, and they hugged, and she gave him a quick peck on the lips.

J.D. then walked over and put the smelling salts under each of the ghost fighters. After they all revived, the agents congregated around Quirk.

Quirk went back into his black operations template, seeing the faces and knowing leadership was what was needed in this moment.

He was distracted by the addition of the guitar to the offensive and had to separate the black operations part of him versus the wet operations, on wanting to strictly plan a mystical psy-operation.

Suddenly, a Claxton rocked the room. They all gave each other deep looks. It was time to face the enemy.

Chapter 30

A noise penetrated through the chamber, followed by earpiece activation. Beth Jones' voice came blasting through everyone's earpiece, shocking everyone caught up in the Death Squad conversation. "Company coming in. Looks like it is another group of 'pro ghost' forces attacking the perimeter, approximately three hundred bodies at first count. It is a full three sixty attack."

There was a pause. "Foxtrot reports a portal opening up in Oswalt's office." Cornelius, Leslie and Mist were instantly lit up by the Bloodstone shooting out three beams connecting the ghost and two ghost fighters. They militantly flared a god-awful mélange of blue-white energy exploding around them.

Leslie's ghost yelled out, "It is the Magi death squad. He is sending them in as a precursor invasion force before tomorrow's full invasion. We will meet them now, they cannot be allowed to port in. They will send half of their squad into Quirk's office. They are trying to knock out the authority beforehand."

With that Mist looked at Bayou as they were disappearing, "I love you Dad," and then she was gone.

All three guitars began to glow a blue-white aura. In a swirling wind they were disappearing along the ghost fighters through a red portal created by the Bloodstone.

Quirk yelled to the agents, “Split in half and cover both offices, check on the operation of your new weapons with Steve Johnson or Jed.

With that all disappeared into a red port that swallowed them whole.

Chapter 31

Razor saw the port first and lay down the cover fire. The port opened even further with three figures materialized.

Razor peppered and fried the portal with a lethal blast of deadly guitar lightning into the poltergeists.

The dark mysterious-looking Death Squad ghosts were quivering in and out of reality started immediately returning fire. A stench dispatched itself with a sickly sulfur smell. It was the worst stench any of them had ever been exposed to in their collective ghost fighting experience. The menacing bastards from hell were shooting back reddish orange beams from the deadly portal.

Razor in his typical kill first, ask questions later, yelled, "Alright bastards, you have just the number spot in the jackpot of things pissing me off. I am going to fry each of you bastards for killing my daughter. Shit, I only hope some of you ghosts are lawyers and politicians. Hell yeah," as he stood up and ran straight at the portal firing the Fender hot blue-white guitar blasts. He was laughing maniacally as he searched for the enemy.

A massive, horned beast with red scales, yellow eyes, and razor-sharp teeth appeared and popped out of the portal. He held a huge axe above him, and his roar was deafening. He was the leader of the evil soldiers. He led the charge through the portal.

Razor had a huge grin and screamed with rage as he blasted him with a blast of light that knocked his axe out of his clawed hands. He charged at Razor with his huge teeth exposed, a mouth the size of a wheelbarrow. Several others appeared behind him.

Bayou and Quirk, a second behind Razor, fired both guitars seeing the pure destructive force of one pissed off Razor Savage. The ghosts were gobbling up Razor's blast with little effect.

Bayou and Quirk shot each a mini look of "Shit, they must have brought the 'A' game." The Death Squad was indeed powerful and was meeting the guitar attack with no problem.

Quirk thought to himself to give Jade a raise if they lived through this. Johnson was a lucky man to have her in his life.

Lights, noise and horrible stenches filled the room.

Razor and Bayou both levitated, flanking the ghosts, leaving Quirk as the center point. All three commanded their guitars to ramp up to full volume, full power, full retribution mode.

The three ghosts stayed centered, firing orange- black tendrils back at the ghost fighters.

Mystical energy squirted into a myriad of colors of attack and defend as the forces sided off. Razor stopped short, hitting some kind of force field. His anger, though, kept the attacking poltergeists in place. No living or dead witnesses had witnessed his rage at this description.

The hideous creature with the axe reappeared and looked smugly at Razor, smirking, and saying. "You have no chance, human. I will eat your liver."

Another burst of deep rage took over, and Razor knew there was no holding back now. Glaring and growling, Razor hit him again right in the throat, and he collapsed and imploded.

Quirk felt the radiant connection to the guitar and was having a hard time staying focused. The guitar power was enlightening and intoxicating. The color undertones turned into overtones with faster picking. Quirk had never played this fast in his life.

A slender, winged woman with pale skin, black hair, and purple eyes, wearing a dark cloak and carrying a dagger, floated into view. When she popped through the portal, the crew was overwhelmed by suddenly seeing illusions all around them of steaming piles of lava and smoldering trees, with the stench of sulpher like a volcanic eruption. She laughed wickedly. "Now I will sing your death song!" she crowed triumphantly.

A slender, hooded figure appeared, with red eyes and a raspy voice. He emanated pure evil. He held a staff to summon forth more of his evil powers, that glowed deep dark-red and orange. He raised his arm to point the staff at them, and the combined forces of the three ghosts were growing in strength minute by minute.

It was looking desperate for all of them, with the demons howling through the portal waiting for their moment to deliver the ghost fighters to the Magi.

The guitars picked up more volume. They shot off rounds of brilliant light straight into the group of ghosts, as the ghost fighters realized they needed to make a move they hadn't ever imagined before. They looked at each other and each could feel the energy of the others. They all knew that Razor would lead the charge.

The ghosts appeared to be agitated, but they were not backing off.

To Bayou they looked like they were reforming their battle plan. Razor had probably not been accounted for in their original plans.

The ghosts decided to attempt a different tack and combined their powers for one blast. They went after Razor, who was moving inch by inch closer firing pure white light.

Bayou saw it and yelled too late. Razor, though, had seen it and levitated up above it. The act only incubated his rage even more. He fired pure rage into them. He yelled, "Come on you see through pricks, is that all you got?" He was far past any form of reason.

Bayou caught on that the ghosts were almost immune to Razor's homicidal onslaught. Bayou was on the verge of pouring more energy into the flanking move. His quality analysis experience surfaced running an algorithm of a missing link. This attack would not work this way. He thin sliced his logic trying to find the missing link.

The putrid stench, the chorus of tortured, screaming anguish of demons in the background, all this was old news. He was not distracted like he had been in his earlier battles.

He kept firing, pouring his physical energy into the guitar and allowed his mind to do the only thing that would work.

He ran a quick "design of experiments" scenario. The screening template was down, and it was time to directly manipulate variables to test cause-and-effect relationships, e.g. alter the music. He figured he had enough time for one mistake, but not two. First attempt, try their own force technique on them and see if the ghosts could handle their own offensive technique of centralizing fire power into a focused blast. He had an epiphany with the thought; all play the same song, same key, same pace.

He yelled to Quirk, “Switch to ‘Eight More Miles to Louisville’ in key of C, open picking. Match Dad’s pace.”

Quirk understood, he wasn’t complaining about direction. He was barely hanging on to this type of wet-ops guitar-offensive operation. The power of the guitar was addictive, but the ghosts had figured out how to nullify their powers. He, like Razor did not believe in faith, he had to do something else to take the offensive. Right now, it was a stalemate, until that last blast that had nearly taken out Razor.

Also, he was having a hard time neutralizing the stench. The damn odor was making him want to vomit.

The female demon kept smiling at them, her wicked eyes glowing brighter somehow. She seemed like the most terrifyingly evil of the group, despite her small size.

Quirk avoided her gaze and focused on the attack plan, and he switched gears instantly.

He, like Razor and Bayou, played guitar by ear. He immediately closed his eyes and focused all his energies, flowing into Razor licks. He could hear Bayou already synching into the song. He silenced his fear of being blasted and stayed on the offensive. He finally felt it; the three guitars all playing the same song, note for note, lick for lick. If the old guitar player Merle Travis was alive, he would be in seventh heaven.

Razor unconsciously managed to suck the entire tour de force and close the gap until the head of the guitar was inches away from the scowling ghosts.

Bayou levitated until he was directly behind Razor, feeding his energy into the glowing and throbbing guitar. Quirk, who didn't have the levitation technique down, ran over and fed his energy, mimicking Bayou.

Razor screamed, "You bastards helped kill her!" Then Razor accomplished a first in guitar history. In his rage he kept feeding his anger. Leslie screamed, "Daddy!" and it drove him over the edge.

He didn't think about it, he manipulated the energy the same way he did at the Whaley House in San Diego when he had pulled energy out of the Bloodstone. His rage went pure primal, he looked the death squad directly in the eyes, and totally took over all three guitars. In a sudden blink, Bayou and Quirk felt the pull of Razor. Both surrendered their power to him and fed him the energy letting him be the rudder to point the power. The heat surrounding them felt like a furnace. The stench was becoming more powerful.

Razor was beyond stench; he was beyond human. The bastards had killed his daughter, and this was his moment of grief. He poured all his energy, all his frustration, all his incredible anger into the guitar. All three guitars redefined their relationship to their hosts. His anger was a fixed point of vengeance.

He screamed L---e---s----l---i---e!!! and concentrated the final blast. They all felt it, Bayou poured his anger, fueling Razor's, and Quirk felt it and joined in. They both yelled her name discharging all the feeling into the rebel vengeance yell.

A sudden change in air pressure and the first death squad member, in front of the other two, the horned beast, imploded. His beady eyes caved in with the rest of his face. The hooded figure was next, screaming in an unknown language as the guitar force imploded him. The winged female smiling, turned her back to Razor. The look and arrogant smile in body language translated to "You wouldn't kill a woman with her back to you, you are the good guys!"

Razor didn't hesitate, letting the Fender guitar neck head pierce the back of the last standing death squad member. As the Fender penetrated, its mystical energy torched and burnt a hole right through the deadly ghost. She turned with a last wicked smile, like something was really funny, and finally vaporized. The last implosion rocked the room.

The guitar was still intact with dark smoke vapor trails coming off the head and neck and the glow started to fade.

Razor levitated back down looking totally out of control. He looked for more ghosts. "Where are the rest of you, you coward son of bitches? Where are the last three?" He scanned the room with a murderous look. Bayou had never seen him this far gone.

"Where are you Magi, come out you son-of-a-bitch!" Razor pointed his guitar, but the magic safety kicked in and the guitar glow faded to normal.

Pure primal instinct now. Bayou and Quirk saw it for what it was.

Bayou walked over and put his hand on the old guitar player's shoulder. Quirk realized that Bayou was probably the only person in the world who could get to Razor in this state.

"Dad, let's go check on Mist, she might need us. They might be trying to kill her; we don't have time to stay here and keep looking for them." Razor turned around, realizing that another family member, another Savage, needed him. He excommunicated the fury and redirected it in a typical Razor rant.

"Good," Bayou thought, "keep him focused."

They all three ran out of Quirk's office and ran towards Oswalt's hoping they wouldn't have to be attending another funeral. Two funerals in one day would be two too many.

Chapter 32

J.D. looked at the results. She checked and double checked. Something was wrong. She had checked Cornelius's DNA from his hair and the sample of his mouth. The last test would be a fingernail clipping DNA test. The blood tests also matched her suspicions.

She ran it and held her breath. The results came back the same.

There was no doubt. Cornelius was the son of two of the staff here at the Institute. It made no sense. She reached over and looked against the two biological parents' medical files. Same DNA, same blood types, it all matched up except for the social history of the two. She had known both for a long time and this really made no sense. As far as she knew they couldn't stand each other and had never been intimate. If they had, the information had never prevailed on the Institute gossip grapevine.

This was serious trouble with a capital T. The consequences of this information going public would be a brew of strong feelings. She reached over to call Quirk. He didn't answer so she left a message.

This was going to a hell of an announcement for someone. She was sure Cornelius didn't know who either of his real parents was. He would have already discovered and dealt with the situation. He could. There was nobody who could stop him.

But he had said his real parents were Jacob and Leah. She had researched it and yes, the birth certificates stated the same.

Then out of a hunch, she decided to do a search on the net on Cornelius and see if anything popped up.

She saw the third article and almost fainted. The time and location were perfect. All the pieces came together, except the how.

The Antichrist? Cornelius had been born to mother who had had a full hysterectomy. This was impossible. Not only had she regrown her uterus but had delivered a healthy son.

The media report stated that she had reported waking up three months pregnant with no idea how she got that way.

J.D. understood. She didn't know how either, but she did know who. That who was going to be a bombshell that she didn't want to ignite.

She put the results back in the folder and put the file in her private office drawer. This would not be put back in the public folders, screw the policy.

Cornelius, Mist and Leslie entered the room through the portal, smelling the stench first. Three ancient beings, the other half of the death squad, were already there, and dead agent bodies were strewn all over. It looked like hell had visited the Secret Service agents. Body parts were strewn all over, no elixir would help this much damage. Mist said under her breath, "This is sucktastic!"

The ghosts were busy wrecking the lab, tipping over tables and ripping out wires. They didn't see the ghost fighters until it was too late.

Mist seized the moment. She fired, first taking the Savage normal course of action, throwing red balls of fire straight at them. An orange shield surfaced deflecting the fireball. She closed her palms into fists and kept peppering the force field looking for a weak spot. Cornelius smiled. He looked at Leslie.

Leslie said "Mist, both of you direct your energy into me."

Mist froze. Her brain temporally scrambled. She had accepted it was Leslie, the Leslie, her aunt, the aunt who had died protecting her grandfather.

Mist's brain tried to emancipate the fright and reconcile the facts. She froze, what little bit of training she had received from Quirk stuck in her brain. Listening to Bayou, she knew that Leslie was now an "entity" with physical and verbal manifestations. Leslie was a ghost. The ghost was the enemy.

Leslie could table tip, levitate objects, set off ectoplasmic emissions, teleport, do materializations, create automatic writings, and Mist's brain hurt.

Her brain was still functioning, she felt the oxygen intake. She knew she was alive. She was curious why Leslie was clothed in the same exact clothes as when she had died.

Mist heard laughter and as she hesitated, one of the death squad disappeared. "Shit!" she heard Leslie scream, "both of you focus your energy on me."

Mist gave in to the command, as did Cornelius who was still freaking on being in battle. He was scared beyond his control.

He knew the death squad was the opening act for the Magi, the Magi who had killed Leslie.

They both focused their energy into Leslie and for a second it looked like she was receiving the energy salvation she needed to vanquish the squad.

Then it faded. Leslie screamed in frustration. She realized too late that as a ghost, she could no longer absorb their mystical energies.

“Mist, feed Cornelius your energy. Now!” she commanded, realizing that being a ghost was affecting her use of the Bloodstone energy.

Mist reacted out of pure instinct and used the Bloodstone’s energy to channel the pure red energy into him. Cornelius understood instinctively. The Bloodstone energy without constraints fed into him and he soaked it up like a battery.

He then channeled the energy of the Bloodstone. It felt intimate. He cherished the feeling, soaking up the power. He then felt the purpose that he had been designed for his whole life. It was the moment he knew was coming, and with no hesitation, he started to glow.

The two-member death squad ghosts saw what was happening and immediately fired orange tendrils straight into Cornelius. They ignored Mist, and Leslie’s ghost, and concentrated their energies into him.

Cornelius laughed, now the mystery was over. He laughed like he had never laughed. The power was intoxicating. His whole life had been one of cloak and dagger, now that was in the past. He was the frigging Magi.

He was glowing bright green and Bloodstone red. Mist kept pouring her energies, all her energies straight into him. He had been a long-lost power of humanity and was now found.

Leslie kept up her own barrage against the combined energies of the remaining two members of the death squad. Cornelius loved the feeling of understanding and finally feeling the power of being a natural Magi. With the strength of the Bloodstone, he felt invincible.

He exercised his full power and fired the red-green power sandwich straight into the ghosts. The ghosts screamed and imploded. The sounds of their screams were that of torture. "Cornelius must have used the full power of the Bloodstone," Mist thought, because she smelled orange blossoms all around her.

Leslie didn't hesitate; "Quick! Port us into the lab, that is where the other death squad disappeared to."

With no hesitation Mist recaptured the Bloodstone energy and ported them straight into Steve Johnson's lab, where she knew Steve, Jade and Jed were. Why the hell would a ghost death squad member port there?

Chapter 33

Steve Johnson was talking with Jed and Jade about Cornelius's power. Steve reviewed the facts that there were only two types of neural connectivity that Cornelius's power could be based upon. He was debating the neuroanatomical and neurofunctional and getting passionate with an arguing Jed.

Steve, laughing, looked away from Jed, who always warmed to a good argument, and started explaining to Jade. The argument boiled down to the difference that Steve believed Cornelius's power came from the neuroanatomical connectivity between Cornelius's brain areas. Jed believed that Cornelius's power came from the neurofunctional connectivity of Cornelius's brain functional connectivity.

Jade was lost in all of this. Jed made matters worse discussing the hypnopompic and hypnagogic experiences that he thought Cornelius was producing.

As she listened to Jed go on this technological tangent, she looked around at all the scientists. Most had on the "Billy the Kid" gun belts loaded with the lethal black Quantum Blasters guns Steve had invented. The whole lab looked like an old Western movie, "Scientists Gone Wild" scenario.

She stopped. Something pricked her spine. She had the feeling that something bad was about to happen.

They all felt the static and smelled the stench at the same time. The air pressure changed, and Steve automatically knew what it was before anyone else.

The damn dream was coming true. A ghost was surfacing just like in the dream, and he guessed he knew exactly where it was going to port in at.

He spun around trying to get an exact fix on Leslie. The Bayou imprint kicked in full alert. Steve knew for one hundred percent sure that a portal was opening, what he didn't know was whether it was a positive or negative force coming through.

Jed yelled as a portal opened right next to him, and before anyone could move an ethereal orange-black outlined ghost hand snuck out and grabbed Jade by the neck.

Jade screamed and tried to turn around to claw and scratch whatever was choking her.

In what seemed like slow motion, the head of the female demon emerged from the portal and looked leering at Jade as she kept squeezing her neck, strangling her blood and oxygen flow.

Steve didn't hesitate. In one smooth move, like a scene from a Western; he reached his right hand down. He was now Bayou Savage, he didn't have the guitar, but he had the quantum disruptor. He knew exactly what to do and knew he only had one chance to do this right.

He looked at Jade screaming, he couldn't hear her anymore. He saw Jed going for his gun and missing it. Jed's hand went too far outside and flew past the holstered gun.

Steve didn't miss. With the experience of an old-time gunfighter, the gun was drawn out in one fluid lightning second, the gun hand was extended low with an imaginary line straight into the center of the ghost's forehead. No hesitation as he shot from the hip. With all the scientists watching, he shot again. The gun had fired two shots in three tenths of a second.

The first blast hit the ghost right between the eyes. The second shot followed the exact path as the first, blowing the ghost's head into an orange ectoplasm hell. The head stay suspended for a second, and then the body imploded upon itself. The experience felt good to Steve, he almost imagined smoke coming off the gun.

He froze for one intimate frightened moment.

He looked for another portal to open; he was now in full Bayou imprint. He snarled and growled, unaware that the other scientists were looking at him. In a low fluid spin on one heel, he rescanned the room looking for a hint of a ghost.

Gone was the pragmatic, logical Steve Johnson. Here was the new scientist ghost fighter. He came up slowly, still on his heels and walked rapidly to Jade.

The other scientists looked in awe as he did a final scan and then dropped to her side.

She stirred and looked into his eyes. Then and only then did he resurface to his old natural self. "What happened?" she coarsely whispered.

They felt the portal open next to them and before anyone could move Steve did a backflip and came up with the gun aimed directly into Mist Savage's frightened eyes.

"Lighten up, Steve! It's me, Mist!"

"Ohhhh Baby, I am so sorry."

Mist saw it wasn't Steve speaking but Bayou, her father. The look, the voice, he was in total Bayou imprint.

"It's OK," she thought quickly, "better talk to him as Steve and see if I can bring him back." She thought all of this in a microsecond.

"No problem, what happened in here? One of the death squad ghosts got away from us and we followed it here after we killed her two friends."

Steve was putting the gun away and walking back to Jade. Jade was staring at Steve. His eyes looked like two bonfires erupting pure energy.

She gently said his name; she had recognized the same thing that Mist had. That Steve had finally given in to his long battle of fighting the Bayou imprint. She felt a cold chill as he touched her. Was he Bayou or Steve?

"Steve, Steve, I am okay. You did what you had to do." Tears started coming down from her eyes. The scientists started looking away. No one had ever seen Jade cry. She was tough, and out of respect they looked the other way to give her a moment of privacy.

Steve looked down in confusion. Why was she crying? He had killed the damn ghosts, what was her problem? He didn't understand.

"I am okay, nothing's wrong with me, it surprised me how lucky I was."

"Yeah," she said without looking at him. It was worse than she thought. He didn't even realize that he had turned into Bayou and was now backing into his Steve mode.

She glanced at Mist who had the look of "don't tell him." If anybody knew what was happening it was Mist. Being Bayou's daughter, it had unnerved her the few times she had seen him fighting the imprint. When he turned into Bayou, he was damn good at it. If not for the physical differences, she couldn't have been able to tell the difference. He literally turned into Bayou.

Steve surfaced and slowly looked around the room.

Jed walked over, breaking the tension.

"Damn good shot, but I had the situation under control, you only beat me by a second!" he had that big grin of his plastered on his face, giving unconditional support to his friend and boss.

Steve understood in a flash.

"Jed it wasn't me, it was the Bayou imprint. But thank God it worked; first time it ever served me any good." With that he put on his own self-effacing grin.

"Damn, it is a good time to be screwed up." He said it with an air of someone who has made peace with themselves.

Chapter 34

The battle was in full force outside. Two full hours had already been fought. The right wing of the Institute was destroyed. The scientists kept working through it all. The elixir making was being used as fast as they could reproduce it.

Steve thought to himself, "The elixir was supposed to be used when the ghosts attacked, not on agents being attacked by fellow humans." He knew they were misguided and in survival mode. For whatever reason they thought attacking the Institute would change the ghost attack outcome.

For the first time the ghost fighters were useless. The guitars would not work on fellow humans, however evil they were. The secret service agents had them surrounded and started moving everyone over to the left wing for safety.

The President was sending backup and the pro- ghost forces were also accepting support just as fast. The Institute was now the sole focus of world news.

The President was going on the air with hourly announcements. The world was watching the West fall apart. The President had the Joint Chief of Staff, all the Directors funneling all resources to the Institute.

The Asheville Airport had been taken over with constant supplies being flown in to support the Institute. The Greenville and Charlotte airports were also closed.

Watching the news, it reminded Razor of when back in his day, Orson Wells had done the famous "War of the World" radio announcement on Halloween. The American public had thought since it was on the radio it must be true, and a lot of people had overreacted.

Helicopters were flying over and being shot down just as fast. Each side was going for the fast knockout, winner takes all, the jackpot. Religious denominations were divided and produced the highest homicide rates attacking each other in pure chaos.

The only thing everyone agreed upon was that the San Diego ghost battle was the harbinger for the end of the world.

Razor sat back in Oswalt's office and laughed. He turned to Bayou with that familiar smile. "I bet you the NASCAR fans aren't even aware that this shit is going on and will be really mad if they cancel a race tomorrow."

His comment broke the ice among the ghost fighters. They felt powerless except for Quirk who was stationed in the set-up command center. Quirk was exercising those old military commando days. From what they heard he hadn't lost his touch.

Bayou looked around to Mist. "Sweetheart, I think it is time we make a plan for tomorrow."

Cornelius, who had been holding the Bloodstone, appeared in a trance. The smell of orange blossoms filled the air.

Leslie's ghost had disappeared after the death squad battle. She had told them she sensed something wrong and that she suspected the Magi might try to sneak in and sabotage something. She could see it, but Mist and Cornelius could not get the Bloodstone to reveal anything. The screens were empty.

Leslie had told them to stick together and then disappeared.

Bayou looked at the screen and saw her ghost flicker in front of a group of attackers flanking around to the left side. Bayou saw her raise her hand and she killed twenty pro ghost forces. He observed that she hadn't hesitated. Was she turning evil?

On another screen he saw Pierre doing the same thing, probably following Quirk's orders. Knowing Quirk, he was trying to save resources and protect loss of Institute life.

Bayou had listened and heard that reinforcements were not getting through. The Institute had been successfully surrounded by the aggressive pro- ghost forces.

The surprise attack would have probably worked if not for Leslie and Pierre. The pro-ghost forces must be in total shock of the presence of friendly ghosts. How could they keep fighting if they acknowledged that information?

The air was growing stale and felt as thick as mud. Razor turned to Cornelius. "Cornelius, use that thing and see if you can lighten up the air. The son-of-a bitches have knocked out the air system." It wasn't a request; it was a demand.

It amused Cornelius. The legend lived up to his name of no nonsense. If you have a power, it better do something practical, or to Razor it was a waste of time.

Cornelius gave the Bloodstone back to Mist and raised his hands. A green aura surrounded both hands and he removed all the negative ions and stale air by transforming the particle composition.

"That will last a few minutes until the carbon dioxide builds back up."

"Good," Razor said, without as much as a thank you. Cornelius could tell he was not impressed, but at least he wasn't at the end of the Razor stare for the cause of not being able to do something productive.

Razor turned to Oswalt and said, "Get us some cots in here." Cornelius smiled, again not a request but a command.

Oswalt turned around and the head secret service agent acknowledged that he had heard the order.

Seconds later the cots were delivered. Razor stood up and walked over to the closest cot and un- strapped the legendary 53 Fender Esquire off his broad shoulders. "Boys," he said surveying the tired faces of the last hope of the human race, "my daughter says that the big attack is coming tomorrow. I want to be awake and see the face of the Magi when I," he hesitated, feeling more tired than his seventy-five years, "when 'we' kill him. My advice is turn in, I will wake up around six and fix breakfast for us."

Bayou smiled, knowing the breakfast would be gigantic. He knew that Razor was secretly happy about being able to feed all the secret service agents too. Sometimes Bayou was envious of his father's lexicons. His passion about cooking and the enjoyment of watching people eat his cooking. Razor always overcooked, you know, just in case other people might stop by. Bayou reminisced about growing up in Waynesville, North Carolina, and the refrigerator that was always overstocked with leftovers. Marynell, his mother, didn't mind Razor's passion for cooking, probably because Razor always cleaned up his own mess. He never wanted anything to interfere with the meal for his guests, God forbid they would get up and start cleaning before fully enjoying the meal.

Bayou smiled and knew that Razor was right, rested minds made better decisions. He walked over to a cot close to Razor. In case of an attack Razor and he could form a defensive immediate nucleus to defend the others until they could take the offense.

Mist looked at the Bloodstone, waiting for something to happen. She desperately wanted the screens to appear and reveal her some clue on how to fight or at least a hint of what was coming. She saw red with hints of yellow floating around, but nothing surfaced. No last-minute salvation. She almost felt impotent, like a skydiver going tandem, waiting for an event to pull the string to her parachute, unleashing her power.

She walked over to the cot closest to Bayou and crashed down face first. She was tired and willed the Bloodstone to cocoon her. The smell of jasmine filled the room as she faded into peace.

Cornelius looked at all three of them fast asleep. It must be a Savage trait, though the legends said Bayou was a terrible insomniac.

Cornelius turned to Mist. He smiled; "You know your dad is a genius."

Mist glanced at him to see if he was joking. She slowly responded, "Both my parents are geniuses in my opinion."

"No," Cornelius said, "I asked Bayou a question that I have heard people argue about for years. I was curious as to his opinion."

"What was the question?" she asked, being sucked in.

"I asked him, how parents get their kids to quit doing obnoxious behavior. An iconoclastic generation problem that has bothered mankind since its beginning. Bayou asked for me to give him an example. I said, 'You're a parent and your teenager wears pants a certain way you and don't like them. All their friends wear them the same way."

Bayou laughed, 'Oh that's easy. I learned when Mist was just hitting her teenage years. Call all parents of the teenagers and have them start wearing the same clothes, the same way. The kids will be so embarrassed, that they will not be caught dead in those clothes.'"

They both laughed as they looked at Bayou.

He looked at them and appreciated the diversion. If he was going to die tomorrow it would be interesting to say the least. He ran the scenarios.

If Cornelius ended up paired up with Razor, it would be brutal and fast. First round knockout and then move on to the next battle. Bayou would be elusive and try for what he called ghost root cause. Where Razor would start on the outside and beat his way in, Bayou would try to start on the inside like a virus and beat the enemy from the inside out. He was a thinker and tried to use his quality thought process to defeat the ghosts.

Mist was Mist. Smart ass and tough, and a recycled combination of Bayou and Razor, and her mother, who Cornulius had heard was brilliant. Mist was the wild card. If she went down, she would fight until her last breath, that much he knew. He had also felt every time she had tried to get the Bloodstone to produce the screens that would inform them of the future. He felt the chronic hunger in her to impress her father and grandfather, and why not? They were truly legendary, though neither one saw themselves as legends.

He could feel the evil surfacing here. He knew the Magi was on the grounds, but he couldn't pinpoint it. Whatever was happening was under his radar screen. He could feel the ultimate evil here in the Institute. He was tired from the death squad battle and figured that Leslie would let him know. If the Magi really surfaced, he would meet him and avenge his, he thought, she would have been his mentor and he had hoped maybe more. Leslie would be avenged; he promised himself and put his brain into monitor mode. The Magi was probably doing some recon to find the ideal launch point.

When that happened, he would meet this dimension's answer to his invasion. As he heavily felt himself crashing, he gritted his teeth. Revenge would be his; he favored the Razor mode and secretly hoped he got to fight next to the old legend. He was in that kind of mood.

The senior secret service agent centrally positioned to protect his charges looked down in curiosity. Razor and Bayou were asleep with the guitars floating next to their bodies, waiting for their master's to wake up. Mist was covered in a red cocoon enshrouding her whole body and producing that pleasant smell. Cornelius was gently snoring while both hands were formed into a tight fist, both glowing bright green auras.

Meanwhile back in the lab, Steve turned the reins over to Jed. He looked at Jade with a look of a man on a sinking ship knowing that even the women didn't have lifeboats. All souls would be lost when the ship went down.

He was extremely grateful for their short time together. He was also grateful that he had made peace with his Bayou imprint. Somehow it all made sense now. Maybe it was fate, destiny, he didn't know but he appreciated saving Jade's life using the imprint.

He looked at her, her body smelled like a cinnamon perfume. He smiled.

"New perfume?"

"Yes," she smiled. "I had bought it for our first anniversary, and it was pretty expensive." She paused and he saw the tears spring up in her eyes.

Yet she stared at him. "Steve Johnson, I love you, we are going to celebrate our first anniversary a little prematurely tonight." She gave a tired, yet mischievous look at him. "I hope you don't mind, seeing how this might be our last night together and I want to spend it in your arms. I have never had an anniversary and I'll be damned if I am going to let some ghosts rob me of it."

He looked at her eyes and saw the love and longing. He couldn't help but to fall more deeply in love with this creature that had Olympic size love and caring for him.

He took her hand with the biggest natural smile he could ever remember producing. He felt excited and tried to smother all the crisis questions running around in his brain.

They both walked with amazing speed as they approached their private quarters. Tears were coming down his cheeks too, and he worked at trying to be calm and stable.

The probabilities were that she was right. They had about a 20 to 25 percent of surviving the upcoming battle, but at least they would die together. He thought her cinnamon perfume would be the perfect memory to share this special night with.

He looked at her, "I, I, ... I don't have anything for you."

She smiled at him while both saw the mutual tears coming down.

She did her best Razor imitation which always cracked them up when she did. "Bullshit, you got the bigggggggg," she hesitated with the cutest grin he had ever seen on her, "you have the biggest "heart-on" in the world and that's all this "countrrrrryyyyy girl needs!"

They stopped and kissed deeply in the hallway, not caring what people thought. It was too late for that.

They reached the door and went in, with the smell of a very expensive cinnamon perfume lingering in the hallway.

The last thing the secret service agents heard were two lovers laughing as they rushed to the bed.

Back at the ghost fighter refuge room, as it was called, the ghost fighters were sleeping.

The senior agent knew he was witnessing history and was glad they were resting. He was high enough up the chain of command to know that tomorrow would be a change to this world one way or another. The phones were all down with the battles and he knew there was no way to call his wife and son to wish them goodbye.

He wished he could say goodbye to both right now. He wished he could whisper "I love you" to his wife one last time before he met her in heaven. He had resigned himself to death; and he sent a quick prayer to God. It was the prayer of every true solder who has ever lived.

"God, please let me die with honor and face death bravely. Please make my death mean something. Thanks, if you are listening and please take care of my family for me. I appreciate it. Amen!

Chapter 35

Quirk hung up the last working phone in the Institute. The President was trying to listen but was too far away to have a true sense of what was happening here.

The President had made the decision of all presidents who must make a judgment without current information. He went with the classic decision to cut your losses.

Tomorrow at twelve, if the ghosts were not taken care of, or the ghosts attacked and breached the Institute, meaning the Institute fell to the ghosts, 3 airplanes would make this place radioactive at midnight.

Quirk knew deep in his heart that this was the last option, but he suspected that even that would just be a temporary stop. They would find another portal and after a while the whole planet would be radioactive.

He knew the President had originally thought of the ghosts as a novelty and any time he spent on it was token and a charity defensive cause. San Diego and Charleston had changed all that.

Quirk had imparted his own words to the President, "Give me until 11:59PM before you drop the bomb. I believe that we will prevail."

He didn't tell the President that he was now a fully imbued ghost fighter himself. He wasn't anxious to reveal that particular detail. The President might suspect him of losing focus and turn the whole place back over to Brown.

Quirk smiled, the last he had heard of Brown was that he was locked up in his bathroom in his private office.

Good. He was so full of shit and had proven so much trouble that he could stay in there all year for all Quirk cared.

The battle was raging on. Quirk looked at all the monitors and knew that his world was changing. He watched one monitor in particular light up with the information that five planes had just been blown up at Charleston Air Force base.

Another monitor showed military trucks being blown up on I-26 and I-40. He knew he was in one hell of a battle, and this was just the opening warm-up for the main act. It was going to be one hell of a concert, he grimly thought to himself.

He was tired; the gravity of the situation and fatigue was making his eyes shut and his headache.

He would have loved to have J.D. next to him. Somehow when he thought of her, the tension reduced, and he saw a light at the end of the tunnel.

He missed her and tried to allow himself the luxury of thinking about her. She had found him. He had forgotten to tell security about her. It pissed him off that he had forgotten to do it. That oversight meant they had lost valuable intimate time. As usual she had turned heads when she had walked into the room, and every agent had to see her identification.

She had kissed him, hugged him and walked over to the most private corner she could find. She was on her way to the emergency room ready to doctor the incoming. She had gotten serious and said, "I am going to ask you a question I have never asked anyone in my life."

"OK," he said expecting a marriage proposal. He didn't know why, but everyone knew the end was coming. He matched her intensity and looked her straight back eye to eye.

She said, "Quirk, I love you. I know you love me." She made the statement a fact, no discussion. "I am not sure if love is an action or a feeling. What do you think? It doesn't matter if we survive. I want an instant marriage and a great honeymoon. Do you accept my proposal of marriage?"

Quirk didn't hesitate, Wellllll, I love the action of feeling your butt!"

They both laughed. "Let me see if I have this right. You want to get married before we, ahhh," she was looking at him hard.

He saw that she was very serious. He felt stunned, like a driver getting pulled over for speeding by a trouper with the bright lights flashing with that really happening feeling.

He continued, "You want to get married before you even find out if I am any good in bed or not."

She met the stare and upped the ante, "Women know these things, now hurry up," she looked at her watch and backed up. "Make up your mind, I have patients to attend to."

Quirk tried to think of something snappy, something romantic, something that would say yes and make her smile.

For the first time in recorded history, Quirk was speechless. Then he shook and the swagger returned with the outlaw smile.

"Wellll, I'll be damned, where do you want to go on the honeymoon, or do I get any say in our honeymoon arrangements?"

She smiled. He smiled.

They gave each other a marriage kiss that promised so much more.

Everyone clapped, watching the incredible romantic spectacle in front of them.

J.D., the impossible catch and everyman's dream, had just proposed marriage to the ancient legendary Director. She was off the market and the news would travel fast. She stopped the kiss and gave him his final order before running out the door.

"Okay, 'Husband', don't get yourself killed till after the honeymoon, that's an order, you got it!"

"Yeah, sure," he shot her a mischievous lewd look not caring who saw it, "My desire, 'Wife', is to live long enough to tame you and that insubordinate streak you have. You have an attitude problem you know, for example, bossing Directors around. We are going to have to fix that!"

General laughter was heard all around the room. They all needed a temporary respite from the constant barrage of attack.

She pecked him on the cheek, socked him on the shoulder hard. "You rascal!" was all she said with a big smile and ran off.

Quirk knew that he would have to live another two hundred years to even get close to finding an incredible woman like her.

Oswalt saw the look and touched Quirk on the shoulder. "Take a break." He motioned to the sofa that he had brought from his office. The sofa had an aged look now. It was the first place that Leslie Quinn's body had been laid when they had ported back from Charleston.

Quirk rubbed his eyes and looked at the sofa. He was on his last leg and knew that Oswalt could handle it. The current situation was a stalemate and Pierre and Leslie had told him the situation was in control.

He made a tired decision. "Oswalt, you have the watch!" He lay on the sofa with an unstable hand and put his head on the opposite end from where he had placed her head. He couldn't put his own head there.

He swayed to his right and rolled on his side. He fell asleep immediately. The Martin guitar floated over next to him with the neck pointed out looking like a wine-colored weapon of defense. It looked like if anybody got close it might fire a bolt of energy.

The agents looked at the floating guitar in shock, not knowing what to do. The guitar had a defensive resolve as it slowly marched back and forth like it was searching for a threat. Everything was quiet but Quirk who had started a low volume snore. The agents tried to just accept it and kept looking out for anyone, anything that might present a danger to the two directors.

They all felt a sense of anticipation. They knew this was probably the last day for the human race.

Chapter 36

Leslie materialized next to Pierre.

Being a ghost was slowly sinking into her consciousness. Before she had died, she had traveled enough dimensions to be comfortable with strange environments. She could adapt to almost anything. Being a ghost, though, was a different deal.

The look that Mist had given her in the battle with the death squad confirmed that she was a ghost. Not only was she a ghost, but she was also now one of the enemies or could be classified as one of the enemies. Mist's hesitation in the battle with the death squad had almost proved lethal for all of them.

Dying was just like taking a different dimension trip, except for the minor things like losing her corporal body and finally finding the lost "death cross-over dimension" on a one-way trip.

Fighting the Magi's evil influence was the worst part. He had killed her physical body. When she crossed over into the death dimension, she found that they had killed the Magi who had killed her. She now had a hand in killing two of the most powerful evil presences in history.

The problem was that this current Magi had been waiting in the wings to take over when number two Magi had died. This third Magi was too powerful for her ghost conditional powers, but she had found out he was the last one.

If not for Cornelius and Mist she would have been assimilated into the Magi's wicked pawns, a heinous puppet to do his whims against her own family and mankind.

She quit reflecting and started focusing on the current situation. She looked at Pierre who was standing vigil at the breach in the Institute's west wall.

They both felt the dreadful badness at the same time. She turned to Pierre, "Do you feel him? She asked. Do you feel the Magi?"

Even for a ghost Pierre looked tired. They had both expended all their energies protecting the Institute. They had both killed over five hundred pro-ghost forces apiece. The irony almost made Leslie laugh.

"Yes, but I can't place it."

They both focused and tried to pinpoint the appalling evil source.

Leslie, being more powerful, looked right at the heart of the Institute. They both turned to look at each other. This was bad; whatever was happening, it was happening in the heart of the Institute. Leslie's death vision before she died was becoming reality.

"You go right, I'll go left and let's see if we can blindside him. Or if you feel any of the ghosts fighting magic, port in and I will meet you. But right now, the Magi is keeping low key like," she hesitated, "like he is spying, but not getting involved."

This made no sense to her, but the awful sick feeling was there, and she knew without any doubt that a Magi was somewhere in the heart of the Institute, but doing what?

They both split into separate directions, worried with the same question. A spying Magi made no sense.

Chapter 37

Brown sat in the bathroom, musing about his life. He was sure that in a few hours everyone would be dead, including him.

He remembered the one woman; make that "girl" who he had gotten pregnant. He never found out what happened with the kid. She hadn't kept it; he knew for sure. He had never been approached for child support and just chalked it to his kismet. He really should have handled that differently. He remembered that she had approached him three months pregnant.

He had told her, tough luck, if she was too stupid not to use birth control that wasn't his problem. It was hers so handle the situation quietly please. Don't do anything to screw up both of their careers.

She had cried and ran off. He didn't believe that she was capable of crying and blamed it on the pregnancy hormones. That spelled the end of the relationship.

It was too sad really; he liked her in a bookish kind of way. He found other conquests and soon forgot about her.

A month later, she looked fit and like she was never pregnant. He knew her too well to think that she had lied. No, she had been pregnant, but the mystery of what happened to the kid never resurfaced.

He took another shot and thought about the Institute agents he had seen ripped to pieces. The ghosts were getting meaner and more powerful.

He looked at the bottle of ancient expensive aged liquor. Why not finish the bottle since death was coming next anyway? He took another swig and noticed a faint smell in the air.

He dismissed it and took another long drink. The smell persisted and he smelled the rim of the bottle. Maybe this stuff had soured over time. It smelled like sulfur and something else.

The light dimmed in the bathroom and then came back on. He took another swig and turned to look in the mirror, maybe he was having alcohol hallucinations. His computer rebooted itself.

He flashed back to what Quirk had called this kind of event. He had said a level five proto-poltergeist could create this kind of unexplainable behavior in electrical and electronic equipment. The effects Quirk reported were flickering lights, sound systems coming on playing weird noises, phones that rang and dead relatives called. He remembered that even computers got odd errors that no programming could explain.

He felt trapped suddenly and looked at the door expecting a ghost to jump out at him.

Then he froze. Little refulgent fires broke out all over and surrounded him entirely. He stared in shock. Something was very, very wrong.

Brown starred in indelible shock. He remembered Quirk talking about that only a level five ghost could start fires. Quirk, his arch enemy now, had stated that pyrokinetic poltergeists were vicious and could start anywhere from three to thirteen fires.

The fires went out. All the fires extinguished themselves at the same time. He looked at how far it was to the door. He had never before felt this flummoxed.

Something moved in the mirror. Slowly, rotating on the right ball of his foot, he turned to look.

The image in the mirror wasn't his. He didn't jump or do anything but stare. The image stared back. It looked like an old weird magician with stage clothes staring back. As he stared, he took another drink. This wasn't good, and he knew for a certainty that grabbing the gun would do no good.

The Magi spoke, "Hi, Brown."

Brown didn't like the fact that a ghost knew his name. "Go ahead and kill me you bastard." He spread his hands. "Get it over with."

The Magi spoke quietly, "I feel your pain, your anguish beckons to me. The agony and embarrassment that Quirk caused and carried out on you should be avenged. Those little ghost fighters on their Quixote Quest of trying to stop the unstoppable, you must admit is amusing."

The Magi slowed down his speech and lowered his tone. "Brown, how would you like to have some of your own 'power' to put him in his place. Wouldn't you like to put all those 'primates' in their proper place?"

With that quote the Magi raised his skeletal hand and fired a blast.

He gave a deadly smile back to Brown. "Power feels good, no need for primate weapons."

Brown liked what he was hearing but decided to be cautious.

"Why should I want power? Especially now, if I have my facts correctly you are going to kill us 'humans' all anyway." Brown asked proud of himself, he was scared shitless of this demon in front of him and barely able to think. His tongue and brain felt slow and hazy.

"Your primates actually destroyed two Magi of the trinity of the Magi. I am all that is left. My time is infinite. This chess game I have been playing almost ended with the death of the second Magi. The portal here closed for two hundred of your years. I will not allow that to happen again. Now is the time to take the next step in my plan in case you mortals figure out a way to close the portal again."

The Magi smiled now as he looked at Brown. "I love to engage in this recreation of amusing myself, toying with your lives. I want to play with the Institute and your ghost fighters before I kill them. I have enough power to wipe all of you out now. But, I contemplated this; it has been an eternity since I had a chance to have fun, especially without the interference of the other two Magi. As you mortals say, 'It is all about me now!'" and he laughed a totally evil sarcastic laugh. He kept smiling as he deliberated, "I want to play with you before I kill all of you."

The Magi's voice was hypnotic and deep. It had a certain mesmerizing somnolent effect on Brown.

He could not think of anything else left to say and asked the obvious, "What do you want from me?"

The Magi smirked with a condescending mischievousness.

"Why, to only make your deepest wishes come true. I want to give you power and let you have some fun before I come through tomorrow night at midnight."

"Why wait?" Brown asked again, confused on why he was still alive.

The Magi looked impatient, but answered, "Because I want one of their own to destroy them. They deserve to be put in their place; don't you agree? I will give you power beyond your wildest dreams. All I ask is that you play with them. Have fun. Especially belittle Razor and your best friend, Quirk. Sink your new mental jaws and claws into them."

"Avoid Bayou," and the Magi gave no explanation. "I will lead Leslie, Mist and Cornelius on a 'wild goose chase', I think you call it. They won't be a problem and I have had fun with Cornelius before. One time I made him kill a whole village by tricking him into thinking he was being attacked, he was so much fun."

The Magi laughed remembering. "Now Brown, how many times do you get offered such power? Tell me, isn't this better than dying, being humiliated by those primates.

"What happens tomorrow night at midnight to me?" Brown couldn't hide the fright in his voice.

"Why, when I finish your transformation, you become my new prime lieutenant."

Brown looked at the gun he held in his hand and then back at the Magi.

The Magi slowly looked around as if seeing through the walls. "Hurry up, Leslie and Pierre are hunting me, and I can only cloak for so long in the mirror before they find me. Choose to die or live now. You either work with me or cease to exist and I will kill you slowly. I can kill you and be long gone before they finally find me."

Brown slowly raised the whiskey bottle to his mouth and took the biggest drink he could handle. He knew it was over, and no matter what choice he made, he would lose all respect for himself. He put the bottle down and slowly looked up to the now furtive eyes of the Magi. This was no time to be garrulous.

"All right, what do I have to do to get the offer for such powers?"

The Magi smiled and said, "Give me your soul."

Brown smiled a sad smile and sold his soul with two words. "It's yours." A thunderclap filled the room.

Brown felt torn as never before. He wanted to reach out and grab the words back, but it was too late.

The Magi laughed and said, "Open your mouth; just like you did for you whiskey a second ago." He had a look of total contempt for Brown and a vicious sneer appeared on the ancient face.

Brown succumbed and opened his mouth. A brackish, orange tendril crept out of the mirror and slid into Brown's open mouth. Brown couldn't control his fright. He wanted to run away, to escape, but knew it was too late. The tendril kept pouring out of the Magi's old gnarled outstretched hand.

It felt like a snake crawling through his insides. He couldn't scream, he couldn't even close his mouth. The snake kept crawling and crawling through; he hurt like he never hurt before.

The Magi laughed and laughed as Brown saw something white and round shaped float out of his chest cavity. It floated up and the Magi grabbed it.

He looked at Brown with a sadistic look. "I love to eat corrupt souls. Yours smells absolutely delicious."

With that he put the white orb to his mouth and started eating. With every bite, Brown tried to scream. He felt his whole being dissolving. The Magi finished and disappeared. Brown could close his mouth, and tried to stand up but couldn't.

Leslie ported in with Pierre coming in the opposite way, and both looked prepared for battle.

Leslie looked confused. "I felt him here."

She looked at the whiskey bottle and then Brown shaking and moving around the floor with a look of disgust.

"He was probably causing the sensations we felt," Pierre ventured.

She glanced at the fire spots.

Brown tried to hang on, but the fire pains inside him robbed him of consciousness. He welcomed the blackness to get rid of the internal demon that caused the pain. Pierre looked at the passed-out Brown with a look of disgust.

"I don't know Leslie, let's keep checking," and they both walked through the wall as if it didn't exist, floating towards the direction of Quirk's office.

Brown's shaking got worse, and he felt on fire. He woke for a second and the pain boomeranged back. It was killing him, and he passed out for the second time. If Jade had been there, she would have understood what he had just done. She even had historical figures that could provide references. Of course, she would have to argue, his name now matched the two names on who would be the top of the traitor list, because that was her nature. But in the end, it didn't matter that the world would be ending in three strange days.

Brown had now joined the ranks of Judas and Benedict Arnold. He had sold his soul for cheap revenge. His formidable brain and disseminating sniper attacks had done him no good against the Magi.

The Magi had disintegrated his will and taken his soul. "But," he smiled through blood bitten lips as the pain took him; he finally found the power that he craved. "Quirk would pay, all the primates would pay." He would kill them, and then kill the Magi.

Jade would have spit on him as he lay there soulless and full of revenge, passed out on the floor. His last thought was "This experience had to be the single malt ancient whiskey. It has to be the whiskey," was his final thought before passing out. He smirked as the pain took over.

Chapter 38

Oswalt sat there, simmering over events, and processed what he was hearing. Pop shots outside the Institute compound were being fired, but the stalemate lasted.

He listened to the sounds of the sleeping ghost fighters. They were all tossing and turning. He figured they were dreaming, and he was right.

Razor was dreaming of making his famous banana pudding for a bunch of hungry fishermen. Razor was dreaming about the recipes he should write about in his cookbook for these bland eaters of this century. Razor dreamed the way he lived, with tenacity for pure focus, velocity, and fervor.

Bayou orchestrated his dreaming. He started with giving a speech to a large twenty-first century executive audience on quality philosophy, talking about risk management. The job was to reduce the possibilities and create a singularity. A singularity would be a predicted future event where progress and change accelerate due to the advent of focused intelligence. We have the ability of changing our environment beyond the ability of television addicted humans to comprehend or reliably predict future sustainable events.

It boiled down to the genius to see through things and the ability to see things through. In a parallel dream he was talking to the ghost of Hendrix Buchanan on strategy to fight the Magi. What guitar licks would bring the bastard down? Hendrix Buchanan suggested the classic song "If Six Were Nine" due to the funky counter rhythms he could pick. Bayou picked up his guitar and played the song with Hendrix working on an attack plan.

Mist was dreaming about San Francisco, a city she loved. She was using the Bloodstone to truly create a city of brotherly love. All pet owners cared and took care of their pets.

Cornelius was dreaming about the master matrix and catching glimpses of several futures. His art-of-war synapses were working in overdrive. He was unconsciously sending out SOS signals to other dimensions and receiving no feedback. In his dream he replayed the news and made instant art of war assessments.

With the Magi about to create Apocalypse, it was not surprising that false prophets and charlatans broke the media surface. They neglected scientific dogma that must underlie all wise decisions. Using an age-old ploy they pretended to deliver "good news" about the Magi. Cornelius smiled in his sleep; the false prophets win fame by telling people what they want to hear and the people hearing what they wanted. The people did their part and turned off their innate ability to critically think when the moment needed it most...

Quirk was dreaming about a tropical hideaway and J.D. being covered by nothing but her nature suit. And after all he was a nature lover. He had two hands now and could serenade with all his natural charm. He had been single for so long that it was a luxury to focus all his love on one person. He compartmentalized the upcoming battle into a small niche in the back of his romantic mind.

Oswalt reflected about the situation. He was incarcerated in heavy mental traffic about the end of the world. Was it all over?

Leslie and Pierre had visited him and were making the security rounds. Leslie was sure the Magi had visited but could not find any solid evidence. She was concerned about the "why" of a Magi visit and they had discussed variables. None made sense.

In his dream he unrolled a piece of paper Bayou had given him earlier. Bayou had said it came from his time and was a poem by a famous comedian, who was named Benny Hill.

Oswalt read it again.

"Please Can I Go Round Again"

"I don't believe that I'll never see your skies or your trees again,

The Women were fine, and so was the wine,

And I shouldn't complain; but then,

You give such damn short rides in this fairground of yours, Lord,

Please may I go round again?"

Would they get to go around again?

The phone rang and it was J.D. asking what the condition was. He told her and she said that she was going to catch a quick catnap. He told her to go ahead and wished he could take one himself.

He checked with the leaders of Alpha, Bravo, Charlie, Delta and Foxtrot. Everyone was accounted for. Everyone was waiting because everyone knew this was the calm before the storm.

This storm was predicted to be not only the storm of the century, but the mother supernatural storm of all storms; his troops were calling it simply, “Armageddon”.

Chapter 39

Brown woke with a start. His head hurt and he felt like shit. He stood up and looked at the whiskey bottle. "Never again," he thought to himself, "what the hell was I thinking?" He felt hollow.

It was then he noticed something very strange. His reflection was fading in and out of the mirror. Plus, he stank; he reeked of a sulfur smell. He turned to go into the shower. He reached out to open the door and orange sparks shot out of his fingers and blasted the door to tiny glass fragments. Damn, that shower door had cost a month's wages.

He sat there in shock looking around at what could have caused it. The only thing that made sense was ball lighting.

He felt weak and thought about calling the lab and doing some blood spinning. That was where the lab took his blood and spun in a centrifuge to amplify its natural growth hormones. It helped him in his sexual endeavors and recovery from skiing accidents.

He looked at his reflection and thought this was way beyond blood spinning. His bouncing pounding headache felt different and ten times worse than anything he had ever experienced.

He started to slowly remember what had happened last night and walked over to his waiting only friend, the whiskey bottle.

He took a deep swallow. His right hand was looking black. He looked in the mirror and saw big black bags under his eyes.

He was doomed no matter what happened. "For whom the bell tolled" was him and his sold-out soul. He was the prime entrée and had bartered himself for a hefty stipend of power. He relived the whole event as a spectator, seeing him over and over selling his soul to the Magi. He remembered the most lethal memory of the Magi eating his soul. He felt cold chills when he recalled the look of triumph on the Magi's face as he ate the white globe of what had once been his soul.

He took another alcoholic hit of guilt relief and levitated himself above the broken glass fragments like it was the most normal thing to do in the world. It took him a second to realize that he could float inches off the ground.

He slowly floated into the shower with a smile. If he was going to die and got to hell he was going to take the primates with them. He would have company in hell and that was a promise! Come Magi or high water!

Chapter 40

Bayou looked around and took a long hard breath. He had something he had to do, needed to do.

"Dad, do you have a minute?"

Getting time from Razor was like an act of extortion. Razor was usually so busy; he wanted a reason for everything, especially his time.

Razor gave his notorious stare at Bayou, expecting an explanation. He looked at him hard. Bayou had been catching the wrong end of some major ass whippings lately. Razor was worried. He never said anything, but nevertheless he was worried and the look he gave Bayou was one of pondering how his son was handling all this stress.

Bayou motioned for Razor to join him in the small private office.

"What's up, son?" he said, his steel wolf gray eyes matching piercing Bayou's diamond blue eyes.

"Dad, this might be it. I just wanted a moment alone with you."

Razor looked at his, searching his eyes. Now was not the time to be sentimental or go soft.

Bayou, after years of knowing that look, met and matched the look. "I'm okay, it's just that if this is it, I want to say goodbye."

Razor unconsciously went into his normal father protector routine. "Look son, it's going to be okay, if we lose, by damn we lose, but we let this mutha know that he took on the Savages. For better or worse we will go down fighting and odds are we will kill the bastard. The son of a bitch can't conceal himself forever, he will have to surface soon, and I feel it."

Bayou looked up tired, yet proud. "I know that, Dad; I have always known that. I just want to say goodbye, that's all."

Razor looked apprehensive, "What do you mean; do you have some kind of plan, son, I need to know about?"

"No," Bayou laughed. To Razor it was a plan or nothing.

"No Dad, I plan on being by your side no matter what happens. I am just saying that it has been great to have a dad like you. No one has ever had a better one. I know the action is going to be heavy and I plan on us winning.

But, listen to me Dad; if, by some damn chance the Magi gets lucky, I just want to tell you that you have been my rock through all of these years. I know that you are uncomfortable with talk like this, but at least you know that I have been proud to have been your son. "

Bayou had tears in his eyes. He took Razor by the shoulders and looked him right in the eyes. He smiled a tough smile for the old man to show he wasn't having a mental breakdown.

"Together we have kicked some major ghost ass. Through all the success and failures, you were there for me, you stuck with me. Dad, you stuck with me through all the women I managed to go through, you stuck with me through Mist's hard times, through all the life poundings we have both taken and we have survived.

You taught me to live and laugh through it all. You taught me a lot that I never got to say thank you for, and if we check out tonight, then we check out. But, although unspoken through all these years I just wanted to say I appreciate all the help you gave me through the years."

Razor and his wolf gray eyes smiled at his son. "Bayou, as I have heard you say, I am a cocky old fart and every time I see a ghost, I do the, what do you call it, Carpe Homocidus Diem routine. Don't worry; we are going to win this battle. We killed two of the sons of bitches already!"

Bayou jumped back in, "Dad, I see that look of fatherly protection on your face. You are not taking on this ghost by yourself. I plan on being by your side and playing my guitar until my fingers and fretboard burn off. We will be responsible as ever and if we go down, we go down taking the Magi with us. If it comes down to it, let's you and I check out and let Mist live."

Razor was worried. He had never heard Bayou talk like this. But the gaze in his son's bright crystal blue eyes showed that he was still Bayou, still his son.

Bayou carried a tall stance, the poignant laugh lines, the look of a warrior, not a chicken shit. It made Razor proud. There was no weakness in those eyes. Bayou looked as strong as ever.

Razor finally understood. It was the warrior's last stand. The one from the Spartans where the last two warriors get back-to-back and fight to the death. He grabbed his son in a big old bear hug.

"Son," he said, if I die tonight, everything I have is yours. I made a will that even this century's idiot lawyers can't screw up. I just wish Wren was here to share it with you."

They had not talked about Bayou's sister in quite a while. They both smiled. Wren had been the biggest hell raiser of all of them. If she was here, they both intuitively knew that the battle would already be over. She would have killed every ghost there was, especially if they were Republican ghosts. She was one of those kinds of people who took no prisoners; she was just that kind of woman. She and her children, Bayou's nephew, and niece, had been killed in the war. They both regretted that they could not have brought her and her family forward to the future.

"Well, if she were here, she would have had all of this shit straightened out already."

They both laughed and the tension disappeared. Wren had always taken the radical stance of killed or be killed.

She inherited a lot more after Razor's personality than Bayou had. Bayou had inherited his father's gift as a talented musician, but his mother's aptitudes and attitudes. He especially inherited the love of science and her voracious reading habits.

Bayou looked at him one last time and reached for the door handle. Dad, if we go out tonight, it has been an enjoyable hell of ride these last two hundred and fifty years and I am proud to have been your son.

Razor looked at his only son and smiled. Not only did he smile, even with the old age and the aches and soreness that rode on his every muscle, he gave his best cavalier look at Bayou, "Shittttt, I don't know about you, but I plan on giving a certain ghost a guitar enema!

They both laughed and walked out the door, guitars slung across their shoulders starting to slightly glow.

Chapter 41

The conference was jammed. Everyone was there, including a smiling Brown. Quirk was stepping up to a prepared podium. He looked around and in a smoldering glance took control.

With no preamble he started, making eye contact with his audience. The room got quiet. Most audience members by now had now heard of his formidable history. One time bad-boy mercenary, training in explosives, martial arts, counterterrorism, avionics and had been one of the elite of the special forces in his century.

Quirk got down to business. "People, at midnight, unless we luck out, this place gets turned into a glow-in-the dark parking lot. I personally find that an unappealing finale to this place that I and the ghost fighters have tried to preserve. The President has initiated a worst-case scenario plan and is going to nuke this place at midnight. I don't have to tell you that the whole survival of humanity is at stake.

The Magi and his minions have made this location their entry port. From what we know, this is the final battle with the final Magi. From our intelligence, it appears that the Magi wants to consume the planet and make his hell or earth a reality he had been planning for the last twenty or so centuries. From our past battles the Magi has a great many resources and twisted, perverted techniques to inflict damage."

Agents next to Quirk started handing out cards.

"If you hear the following numbers, know the level of attack." Before all the cards were handed out, he did a quick review.

"Listen up!" he yelled going into a command-and-control measure.

"If you hear Alarm 1, it means we have detected a sensory attack. It is the early stages of a poltergeist attack. If you feel cold spots or hear strange noises or smells, radio in immediately, don't blow it off.

Alarm 2 means The Magi is getting closer. If you hear weird noises coming from nowhere, whispers, moans or shrieking or see white wisps, what we call base apparitions, call it in.

Alarm 3 means lights and other electrical appliances turn themselves on and off. If you feel unseen hands grabbing or touching you call in ASAP. This is where we see full apparitions.

Alarm 4 stuff starts flying and moving. Fires start, you feel air pressure change, feel dizzy and sick. Stuff breaks around you, windows, mirrors, you will know, trust me.

Alarm 5 This is Armageddon. Hopefully we at least get some warning before this stage. This is full attack, raped; flying knives, biting and now, he paused. Everyone got quiet, he pushed a button and a picture flashed upon the screen.

There was an audible gasp in the room. Quirk didn't care, these were soldiers and they needed to see the truth.

The picture was of a woman, apparently dead, lying on a sofa. She looked familiar with the red hair with the white streak. Everyone stared at the big hole where her left lung and side used to be. The gruesome sight made even the hardest soldier tighten up.

Quirk in a sad powerful voice proclaimed, "This was Leslie; one of our ghost fighters and the most powerful offensive weapon we had. This is what the Magi did to her.

If any of you want to quit and go home to be with your families, I will understand and have no hard feelings. If you choose to stay and fight, I promise you that the Magi will have his hands full with the best fighting troops the neo-federation has to offer. If you die, you will die saving mankind. If we fail, we all die, or," he paused, "or you will have wished you would have died. No telling what the bastard will do. It will be like a German panzer tank fighting us, the inferior Sherman tank."

He saw the looks of the confused agents.

"Wellllll, what I am saying is that we have a plan to overcome the Magi's superior fire power. We have a plan on using our guitars a new way. It will be like a concentrated laser attack instead of our regular 'chainsaw' approach."

He knew he was lying with the strategy, but he had to give them some kind of hope and act like they had an offensive coordinated plan. In reality, they were playing defense.

He paused again. Not even one left. No one took him up on his offer.

He felt a sense of patriotism he hadn't felt in a long time. He was proud of the young soldiers in front of him. His eyes misted for a second. Without turning away, he let them see how much he appreciated the sacrifice.

"Now for the battle!" he said with the steady voice of a supremely confident kung fu master. "If you see, feel, sense any of these call in. Our intelligence predicts an Alarm 5 will happen before midnight. I only hope that we get some kind of warning."

He gave a quick smile.

"Here is the good news, Mist and Cornelius will be our recon and first line of attack. We think that the big attack will happen anytime between now and midnight." He gestured at them, "The later the ghost attack, the bigger the chance that we risk nuclear death. You all signed on knowing that this was that kind of mission, that was all or nothing.

Once Mist points out where they will begin the attack, then the first and second line of offense kicks in." Quirk deliberately chose the word offense versus defense for the psychological edge.

"Hopefully, with enough notice, Razor, Bayou, and I can kick in with the guitars and go for shooting down the portal and hopefully killing the Magi and what's left of his death squad in the process.

For defense purposes Steve Johnson has distributed the just released the pistol quantum disruptors. Wear them, that's an order, shoot just like a regular hand pistol, they will kill a ghost. Steve, though I imagine most of you were already updated, killed a member of the Magi's death squad with his pistol, so it can be done." Brown let a giggle slip out, which was ignored by everyone except Quirk. "Is there something funny, Brown?"

Brown glimpsed up and gazed around. "Why no", he said with a big grin.

Quirk hated insubordination. He said, "Brown, I need to see you after the meeting."

Brown responded sarcastically, "Quirk is that a, "You need to see, or want to see me?"

Quirk didn't have time for this bullshit, and he ignored the question, a response he would later regret, though at the moment he didn't think about it. His intuition was screaming something was wrong, but he hit the off switch and slammed the intuition door.

What he focused on was trying to outthink the resistance to his next statement.

He took a deep breath, expanded his chest.

"I want everyone to listen. I have already called and told the President what I am about to tell you. He disagrees with me 100%. Sometimes when you are in the field you must trust your instincts." He slowly looked around the room at the face of hardened warriors. "I am talking about a new chain of command." They knew what he meant by chain of command, and they also knew whatever he was about to say had pissed off the President.

That didn't bother them as much as the curiosity of what he was proposing. Was it feasible, and why did he look like it would be bombshell, was all they wanted to know.

Quirk's expression turned very serious. "If anything happens to me, if I get killed in battle," he paused. He was glad that J.D. wasn't in the room. "The next in charge is the only logical choice based on my analysis and having first-hand experience with the Magi in two battles. I have helped kill two of the bastards with one to go. This one I might not make it through."

Most agents assumed Oswalt, Bayou or Razor, due to their Magi experiences. All three had great credentials though most chose Bayou who was a combination of Oswalt and Razor. Bayou was famous for quick analysis, quick humor and quick not to blame people but look at the system that created the mistake.

Quirk had not had the chance to discuss this with anyone but the President but felt confident the ghost fighters, especially Bayou, would support him. He took another deep breath and dropped the bombshell.

"That would be Leslie."

The ghost fighters entered the room and came upon the platform behind Quirk. They all heard Quirk's announcement. Not one of them second guessed the decision. Razor looked like he hoped somebody challenged Quirk's edict. Bayou looked at Quirk and thought about the President's reaction and smiled. Mist was glad that she hadn't been chosen, and choosing Leslie made perfect sense.

You could have heard a pin drop among the agents.

The leader of Bravo stared around and slowly raised his hand. "Sir, do I understand that you want us to take directions from a ghost?"

Quirk had been waiting for that response. Then Quirk released the second bombshell.

Leslie appeared and materialized by Quirks' side. The ghost fighters intuitively came to her support and surrounded her and Quirk. The guitars remained dormant and pointing down. They all understood the risks more than any of the other fighters in the room.

Quirk's face broadcast the choice with finality, "It was not only the right choice, but it was also the only choice!"

Leslie saw the related looks and took the lead. She made sure that her feet were appearing to touch the ground for appearance's sake. She felt human and it was disconcerting the looks she was receiving. She wasn't used to being a ghost and she understood the looks. It was like being turned into a vampire and going to a vampire killer convention as the guest speaker.

The agents stood transfixed, and the full impact of a ghost was right in front of them. Not only a ghost, a former one of them, and one of the most powerful humans that had ever lived. The ghost fighter who had survived the legendary Woosley Heights battles, one of the decorated saviors of San Diego. The hero who gave her life in the Charleston battle to save Razor.

Most of them had warning signs going off in their battle-ready brains. Fingers were itching and the tension was palpable.

Bayou knew the mental term, cognitive dissonance. It was where your brain tried to process two conflicting thoughts. He stayed calm and kept his guitar pointing down. It was unbelievable to the agents. They could see through her in a vague whitish grayish coloring. She was a damn ghost! She was now part of the enemy that was on their way to kill them and massacre the whole planet.

Many who had known or met her were stunned also. She radiated her familiar smile which made this appearance easier to digest. Even in death she looked impressive.

The delicate moment was shifting to their side, Quirk thought, she is a familiar warrior who just now happens to be a ghost.

Leslie had made sure to ask Pierre not to show up. That would have created a riot. To pull this off she had to prove herself trustworthy, and she decided on an unusual ploy which she had discussed with Quirk.

She shimmered and started speaking, her voice sounding ephemeral and ghostly light.

"Traditional warfare won't work. Somebody had to get inside intelligence. I came up with the plan and didn't tell anyone. By sacrificing myself I was able to find the secret dimension where the Magi was coming from. Had I shared my plan with the others they would have tried to stop me. There was only way to get that inside information. I took the risk of being turned by the Magi into one of his evil minions. But I knew I was the only one who had a chance. When you die, you can't take your guitar with you." She smiled at Razor, who smiled back.

There was a small laugh around the room as agents digested the information. "My powers gave me the short straw."

There were deadpan faces on the stage. The ghost fighter themselves were having a hard time digesting the information. Had Leslie really taken this covert operation as she said?

Razor was having the hardest time. If they had been in private, he would have killed her again. Mist got tears in her eyes, since she knew the truth. Bayou thought about his half-sister and knew that she was capable of a drastic measure such as killing herself to get entry to the Magi's secret port. She had complained about what it would take to get to the Magi, to take it to him in his own dimension.

Quirk was numb. What had she said? It hit him hard, a damn reverse bombshell. Leslie's announcement took him totally by surprise. He fought hard to keep in control.

No matter their private thoughts, all the ghost fighters stood by her. Still, they were all mentally rocked. Her words were hard to extinguish, and their mental emotional carryover hurt. Her sacrifice discussion had opened up scars that were not healed.

Leslie continued rapidly.

"Reality is merely sequences of events that happen relative to one another. I used to travel the macroverse going from dimension to dimension. I was able to do that by using a form of mental calculus. As long as I had fixed before-and-after positions I could connect to another dimension. The other dimensions are right next to us. The difference is the thickness of a piece of paper.

We are oblivious because it is only a fraction of an inch away. Sometimes a portal is created because huge clumps of shadow matter pull on matter in our own universe. I have the ability to sense these "Portals" and have learned to cross over. I spent a long time trying to find the Magi's dimension.

His portal is so tiny. The dimensions with those tiny portals are three. Heaven, Hell, and Purgatory, as far as I can tell, are where these tiny portals lead too.

Somehow the Magi, who is what we call a Zeitgeist, a most powerful ghost, has taken over Purgatory and wants to take over this dimension as well. What we need and will do is to send our wanna-be conqueror on a one-way trip to the Hell dimension. I have found out the Heaven and Hell portals are one-way trips.

I have found that the Magi can be killed. We will kill him. We will win for the sake of humanity!"

To the agents she looked like a medieval Joan of Arc come back to life as a ghost.

She paused, "I am not sure exactly what God is or does, but I do know that he, she, it exists and has a heart. I know that God is behind us in this battle so we might get some unexpected help."

That news was a welcome relief to all the bad news they had been receiving lately. She just wished she knew it to be true.

Leslie continued, unrelenting in her passion.

"I died, that's a fact, the good news is that I have found the ghosts' hiding place. They are being controlled by an entity we call the Magi. There were three Magi. We killed two and the last one, the one we need to kill to finish the war. Killing the second one consumed most of our ghost fighting energy. I know, that is how I died. I could have fought and lived. But I chose to die to save mankind!"

Silence, it was like being underwater for a second. She personified every fighter's hope, to die in battle making a good stand.

"The third Magi is the lone surviving 'enemy' if you will. From when I crossed over, I found that he can selectivity grab emotionally tortured souls when they come through the death portal and turn them into one more soldier of his army of zombie ghosts.

Swirls of white ether floated off her body as she talked. A pale bluish luminous glow surrounded her.

The Magi confiscates their goodness and releases the evil in them. If we ghost fighters can kill him, I believe the good side of their nature will return and they will ascend back to where they are headed to begin with. They will reconnect to where they are supposed to go. I suppose that is Heaven, even though I haven't seen it. There is a place you go, I know that. But that is not our problem. Our problem is killing the bastard to let the souls progress to their final destination.

Fight to the death! If you don't, he will kill you anyway and then eat your soul. His plan is to subjugate the human race and take over this dimension.

In my head I have seen two futures. His is beyond what I can describe to you. The pro-ghost forces don't have a clue as to his true intentions."

She brought her gaze to each of the squad leaders. She radiated a sense of staggering purity and intensity.

"Like Joan of Arc, I come to you with a message. I can feel where he is, and with Mist and Cornelius's power we are going to kill him and his lieutenants." She looked around, feeling evil somewhere in the room. There were too many people to pinpoint, but it was here.

Her aura turned azure and gleamed an iridescent ethereal effect.

Brown felt some shadows like worms' slither around his mouth. He felt a bloody caterwaul starting to escape from his lips. His spine tingled and parts of his body started to shake. He fought it off as best as he could and excused himself. He felt like he had a demon inside of him trying to get out. He listened to Leslie and as he exited, he heard her say, "When I crossed over, I found the Magi can take a human host and infect them.

They will be given a dose of power but will die from it in a short time.

I didn't find out how he did it, but assume he gets traitors who want to fight on his side to be spared. I have strong reason he visited us here last night and turned one of us into a traitor. If you see anyone that starts to unexpectedly stink or glow with an orange-blackish glow, shoot immediately, I repeat," she said while staring at all of them, slowing turning her ghost head to make contact. "Shoot immediately or you will die an unearthly horrible death."

Brown was feeling cornered and ran out the door. He knew the supernatural possession was causing him to stink and that some of the agents had noticed.

Also, the overheard remark she tossed out at the end of her speech really bothered him. What exactly did she mean about dying in a "short time?" What precisely did she mean and how accurate was her information? It was a matter of life and death. He was so anxious about it he became inattentive to the ruckus he was creating as he exited.

The FBI agent noticed the stench coming from Brown and the unusual way he was acting. "Code 1," he thought and silently backed towards the door, and as he opened and walked through, he again smelled the smell. No way was this a normal smell. He saw Brown walking rapidly to his left and picked up his radio. He checked his sheet of Institute personnel and recognized Brown immediately. It was easy, he was high on the organizational chart.

"Control, Bravo 13, Detect stench smell coming from civilian CFO Brown.

"Request permission to neutralize the threat." The controller looked at the receiver, then the mike.

"Permission denied," she said, engrossed, then rethought her command after a pause. Her thoughts were like dark clouds about to burst. If he is wrong and shoots the CFO the manure will hit the fan.

"Contact Director Quirk immediately."

"10-4" came the answer and then a click off.

In the control room she did a quick squat on the closest chair surrounded by five other agents. As she sat there, she hoped she had done the right thing. It was okay, though, he was only one man and they all had on the toe-to head body armor.

Brown made his way straight to the control room. Stupid idiots, trying to stop him was lunacy. Their childish weapons no longer worked on him. He still felt pensive about the guitars and Bloodstone though.

The power felt good. Screw the odor, if that was the only price to pay for this feeling it was well worth it.

He was about to try his first demonstration of his powers. He looked in the control room. The person looking back asked for his biometrics.

Brown laughed, he could easily blow the door open, but he had better save his power for the ghost fighters.

He punched in his identity, with the matching speed and rhythm, and the door slid open.

The controller and five other agents didn't notice the stench smell until it was too late. Her last conscious thought was wondering where the smell was coming from. Then as the killing orange blast came towards her, she recognized the face killing her, she had put the pieces together too late.

Brown smiled as he killed them. His powerful newly gifted arsenal felt good! The evil power and spattered blood soaked him with pleasure.

It was just like the Magi had promised him; the power was rightfully his now!

Chapter 42

The FBI agent of Bravo group was irritated that he had been ignored with a report of a potential death threat. He walked rapidly through the exiting agents, feeling more anxious every second.

He wasn't sure who to go to, now that Control had opted out of doing the right thing. He saw the circle around Quirk and decided.

Quirk, with the ghost fighters was explaining exactly what a ghost was to a group of agents. The FBI agent heard him say, "Ghosts are believed to be caused by the residual life force of a deceased human."

Bayou jumped in, "Their appearance goes in cycles usually from a low intensity to high. They get more dangerous the higher the intensity registered. We have proof now, due to Leslie and Pierre's presence, that ghosts are based on the energy of a once alive human being.

The FBI agent stood on his toes and raised his hand; he interrupted Quirk as politely as he could. He finally yelled when Quirk ignored him.

For a moment the FBI agent was stunned, looking at him as an unwelcome interloper were three bad-ass looking guitar fighters and three Bloodstone fighters. Oswalt also starred.

The agent looked straight at them, choosing Oswalt to due to his rank to deliver the message.

He looked at Oswalt, “Director Oswalt, I called into control. They postponed a decision and said to get the message to you.” He shook his head in disgust. His look said this run around was all bureaucratic bullshit.

“Sir, Leslie in her briefing said to immediately kill anyone who had an unusual body stench. During the conference I noticed one person, a man whom at the close of the briefing really started to stink. It wasn’t psychosomatic sir. I don’t brainwash easily. As I watched him, he grew nervous. Leslie said look for bad body odor. Her words were, ‘If detected, throw the knockout punch and don't hold back.’”

The agent looked for and got approval that that was the same message they had heard too.

Razor jumped in, walking straight toward the agent knocking the cluster around the agent to the side.

He gave the agent his famous stare and grabbed the agent by the arm, “Damn son, did you kill him?” His look said you better had killed the bastard. Razor didn’t care who it was, “what” it was, and the “what” had to be killed.

“I went to..., the agent hesitated and finished the unanswered question, “No sir, Control,” he said the word with disgust, “said to notify Oswalt, because of the man’s high position. I am here waiting on orders.”

They all felt it; all the pieces started coming together. “Shit,” was all Quirk could say. He looked away in disgust and muttered an unkind profanity.

They all knew who it was before the agent said it said it.

Bayou said it for all to hear.

"Brown".

Chapter 43

Brown looked around the control room and could feel the evil power increasing. He had never had personal respect for anyone, only positional respect. He now had earned the highest positional power on this damn measly planet that could be achieved. He knew and felt it.

With his right hand he had already killed six agents. It felt good having power like this. After he killed the primates, he would kill the Magi and then take over the world. The archeology of his life was about to change. He would take over running the whole planet. He laughed and he felt the power growing.

He noticed the slithering thing in his mouth kept moving about, but he downplayed it. He reasoned, feeling his head growing hotter and hotter, "It's probably just a big parasite. I'll deworm it when I am finished killing the apes." The fever was really kicking in now. He saw a pitcher of water and with just a look sent an orange tendril out from his hand to gather it and bring it to him. He drank all of it, but still felt dehydrated. He felt a compulsion to drink all the time.

He knew he didn't have a lot of time. He wasn't sure how powerful the Magi was, but he did know that a nuclear warhead was not a conventional weapon.

Everyone wants to control someone; he smiled at the familiar thought. See, he still was himself. The odor and thirst were minor issues. Leslie hadn't known what she was talking about.

He thought about the approaching nuclear deadline. He didn't know exactly how much power the Magi had given him, but he didn't want to test it with a nuclear showdown.

He intuitively knew what he had to do. He had to open a portal from this side to get the ball rolling to increase his energy to beat the Magi and then get the hell out of Dodge.

He concentrated all of his energy and lashed both hands out. Four orange, and then turning into ink jet black color bursts shot from his hands. They formed a nasty ball floating in the middle of the room. The ball pulsated looking like a big sinister embryo.

His fear started to surface, and he realized the thing that had been sliding out of his mouth was now attacking his ears. Something was trying to crawl out of his ears. He screamed yet kept to task. Some program architecture told him he had to finish the task.

The embedded program told him to crave the embryo, to nurture it, to give it all his power. He kept feeding it, feeling weirder and worse by the moment.

Chapter 44

Leslie, Pierre, Mist and Cornelius all materialized in the control room.

Brown laughed, "You apes are too late," and with that the embryonic ball exploded. The shock wave threw Mist, Cornelius, and Brown to the floor. Leslie and Pierre were unaffected.

They all stared at the dark portal that was ten feet by ten feet floating in the middle of the room. They could hear the sounds and smells about to come through.

A second later, the door burst open and the three ghost fighters levitated in with the guitars at the firing position.

Bayou took the center position according to the plan. Razor flanked him on the right, Quirk on the left.

Mist, Cornelius and Leslie waked in front of them holding the Bloodstone above their heads.

"On three!" Quirk yelled, the guitars all strummed E chord major at the same time, the three energies hit the Bloodstone in unison.

The putrid stench of evil permeated the field of battle, and the chorus of tortured ghosts could be heard throughout the entire Institute.

Brown looked up and saw the Magi enter through the portal. Ghosts with ghastly skeletal bodies started streaming through the portal.

He laughed and created a tiny portal for escape. He knew he didn't have the arsenal to kill the primates and the Magi. It would be better to let them kill each other, then whoever survived he would come back and kill. As the portal started to open, he saw that his hands were now black and the fingers resembling claws. He didn't care about that; he could reverse all that later.

The portal opened and he jumped in, thinking he was going to project himself down to the basement.

Quirk and Cornelius, who was closest to him, instantly jumped him behind him. Bayou and Razor watched the portal close. That left the Savages collective to fight the Magi.

In the alternate electronic communications room J.D., Jade and Steve saw where Brown had ported to. They ran with J.D picking up a gun belt on the way. J.D. knew Quirk was about to die, she knew that he was her life mate and by God, she would defend him with her last breath. The selfish son-of-a bitch would not sacrifice himself for mankind without her by his side.

They didn't have time to send a message for alternate backup. The time was 11:50 pm and the bomb was mere minutes away.

Chapter 45

Razor smiled. It was him and the kids taking on the bastard. He wouldn't have planned it any other way, except to have himself and the bastard mano o mano. Razor, who had the highest evil ghost kill history of any agent in history, followed in second place by his son Bayou. Leslie had been third place.

Four living Savage legends, Razor, the logical ghost killer, Bayou the son, the Renaissance ghost killer, Leslie, the newly apparitional daughter, the most powerful human who had ever fought ghosts and now a ghost herself, and the granddaughter, Mist, rightful heir to the Bloodstone.

Mist yelled, her frantic hazel eyes' looking at Bayou. He caught her glance. "Dad, Brown is porting to the basement."

Bayou yelled back, "Send a psychic message to Steve and Jade to get there ASAP. He might be trying to open more portals." Bayou didn't know that Steve, Jade and J.D were on their way to the basement already.

They felt the air pressure change and the smell was overpowering.

The Magi, the third and last of the evil trio, had come completely through the portal. This portal was the biggest portal any of the ghost fighters had ever seen, a swath of pure evil the size of four-story building.

Leslie knew what the others didn't know. She had seen this future and knew that there would never be another scene like this in history. The size of this portal was a once-in-a universe event.

Oswalt had finished talking with head agents of all the units. They were the best of the best. He smiled a doomed smile.

They were shooting all the ammunition left, firing with all safeties off. He had given the order to abandon posts five minutes ago. The nuclear holocaust was now unavoidable, and he ordered to abandon posts. None had left their posts. He suspected the real reason was that they were surrounded, like the Alamo, by pro-ghosts attacking forces and that there was no escape for any of them.

He had never really thought about his own death, and he was surprised at how death snuck up on you. His instant conclusion is that you are never ready. He looked at his watch and started running. Damn, at least if he played guitar he might have a chance, he rationalized as he turned to move.

He ran down to the alternate control room and saw instantly that it had been abandoned. There was no time to wonder where Steve, Jade, and J.D. had disappeared. He knew that they wouldn't leave their post unless they had a damn good reason. Maybe they were already dead. The perimeter wasn't yet falling; the pro-ghost forces were trying to get through, but he was sure the perimeter was still secure.

He hurriedly looked at the psychic Richter machine. His eyes widened. In front of his desperate looks the machine first slowly red-lined, then quickly blew up.

He stared in shock. The nuclear bomb had better go off soon, or humans were doomed. No director in history had ever seen an infestation of evil as bad as this.

No reading or recordings in Institute history had matched this. You didn't need for ghost-radar to know the end was here, the attack on the institute and ending was now a foregone conclusion. Nothing could stand up against a level 10 hurricane ghost such as this latest Magi.

Oswalt looked at the smoking remains of the Richter machine. Flames were sputtering, and the acrid smoke filled his nostrils. He could feel time ticking away and looked at his watch. A few more minutes, could they hold on till the nuclear bomb gave humanity a final redemption? He thought about the Texas Alamo story and how the reprieve they hoped for never came.

He knew his reprieve would come, but no human hosts would survive. He only hoped that it would be enough to kill the Magi.

How much power would it take to kill the Magi? He sat down looking at the monitors flickering and waited for the world to end. He stole a look at the emergency phone to the president. He knew that he wouldn't pick it up unless a miracle happened and they were out of time for that now.

Chapter 46

The inter-dimensionally controlled evil ghosts and banshee demons seemed frozen in motion. It seemed that they were waiting for some signal from the Magi to attack. The army of the leftover dead retreated to all sides of the portal.

The emergency secret service agents slid into the back of the room. Everyone sensed this was the end of humankind. They were outnumbered a thousand to one. The Magi looked at all of them.

One of the sniper agents fired a shot. The bullet got about two feet close to the Magi and then melted. The Magi's laugh was so loud on the eardrums that most agents put their hands over their ears. The volume was excruciating.

Time slowed for the humans. All inertia came to a stop.

If they could have seen outside the monitors showed pro-ghost fighters outside the Institute pouring in for what was going to be the final attack. The signs would have shown, "Fight for the Dark Angel" and many such other signs. The Pro-forces collectively gave a yell and charged. Their final sign had manifested itself, their savior; the ghost of ghosts had come to grant them an eternal place in the afterlife. Their rights for eternity would be protected by this death charge.

All the Special Forces troops felt it too and placed all the remaining ammunition next to them. The piles were small and not enough to survive more than a few minutes at best. All agents looked Those seasoned with combat experience automatically went into instant force release mode, all weapon safeties were taken off.

All the ghost fighters felt their impending doom surrounded by the ubiquitous beasts of Satan. They were outnumbered, outmanned, out resourced. Bayou smiled and felt himself sweating. He never sweated. The sweat he realized was from the stress of what he was witnessing: the end of human history.

Bayou smiled; he had always loved history.

He thought of Bon Jovi's song "Blaze of Glory." The words "Let me die like a man, looking down a bullet let me make my final stand." The song rang off his lips as he sang the lyrics.

The smile returned as he grabbed his guitar, time for a final rock and roll song, and this time it would be followed by death.

Chapter 47

J.D. was talking through rushed breaths with Jade and Steve outside the basement door that they suspected Brown had transported to. They had run at full speed, and getting there they heard nothing.

They all looked at their watch and knew the end was here. J.D. looked at both of them. The decision to reveal the secret information she had was tearing her apart.

If Brown was in there and used the information to stall Steve or Jade, then the battle was over before they even had a chance to fight. She looked at both.

"Before we rush in, I need to tell you something." They paused, "I got the results of Cornelius's DNA search."

They both looked at her wondering why she would bring this up now. They listened to the door as they drew their guns but looked at her due to her severe urgency tone in her voice.

J.D. took a deep breath as she let the revelation that she had been protecting, holding onto, and flow in a quick cluster of information. "Jade is Cornelius's natural birth mother."

Steve looked at her with one of the most intense looks she had ever experienced. He knew that he had heard her, but his listening might be off. "Please say that again." She repeated the bombshell.

Steve stared hard at her and then dropped his head, wondering who the father might have been.

Jade broke her shock freeze, "No, no, no, that was a long time ago, my pregnancy ended in a missing uterus after the first trimester. I never delivered a baby. I, I, I.... woke up one morning and I wasn't pregnant, and my baby and uterus were missing.

I know it sounds impossible and it was, but we, the doctors and I never figured out what and how it happened. Someone stole my baby. I compartmentalized the loss and put it behind me. It was a long time ago."

Jade looked ashen as she spoke, and Steve looked like his spirit had broken with a downcast chin.

J.D. felt the way she always felt when giving a person a death sentence of short death.

She grabbed both by the hands and made eye contact. "The only reason I told you is that Brown might use the information against you if he knows and we can't allow that to stop us from killing him." She wished she had some kind of mind share software that she could connect to.

Steve tried to stay calm and rubbed his forehead with his gun hand. Sirens were going off all over and he knew that the pro-ghost forces were attacking in full. Armageddon was in full play. What a time to find out that you are a stepfather.

He looked down to do a reality check. None of his ghost reading equipment was working; some kind of interference was at play. Light and sound manifestations were occurring, distracting them. It reminded him of San Diego.

Steve looked at J.D. right in the eyes. "Are you sure, J.D.? You are saying that Cornelius is Jade's son. Did you double check?"

Jade's mind was still in turbo shock. The economies of neglecting a search for her son and the now unintended consequences were coming home to roost.

Jade spoke, "I didn't know, I was pregnant for the first trimester and somehow Cornelius was.... was transferred out of my uterus and transplanted somewhere else. I don't know how it happened, but I always thought that my son had survived."

Steve reached over and took Jade's hand. Jade had a son, he had a stepson, it registered and felt good.

J.D. appreciated the fact that both Steve and Jade dissipated the emotional blame storming in situations like this. She was holding back the information on "who" the father was. It would be better to let Jade bring that up. She had reached her cut-off point.

Steve looked incredulous and restless, he stared at Jade, "I know that you told me you were incapable of having children, you had no uterus. I thought you had had a hysterectomy."

Jade couldn't help it; she went on a dogmatic defensive. "I never told you I had a hysterectomy. I told you I had no uterus. When I first came to the Institute, I had an affair with a person here." She paused. "I never told you, Steve. I was embarrassed by the whole twisted ugly incident. It baffled and confused me. I made a covenant with myself never to talk about it. No one would have believed me anyway and I would have had to append the story if told or found out. So, I promised myself to never think about it, or discuss it. The event robbed me of all my past spiritual feeling of being in the protection of some great creator."

"Don't panic," she thought. Her rising panic about Steve's reaction when he found out the father was would be unbearable. She loved him, only him and if she had to die, to be with him. Maybe she hoped that wouldn't come up.

She was beyond mad at J.D. for bringing this up with the end of the world happening. "Why?" she looked at J.D. imploring her to quit this inquisition.

She asked, "Why now, J.D., and how sure are you?"

J.D. handed over the test results in the manila folder. Both Steve and Jade were professionals. They looked over the materials. J.D. had deliberately left off the father's name. Jade started explaining it as they looked at her medical records. She needed to do damage control and fast.

"Steve," she couldn't look at him and kept staring at the contents of the folder. "When I first arrived here twenty-one years ago, I was single and young. A man made some passes at me and seduced me. I thought I was in love."

She continued speeding up, listening to the alarms sounding.

"Steve, at that time I was a girl that men read but didn't subscribe to. This man here at the Institute promised that if we had sex, he would love me, and we would be together forever. I got pregnant. I told him and he started avoiding me. My skepticism hardened to cynicism when I tried to discuss the baby with him. I decided to keep the baby. He finally got up the nerve to talk honestly with me. He told me that I was stupid for getting pregnant and should have known better than to think he wanted to raise a kid. He said I was trying to trap him into marriage.

It hurt, but I had thought it out and thought that would be what he was saying. I told him the conditions and how this was going to work."

Steve and J.D. knew Jade well enough to know that she had been emotionally scorched but were curious to what her "conditions" might have been.

Jade saw their looks and revealed the past event. She talked like it was happening now. "

"The conditions were, I would raise the baby, the baby would never know who the father was, I would never ask for any form of child support, and lastly our relationship would be strictly professional. He was to make no contact with his son, period. At the end of my first trimester, I...she hesitated. I told the doctor about what I thought had happened. I see it is not in the record, except for the mental evaluation."

She ignored all the commotion and continued.

"I went to sleep and had a nightmare of a demon trying to steal my baby. I woke up and the baby and my uterus were gone from my body."

"I," again she hesitated as tears started to pour from her eyes. "My baby was gone. I went to the infirmary and the doctors couldn't believe it. No one could explain it." The exasperation in her voice was barely audible.

"I went to the father and accused him of stealing our baby. He denied it and I believed him. He was too egotistical to get involved in anything that complex, plus I believed that he didn't want anything to do with me after the pregnancy. I saw psychics, but I knew from our records that they were all pseudo-tricksters. The psychiatrists I saw doubted my sanity when I told them of the event. I was given every mental test that applied. Most mental counselors practiced something called supportive therapy. I talked and they just listened."

Steve tenderly reached over and held her hand. J.D. looked at them and felt the bond between the two.

"Somehow, your baby transferred to a couple named Jacob and Leah. Leah delivered your baby." J.D. said loudly, "I believe it was the work of the Magi. I wondered and pondered about it, the how, the why and it is the only option that makes sense. Occam's Razor, you know, the simplest option. She spoke directly what was on her mind.

"Maybe the Magi used a surrogate here to impregnate you. If the Magi did this, was behind this, then that would explain Cornelius's powers. It would make sense if he is actually the son of the Magi and a human father surrogate. I think that explains what he really is, a raw Magi."

Steve and Jade listened. Both were reaching for a logical, emotional analysis.

Steve said, "But somehow the plan backfired. When they met last year, something went wrong. When the Magi tested Cornelius, he had a bad reaction. He hated that he killed the townspeople. He swore he would kill the Magi if he could find him. He came here to align with Leslie to find the hellish dimension he came from and kill him."

Steve paused and asked out loud, "What asshole here could the Magi have used?"

Jade looked down and J.D. glanced over at the chart. It had been on the chart that she had erased the father's name on.

Steve followed her eyes and then it hit him. Tears flooded his eyes, his temper flared, and he wanted to be wrong. He grabbed Jade, "Please tell me it wasn't who I think it was."

Jade, with tears in her eyes, whispered the one secret that she had kept from her husband. The one memory that she had tried to repress for over twenty years.

"Yes, Steve, it was... Brown."

Steve Johnson looked at her stomach and let out a yell. "Aggghhhhhhhhh," he screamed and felt his mind going nova mad. His brain felt caught in a crossfire of emotions. His love for his wife, the betrayal by Brown and the Magi using Brown to get her pregnant. "I will kill him!" He said quickly depleting his calm control capacity. He hugged Jade.

"So what," he thought, "Cornelius was Brown and Jade's son, that had happened a long time ago", and Jade looked as much in shock as he was. He was her husband and he had to take care of her.

"Honey, we will work this out. This changes nothing between us. That was a long time ago. If we survive this, we can adopt or do anything you want to do. I love you."

Jade broke down crying and hugged him back. They didn't notice J.D. cocking her head in a weird fashion.

Their moment was interrupted when J.D. leaned on the table looking strange. She froze as if listening to an unheard voice. Steve and Jade, still hugging each over, looked at her concerned.

J.D. stared at them. "Grab your guns, hurry, Mist sent a telepathic message to me. Quirk and ...your son, Cornelius, are on their way here to help us fight Brown. The Savages are taking on the Magi." She flashed that beautiful mean smile of hers. "I will not lose my man to that asshole," she growled. "Quirk is my man and it's time I know how to shoot." With that she quickly drew the pistol out of the holster.

Steve and Jade brought up their guns as they went Quirk and Cornelius rounded the corner. They all felt the same way. Steve thought about killing Brown as they opened the basement vault door and rushed into the room.

Jade thought about protecting her son.

Chapter 48

Brown looked around. He had had to fight to get here. The Magi saw what he was doing and almost trapped him in limbo when he was transported. Brown used his new powers to teleport through the trap. He reasoned he now had the combined powers of the dead Magi lieutenants. It made sense.

He didn't know how he knew it, but it explained his increase in powers. Like a battery, he was charging and getting more powerful. The Magi had tried to block his transport but hadn't been able to do it.

"Dumbass Magi, you should never have given me the powers." The effort to escape from the Magi had taken its toll, but he had won. Now he was tired and needed to rest for a second. He could feel his powers still increasing, but he was not powerful enough to stop the bomb.

He sunk to his knees and took a deep breath. He looked at his hands and stared. His feet now had burst through his shoes and looked like black giant goat feet. His head was still burning and something had grown from his head. He reached up and touched horns on either side of his head. He now had two tongues; one was a black serpentine bi-furcated long tongue that constantly flashed out of his mouth. He could smell the air better with it. He could smell the primates on the other side of the door. He liked this tongue. He would keep it when he reversed the other effects that the Magi were installing into him.

He needed to teleport fast. As he raised his hand to create a new portal, a portal opened in front of him. Pierre came out shooting a donut right at Brown.

The donut stopped and reversed itself towards Pierre. Brown loved the new power. Pierre laughed at him. "I have already died once and have no fear of death. Razor will make sure you will pay for this. To kill a chef is the ultimate depravity."

Brown had always hated Pierre's monologues and had heard too much about them to listen.

"Pierre, you are a compulsive talker. I have turned into a compulsive killer. See, nature balances things out. I am doing the world a favor by banishing you. I am going to see if I can kill a ghost."

Pierre felt the ley line to his right, he was too far away. Brown made the donut squeeze and squeeze the poor French chef.

Pierre felt pain for the first time in his ghost life. He fought it but knew Brown was going to kill him.

As he died Pierre screamed, "Razor, kill this bastard for me!" He hoped Razor heard, because he knew that no one would kill a chef with Razor around.

Pierre saw a new portal, a white portal opening in front of him. He reached for it as his ghost body died.

Brown laughed, "Finally getting him to shut the hell up! I should get some kind of medal for that."

The vault door flung open as the Institute fighters broke in.

Steve Johnson was the first one in. Steve didn't hesitate and fired straight at Brown. Steve wasn't sure it was Brown, since the creature he fired resembled a human, but just barely.

Brown's right claw threw up a force field which deflected Steve's shot.

Jade and J.D. came through next. Jade fired at the center mass, while J.D. went for a head shot. Both shots were deflected.

Quirk levitated in and strummed his guitar, the lightning bolts off the old Martin, lighting up the force field in a nova of light.

Cornelius came through next and raised his hand and fired a red ray. His ray penetrated the weakened force field but missed Brown.

Brown laughed and with a coaxing claw movement, motioned for a time out. He yelled, "My son, forgive him he knows not what he does."

Quirk didn't know what the hell the now demon Brown was shouting about and didn't care. He fired point blank into Brown.

Brown glowed with an orange aura, intercepted and deflected Quirk's attack.

Steve and J.D. shot again and again pummeling Brown with a constant barrage. Jade turned around facing an astonished Cornelius. He had a look of anguish on his face.

Cornelius looked straight at her, he yelled above the noise, "Brown,...He's telling the truth, I can feel it, and.... he hesitated, eyes opening wide, you are my real mother!" He looked in shock, like his soul had just experienced an exorcism. Two sets of parents were now imposing on his mind. His biological parents in this room were on opposite sides fighting for the future of humanity. It all made sense. This was the moment he had been destined for.

Do you go with Dad or Mom? Don't worry only the future of mankind is waiting on your decision. By the way, we don't believe in split custody, you have to make a total choice.

All this sank in within a second. His high I.Q. grasped the situation instantly. It was distracting, vivid and fulfilling all at the same time. He had grown up accustomed to making instant decisions.

He looked at his biological father fighting Quirk. This was the father who had chosen to become a demon. This was the father who had deserted him. This was the father who had been nothing but a pawn in the Magi's long-term plans.

He had pulled the event from Brown's mind. He knew the truth. His mental carburetor was being blown clean of any guilt in the choice.

He looked into the deep hypnotic eyes of Jade. Her smile lacquered his choice. He felt compelled to hug her, but confusion was still wreaking havoc on his emotions as the revelation unleashed in his consciousness.

Time seemed to slow down, and the doors closed in his mind to a single door.

He made the choice. He walked to her with outstretched hands and blissfully walked straight into them. He enjoyed one of the few real smiles he had ever experienced in his short life.

He had found his real mother. His inner dialogue finally went quiet, and he enjoyed the hug. They were oblivious to the battle going on around them.

Quirk looked at his watch and he saw it was three minutes until twelve. The bomb was almost here.

Brown looked like a living nightmare. He had ten-inch horns growing out of his head and he was morphing right in front of them. As he morphed his powers became stronger.

Oswalt turned to look at Steve and J.D.

Quirk became alarmed. Brown had now become completely demented.

"Johnson, I hate you." His big claw flashed a deadly orange burst straight into Johnson. Johnson saw it coming and ducked. The orange-blackish ray hit the wall where Johnson had been standing. The ray hit the wall with a force that let Johnson know if he hadn't ducked, he would be dead.

A brick from the wall façade dislodged loose and hit Johnson in the back of his head. The pain was a killer and the last thing he saw was Jade hugging Cornelius as he lost consciousness. The Bayou imprint implored him to stay awake, keep fighting, but the unforgiving pain was too much, and he blacked out.

J.D. watched out of her peripheral vision as Steve went down. She didn't think he was dead, but he would have a hell of concussion when he woke.

It must be approaching midnight, and she knew she only had one option left. She ran to Steve's gun and picked it up.

Brown watched her with amusement.

She put a gun in both hands and ran towards Brown yelling.

Quirk knew a suicide charge when he saw it. He knew the time; he saw the time. This woman had more grit than any woman he had ever met. He discovered he could fly pretty fast when he wanted to. He levitated towards her, getting in front of her at the last second as Brown fired both hands towards her.

Quirk could hear voices surrounding the guitar, he had never heard that before. Adrenaline and all the fight or flight chemicals flooded at the same time.

He would not lose this woman. He wouldn't let this son-of-a-bitch hurt or desecrate this woman he loved.

Brown was screaming repeatedly, making no sense whatsoever. The blast hit with the impact of a bomb and went through Quirk's force field like a knife through warm butter.

Quirk had always been prepared for death, it had always been just another demand, a debt he would eventually have to pay.

When the guitar force-field gave way, he was shocked. The guitar had interceded and gave him new life. It couldn't give way, it was his sanction, a gift from the gods.

The guitar was slaughtered. Wood impregnated itself all throughout his body and he slammed into J.D. They both seemed to float in slow motion towards the wall where Steve Johnson's body lay dormant.

They hit and fell to the floor. Quirk, damaged, bleeding, grabbed J.D. the way he had many a football in his sports years, twisting so that her body would fall on top of his massive torso.

Like a big bull, he felt the bones breaking as he hit the floor. The mighty Quirk held onto J.D. with all his remaining energy. He knew the bomb was on its way. J.D.'s conquering hero was wiped out and she was either knocked out or dead. At least they would die together.

He saw the stars floating in his eyes, with the last remaining energy he yelled the only word that might save them. There was only one person who could bring down Brown.

He screamed at the top of his lungs, with all his energy, "Cornelius!" and then surrendered to the blackness.

Chapter 49

Jade and Cornelius' spell was broken by the yell. They turned and saw Johnson laid out with J.D. sprawled on top of a massive Quirk whose head hit the cement as they stared.

Brown laughed, "My lover and my son, a family reunion. Son, I just found out, but I am glad to have someone to share my legacy with. Join me, let's get out here, come back and kill the Magi if he survives, and take over this planet. No one could stand against our combined powers. Son", Brown looked accusingly at Jade; "she can come with us if you choose. After all, she is your mother."

Cornelius pulled the arcane powers forward to his fingers. "You were noting but the Magi's stooge." He spit out the words as though tasting something awful. "You threw your life away, Brown. I might be your favorite off-spring, I don't know how many others you have out there, but this one is going to kill you."

With that the two launched a full-bore frontal attack. The impact of Brown's assault knocked Jade 20 feet into the wall immediately behind Cornelius. Cornelius withstood and started slowly moving the orange blackish force back into Brown's face. It was obvious that he was the superior power.

Jade hit hard and went down but was not out. She started crawling towards her son. She would not let that bastard kill him too. She assumed he had killed Steve. She reached into her holster and still felt the gun. She pulled it out and aimed at Brown.

Cornelius was tapping all his powers. He moved to the right, feeling a ley line there he could further tap.

Brown's response was to yell at him. "Come on son, is that all you got, you deserve to die, you are not worthy of being my son."

Cornelius avoided the conflict. It was Art of War stuff and bereft of any real emotional meaning.

He focused on Brown's attack.

Jade could see Brown shadowed against the glare of his hand shooting power. Her legs wouldn't work for some reason, but she kept pulling herself forward.

Brown kept yelling, "Come on son, give the old man your best shot, is that all you got."

Cornelius contacted the ley line and sucked the power of it, adding it to his own. The addition to his power caught him off guard and his deflector shield wavered. Brown saw this and summoned all his powers for the coup de grace. He pointed his claws at his son, bright pulsating orange power globes surrounding each claw. He had a triumphant smile on his demonic face.

Jade would not concede to the agony wracking her body. She saw the phantom shape of Brown materialize as he readied to kill Cornelius. The opening in his protective barrier helped her pin down his position. "He thinks I'm dead," she thought and smiled despite the pain shooting through her body.

This bastard had screwed her, left her, and abandoned her. She was now numb from the waist down and the asshole was now trying to kill her son. She couldn't feel her legs. She glanced at Steve, her husband who had died to save her and mankind.

She pulled strength from the hate. She hated Brown with a hatred she had never known. She gave way to it, used it as strength.

She took a deep breath and aimed towards center mass. The way she had always been taught to do. Don't go after the fancy stuff, the probability of a hit increases with center mass.

Brown yelled, "Come on son, is that...."

Jade pulled the trigger. No woman will put up with someone trying to kill her offspring. Her maternal instincts flooded her brain, then an unconscious hurricane of pain hit, and she passed out. Her last thought was an expression she had learned from Bayou, he called it a "Smith and Wesson Divorce".

Chapter 50

Cornelius filtered the fact that he was about to die. He had made a mistake in trying a too-risky move in this battle to the death. His natural gift of warfare and operational battle had led to a fatal major miscalculation. He had needed more power to defeat Brown.

The ley line power, the natural magnetic earth power lines, collected and connected to his arsenal would tip the balance of power. He could easily neutralize Brown.

In slow motion he had drawn the power from the ley line. What he hadn't accounted for was that now the Magi was back, the power of the ley line was double its normal strength. All magic on the planet was doubling in power.

"Shit," he growled in frustration, and did the only thing he could.

The increased power short circuited his command of his own power and he had to cut off all power connections or be electrocuted by the increased ley line's power.

When he cut the power off, wild energy burst all around him. He stayed grounded by staying still and throwing an insulation psychic barrier around his feet. He had to break the conduit of his body to the ley line. He barely succeeded.

The multi-color energy burst surrounding him would prove fatal if he moved off the insulated spot that he had glued himself to.

Then he tried to duck, relying on his old defensive football skills. He knew it was too late, he saw and felt the power surge Brown was pulling in. He was impressed and reading Brown's mind he saw the strategy of why Brown hadn't already fired. Good ole dad, Brown, was going for a shotgun psychic blast. There was nowhere to run, he would be shredded like spaghetti.

His adrenaline flooded and he knew it would be too little, too late. He growled and got prepared. All of this was happening in an infinity of microseconds, it seemed.

Then he saw a purple ray shoot out from somewhere on his left from the floor.

He stared in surprise as the beam shot straight towards Brown and hit him in the chest in a spectacular bloody explosion.

Chapter 51

Brown laughed. He was proud of his son. Tapping into the ley line had been a good move and Brown had halfway hoped that Cornelius could have pulled it off. He saw the strategy and felt the power. It had been a smart move by a brilliant young man.

For a second, he felt remorse. He felt the changes in him accelerating and wanted to die. He now had three tongues, and something was growing out of his lower spine. He suspected it was some kind of tail by the feel of it.

He couldn't lose focus, but he watched as Cornelius made the mistake that would kill him. He was going to kill his only son.

A flash of sanity surfaced in his consciousness. He should have killed himself when he had the chance. You don't kill your son. If he had the chance to meet him in different circumstances, he could groom him for success; introduce him to the right people. He could share with all the collective experiences he had learned from. He could raise a son that would one day be President.

His body lurched and he felt the tail thing growing a few more inches. These physical changes were going to be a bitch to reverse, and he now suspected he couldn't. He felt sad.

The program the Magi had embedded in him mapped its way back to his mental surface.

The evil in him took back over and he saw that his son had screwed up. "Well, well, well, better kill him and then teleport the hell out of here." He knew that it must be the midnight hour and the bomb was already falling.

He paused for a second knowing that Cornelius was soon to be dead. After killing him should he go back and kill the Magi for doing this to him?

The last thoughts he had was, "Kill Cornelius first, get the hell out of here, then come back and finish the Magi if he survives the nuclear attack. It was time to kill and eliminate the one mistake he had made with his lovers in the past. Kill Cornelius!"

His mind fought and he tried to delay the impulse to kill his only son, but felt his resolve give away.

Finally, the impulse to kill peaked and he sent the command to his brain to fire at his one and only offspring at full force.

He didn't even see the ray from Jade's pistol coming at him. He felt a pain interrupt his firing impulse and deliberately fired to the left of Cornelius.

He felt his body die and let it happen. He made no attempt to stop the physical carnage and resigned himself to finally be out of the prison of the unholy marriage.

His last fleeting was a silent thank you to whoever had put him out of his misery, and he felt grateful that he hadn't killed his son.

He lay there looking straight up at the ceiling until his eyes became lifeless, the orbs turning from black back to their normal color.

Red colored irises across the room stared at the remains of his biological father. Tears were streaming down Cornelius' face;

he had mentally heard the command to miss him that Brown sent. He knew that Brown had tried to save him with his last act. For some reason that meant something, it was a little thing, but it meant that Brown hadn't totally hated him.

He wiped the tears away and teleported back to the Savages, there wasn't time to do anything else. The bomb was already dropping, he could feel it.

As he teleported away, he didn't see Quirk's guitar reassembling itself. It took only seconds, and then the old Martin was back to its original condition.

It floated over and rested on top of Quirk and J.D. A bluish cocoon slowly emitted out covering Quirk, J.D. and then spread to Steve and Jade.

Chapter 52

"Retreat, retreat!" Oswalt yelled through the microphone. All the monitors revealed the Institute was completely being overridden. He saw the best of the best retreating obeying his orders.

The booby-trap explosions were going off like July 4th fireworks show. The Institute walls had survived for hundreds of years and were now being obliterated.

He saw one group that hadn't made it to the gate and were now completely surrounded. He saw them keep shooting till they were overridden.

Commanders and troops were flowing into the alternate control room. Here they would make their last stand. The red phone rang, and he picked up with a sense of relief. This option would be faster and better than the one he was currently facing.

The President said. "We are dropping the bomb in two minutes; can you tell me anything to abort the mission?"

Oswalt thought if there was any information that would contest his next words. He gave the most emotional feedback he had ever given.

In his most serious voice he started, "No sir, if anything, please release as soon as possible. The pro-ghost forces have completely overrun our outer perimeters and are closing in. I haven't heard any feedback from the Savages, or the others, so I assume they are dead or are still fighting. Thank you, sir," Oswalt cynically stated, "For giving us the chance to try to eradicate the ghosts first. I only hope," he said as he surveyed the group of agents running in reinforcing for the final attack, "That the bomb will abolish the Magi and purge the planet of his and his minions' influence."

The President said the only thing he could say. "Thank you and the Institute for your years of service and loyalty. Your country will remember the brave agents who sacrificed your lives for the rest of us.

Oswalt felt like saying, "Don't count your chickens too soon, you might be joining us if the bomb doesn't work." He felt like saying, "You could have been more proactive on this threat when I warned you after San Diego." He felt like saying all that and more. Instead, he said the mantra all lost leaders use when talking to their Presidents. "It was an honor sir, to serve our country."

The President said, "The feeling is mutual, good luck, I hope this wipes the bastard out."

Oswalt sounded his agreement. He hurriedly put the emergency phone on the receiver and ran to help organize and construct ramparts against the encroaching forces. Oswalt thought, "Well, it will be an organized Armageddon."

Chapter 53

The Magi's portal kept growing to epic orange and black proportions. The smell was a swamp of unbearable brackish sulfur-laden odors.

Bayou looked on. He appraised the situation, an endgame of evil with an infested ghost malediction. Good, his old Mental Judo and gift for coming up with big words was still working.

He focused on the Magi who appeared to be in jocundly good humor. Why not, the bloody odds looked in his favor, and Bayou had always been about probability. Bayou did a rough estimation. He figured the earth had a better chance of being ejected out of the solar system than of them winning. Not bad odds, it could be worse.

The Magi looked through the portal at the puny ghost fighters in front of him. They were warts on his plan on manifest destiny.

He focused on the old timer holding the yellow musical instrument, the one called Razor. He glared at the old man who was staring back with a hard combatant look. He hated Razor, who had killed the first Magi solely by himself at Woosley Heights, the portal that had been the original crossover point. Razor had taken over as Bayou fell, and with the help of the witch had killed the first Magi and closed the portal. It had taken two hundred years to come back to necessary strength. The Magi craved revenge and watched Razor intently.

He laughed a horrible screech, a loud echo that crossed through the portal. Bayou thought it sounded like a madly crazed donkey braying. The ghost fighters had seen versions of this all before, except this was an ominous David and Goliath fight until death.

The Magi swore that Razor's killing days were over and he would take great delight in torturing this old musician warrior. He and the other Magi had assumed that there would be some kind of resistance. But they never expected the resistance to have come from magical musicians. To add insult to injury was that Razor was ancient in years and shouldn't have been able to accomplish what he did. Razor and his son, Bayou, had killed some of his prime lieutenants and would pay the price today.

He enjoyed the waiting and appraised the fury of the ghost fighters. They all appeared to be strategizing except the one called Razor. He fury reached through the portal; he truly was a primal creature as Brown had called him.

The Magi smiled. He knew Brown was about to be destroyed by the demon growing inside him. Brown was expendable, but Cornelius had to be kept alive. Cornelius was his mystical offspring; Cornelius was the true Antichrist. He had all the magical powers a human could stand. So far, he had been confused, but all that was about to change, as soon as the cross-over was complete.

The Magi had chosen Brown as the surrogate based on his DNA, and he had made a good choice, in his eyes. Brown was as evil as a human was capable of being. Now it was time for him to be out of the way.

Brown had served his purpose, and all was going according to the Magi's centuries-long plan. The first two Magi's dying hadn't been part of the plan. The plan had been to break the planet up into three kingdoms with a Magi in charge of each.

The Savages had destroyed the first two attempts at that plan. They also had contributed to both Magi's deaths and would now pay the price. As he surveyed them, he knew how he would avenge the other two. Their torture would be slow and painful and an example for all resisters to his domination. They would be his ambassadors of pain to what happens to those who don't comply.

He could feel the full powers of hell waiting to cross over. It felt good to have all this power at his disposal. The moaning of the demons only excited him more. He could see the bloodshed and butchery that would be created when unleashed in this dimension.

His powers allowed him to assess the readiness of the portal properties and everything happening close in proximity.

He saw the Institute being overrun by humans who thought they might be saved if they fought in his service. The pro-ghost forces provided him humor. The irony made him laugh. The curse of that group is that they would be his second group of victims, after the ghost fighters.

He would humor them at first, making them feel like they had been the difference in this Armageddon moment.

Then he would play with them; make them do grievous things to each other for his amusement. Then when he was bored, he would massacre all of them, or let his demons do it for him. He hadn't decided what to do with the hostage ghosts he had under him domination. That was trickier.

Razor, Bayou, Mist, Leslie looked on as the seconds ticked on wondering what was taking so long for the Magi to attack.

It was an awesome sight. The agents who had come in for support stood on the side watching, cloistered close together, tactically set for the final fight. The Savage collective versus the most powerful supernatural force in history stood before them. Winds were now whispering evil noises and blowing from the portal. The blustery wind stream was making the ghost fighters' hair blow backwards, stinging their eyes as they faced into the portal.

The tension was palpable, yet none of the Savages appeared alarmed. They had all fought ghosts before, granted no ghost like this. The basics were the basics. Find the weak spot and hit it hard.

Razor, all 76 years, tall, steely-eyed, positioned the '53 Fender Esquire and himself at center point. Bayou, tall, handsome crystal blue eyes and devilish smile took the right with the old Hendrix Buchanan Fender Telecaster. Mist, blond hair, the challenging iconoclastically youngest Savage, held the Bloodstone to the left. Leslie, the pale and beautiful dead champion, the most powerful ghost fighter, now ghost warrior aunt floated beside her.

It was a biblical apocryphal moment for all attending, with the wind increasing in intensity.

Razor looked at his watch. Two minutes before the bomb hit. That was plenty of time to get rid of this overblown supernatural panhandler. The Magi was a power bum, the same as the last two. The Magi was a demon shark eating the less fortunate. Somehow the shark had found a way to stray and eat on land. The Magi had crossed over and was hungry.

Razor looked and thought, "God, if you are out there you better get your ass in gear." He never assumed God would show, God gave him the guitar and that was it.

Razor tried to figure it out. Would the guitar fit halfway or all the way up the Magi's ass, he was about to find out. This was a challenge finally worth a good fight. He smiled a grim deadly smile, ready to get it over with. Bayou looked at his father. The old man was truly incorrigible. He always had been. Razor always homogenized all strategies in one. Slaughter any ghost in sight. Period.

Razor loved these moments. Bayou somehow knew that this time it was different. He also knew that Razor was meant for this moment, this was his destiny.

Bayou looked over at Leslie and flashed a remorseful smile, a sister so powerful that she came back from the dead to help them in the final battle. No one, except Pierre, had ever been able to come back and stay to fight. She had sacrificed her life for Razor and them in Charleston. The second Magi had blown out the left part of her upper abdomen. His agonized memory of Leslie's slow painful death momentary resurfaced.

Her forfeiture of her own life had demonstrated a strong sisterly love. The onslaught of selflessness overwhelmed him. In that final battle, on her deathbed she had surrendered her secret that she was his half-sister. His regret was that he wished he had found out about their brother-sister bond earlier. She had kept the secret from all of them only revealing it upon her approaching death.

Mist looked scared, doing eye aerobics, but in control. Bayou was proud of his daughter, always had been. Bayou did a quick glimpse, looking at her uncorked all kinds of memories in Bayou.

He remembered her birth. She had been born in Germany, her different growth spurts, her adventures as a bohemian teenager all flashed through his head. He peeked at her life history as it flashed by like a fast rolodex. She had always tested the system as a life soldier of fortune and been an independent thinker. A true shero in every definition of the term.

She was an original for damn sure. She was also the first ghost fighter to control both the Bloodstone and the guitars. She was the vagabond avatar, and the hope of the future, if she survived this battle.

She had always managed to speed and finesse her way through life fighting domestication the whole way. If any of them could survive this, it would be her. She had captured the respect of all the agents with her stand at Woosley Heights. She had almost died but had not backed down and fought a hell of a fight with no education or experience. She had crossed the frontier of the Magi world and understood the price for failure. Without the Bloodstone she would have died. It resurrected her, turned her into its shaman and now shared with her its wealth of power. The word agents used to explain her fierce independent behavior said it all; "She was a Savage", plain and simple. That underscored the truth but was an acceptable working explanation.

Bayou smiled; his little girl had become a woman. Her legacy would probably outshine all of theirs. He thought about his own life. He had been a quality philosopher. He had audited and trained many people in three different centuries. He had shared the secrets of chaos control.

He remembered his screw-ups like the time he got into trouble for saying that "customers don't bitch, they switch" in front of a big audience and got censored.

He felt he had left all kinds of legacies, but it all came down to this moment. He regarded the Magi. The Magi was growing, and the portal pulsated behind him.

Bayou was exhausted and thought about Aristotle's theory of means. He figured out that his chances of success depended on the first few moments of battle. He would mortgage his mortality to save mankind and he knew it in the first thirty seconds of the battle.

He felt the guitar glowing and focused his attention on the upcoming battle. The old Hendrix-Buchanan Telecaster blazed at his stroke. It was truly time for mankind to rock and roll. Would Mist survive this, could he protect her? His father protection gene was not relenting.

Mist surveyed the waiting train wreck. She respected the predicament and prized the rush she had gotten from her battles at Woosley Heights and Charleston. She had a pretty good clue on their odds.

Her rebel bittersweet philosophy was simple; live long enough to learn from her experiences. She had paid a price of lost innocence and this battle harbored death. Her remaining innocence was shattered, and she was ready to use her full mystic arsenal to finish this bullshit. The Magi was nothing but another power pimp.

The flickering Bloodstone wasn't showing her anything and the guitars were nothing but static resonating throughout her brain. That was a first. The divine Magi was sending out waves of black evil power that prohibited her normal power control. The word shit was invented for situations like this was her only conclusion.

Grandpa looked like he always did in battle, kill it, cook it, and go home. Dad had that look she knew too well, it was his system audit mode, taking everything in, looking at his probabilities for success. He was a paranormal actuary, and the mortality death odds looked pretty good she knew.

Leslie was purely focused on the abomination in front of them. She knew she was a ghost. Somehow, in her fighting instinct it made a difference. But damn, being a ghost on the Apocalypse front row battle created a different tactical plan. Her weak link at the moment was her emotions, not her logic. She knew what had to be done. Her emotions were in overdrive because of her love of her family who looked like they were about to become ghosts in a few seconds.

Mist was sharing the exact same thought. She couldn't let father and grandfather commit suicide on their own. She had learned to proselytize the use of the guitars and the Bloodstone. If anything happened to Razor or Bayou, she could assume control of their guitars. But she didn't want to be an orphan yet. Together they had a chance to win. Like the rest of them she knew an instant offense was their only chance.

Why not? It was the Savage way. The Bloodstone started to throb. When the Bloodstone had chosen her to be Leslie's successor, she had been grateful. It had provided her life. Now the burden of that responsibility lay heavy on her. No time for frivolous pity thoughts, she grabbed the throbbing Bloodstone and thought of all the times she had cheated death. At least she would leave a good-looking corpse, and she smiled at her death humor.

Leslie inspected the layout. She had been so powerful while alive and was now haunted by the truth. The truth was that the Magi was more powerful than she had told them. They were all that humans had to offer, and she was hampered by the Magi governor control of her afterlife. The Magi blitzkrieg was about to begin. She could smell the evil coming forth.

The Magi was a mammoth force compared to the ghost fighters. He was like a Class 10 Hurricane, knowing the system normally tops out at 5. The precariousness of the battle was overwhelming. She had helped kill the second Magi and knew if given the opportunity she would kill the last and final one.

The problem was the ghost fighters had had no rest and were burdened with crisis after crises. Travel fatigue, battle fatigue, decision fatigue, non-stop. Three days of no rest and then fighting the final battle for the survival of mankind did not bode well.

The pain hit her psyche. "Pierre!" her mind screamed. Ghost tears flowed down her face. Damn Brown, she forced her attention back to the Magi.

She couldn't tell them that she had just felt Pierre die. That would only demoralize them. She assessed her options. Her raw powers could only provide a slim chance of surprise to the Magi. She had spent most of her energies in her initial contact with him when she had broken free.

Even though she had transcended her human form she still felt human. She still felt like the old Leslie. A ghost tear came to her; it was her family, the Savages. They were the fated ones that were on point for the Magi counterattack. They would either save or destroy mankind. The fight for mankind, and eternity, would be over in a few minutes, she thought, knowing this battle was beyond just this dimension.

She could feel the Magi's sinister despicable powers increasing by the moment. He was getting ready for his nasty big move.

She padlocked her fears and got ready for battle.

Razor had naturally chosen the strongest offensive point. Bayou, Mist and Leslie flanked the sides. It was a good offense by combat standards. It was called the Admiral Nelson suicide attack mode, which had left the old boy immortalized back a few hundred years ago. It took courage to set the deadliest offensive tactic, with tired, exhausted ghost fighter warriors.

Yet none had questioned the formation and they fell into it naturally. After all, if you are going to fight to the death, take every advantage you could, especially the advantage of thought-out contingencies. This formation allowed for all their specialties in combat.

If Razor got hurt, Bayou could come up and harness the energy of both guitars. If Bayou got hurt, Mist could control both guitars and the Bloodstone for the final attack. It was a strategy of contingencies and surprise attack.

It had probably been unconscious that Razor had positioned himself in the middle. The Magi would see it as a challenge. Now if Razor could irritate the Magi enough to make the Magi cross over by himself, they might have the remotest of chances to pull this out.

The demons of hell, and all the captured souls the Magi had made his indentured evil unholy hosts, might be trapped on the other side of the portal if the Magi could be summoned solo across.

In the annals of ghost fighting there had never been a situation this bad. No portal in history had a virago hellish nature like this.

Razor looked around with the deadliest look Bayou had ever seen. He looked at his son, daughter, and granddaughter and smiled a malicious smile.

"Where's Pierre?" he barked.

No one knew, shaking their heads in the negatives. Razor responded, "He could have talked the ghost to death," and laughed.

Razor, as usual, displayed no fear and had a callous look about him. Bayou knew that Razor would ask, if questioned, what value would there be in showing fear.

Bayou looked hard at Razor. "Dad, any particular strategy you have in mind?"

"Yes," Razor said, "try not to lose, don't worry about winning."

Mist looked and listened. This was a first. Razor thinking defense, the thought of that scared her. Maybe he was saying that they were all expendable. If Leslie could be an independent ghost, maybe they could all die and keep battling, for eternity.

The thought gave her some comfort.

Razor looked to Leslie. “What do you think?”

Leslie was standing next to Mist, who was holding the Bloodstone. Leslie psychically beamed the thought to them, “Whatever we do; we need to do it in one minute. Time’s running out!”

The Magi spoke as if listening to their thoughts, “Your desperate craving for survival is amusing. Your time in paradise is over. You could save yourself by swearing devotion to me.” He paused and read the faces and laughed at the obvious conclusion. “Oh well, please put up your best fight, I will enjoy it in a,” he paused,

“in a sentimental way.”

Razor spit in the direction of the Magi, taunting him.

The Magi’s mood swung like a pendulum. His rage surfaced looking at Razor.

“Even though my hungry demons are limitless, I will fight you by myself.” He stepped out of the portal.

Bayou smiled; all the ghost fighters smiled. Bayou caught the beamed thought that came from Leslie. “At last, a break!” The ghost fighters closed ranks. This was it.

As the Magi stepped through, Razor floated up and fired full volume the force of the Fender Esquire. The guitar sounded like a sonic cannon going off. The walls shook, threatening to crack under the strain.

Bayou levitated and closed in on the right, firing the Telecaster, shrugging off the tiredness, flooding his body with adrenaline. He had tuned to a regular E tuning and hit the opening chord of Guns N’ Roses “Welcome to the Jungle!” The guitar became a sonic mystical cannon fired straight into the Magi.

Spots surfaced, scarring the surface of the Magi where the guitar's mystic energy hit.

Mist and Leslie both soared up and used the full force of the Bloodstone to fire into the Magi. Leslie channeled her energy with Mist's resonating with the Bloodstone.

The Bloodstone, instead of a red light, shot out a bright white-pinkish light with the combined energies of Mist and Leslie. Neither one had ever seen or felt their combined might affect the Bloodstone like that before.

Chapter 54

A three-way barrage of light and sound assaulted the Magi.

Loud music bombarded the air. Razor and Bayou's fingers were blistering the fretboard with white lightning streaking into the Magi. Both machines and fret boards turned solid brilliant white, and the lethal energy was electrocuting the Magi where he stood.

The Magi soaked it all in and made no attempt to defend himself. He felt the blows but had enough energy reserve to wait it out.

The ghost fighters poured it on, using the last of their remaining strengths. The room was a nova of angry energy like big wasps going after an intruder.

The assault was jammed by the Magi appearing not to be affected.

Razor knew that time was running out. He turned to Mist, with a look that she knew. "Read my mind. I am broadcasting an emergency thought. This is it, pay attention. When the bomb drops, shoot the bomb into the other portal. When you do that, I am going to try something to distract the Magi. With any luck we will kill him and the incoming demons he wants to bring in with him."

He didn't wait to see if she got the message, and he resumed the battle, not missing a single lick.

Instead, he did something he had wanted to do his whole life, he unleashed his full fury. It was his time to die, and he knew it. No use getting the kids killed in this bullshit power play by the Magi.

Razor had always suspected that if he gave totally in to the music there was a place too far, that his power could go. Some warning had always gone off in his brain to release the power before he hit that junction. This time would be different. Old, tired, but still damn good at finger picking. This time he picked with everything still left in him. He didn't think about trying to save mankind, save his family, he was well beyond that now.

He heard something he had never heard before, knowing that he was hallucinating. His guitar heroes, the ghosts of those old pickers from his past, whispering to him to kick some ass. He could feel their rage adding to his own. He smiled the angriest grin in musical history!

He let his fingers find the song for the last time, Eight More Miles to Louisville, his old time favorite.

He started picking and increased the speed, feeling the power grow in him.

He played and prayed harder and harder, letting his full impressive muse go. Like Samson from the Bible, he prayed, "God I have been a lifelong sinner, but please grant me this one wish, the power to bury this bastard!"

The first wave of fatigue hit him. He could feel the toll it was taking of his body. His body luminosity was flaring hot white now like the guitar, willing it to give him more, just another few seconds.

Bayou glared and couldn't believe what he was seeing, it couldn't be done. He calculated the resolve and energy being put out. He too knew the secret of the guitar.

He smiled and thought about dying with Razor. Father and son had been here before. Bayou knew the part of the brain he had to activate to full, it was called Heschl's gyrus, and it released all governors. The pain and pleasure transcended all the previous battle experiences. He grinned a death smile matching Razor's.

He started to match Razor's speed, growling, and spittle flowing out his mouth with gritted teeth, he poured it on. The white, super bright power was coursing through him streaming out the end of the guitar into the Magi. He heard Hendrix-Buchanan adding their legendary crossroads power.

Razor felt another wave of tiredness hit his body, it was hurting somewhere, everywhere, damn old age, he blanked the pain and turned it up, keeping on playing.

He felt intense pain and his eyes melting, eyes gone blind. He got angrier and kept playing. His eyes disintegrated and he felt the hair burning off his head and body. He kept playing, pain coursing through tearing him apart. He felt physically worse than he had ever felt. He sucked a deep breath, blind, yet focused; the son-of-a bitch was going to die. Pure rage poured forth out of his fingers.

The music had never sounded sweeter. He was in the key of C and he heard Bayou in the key of G major doing some of his rock music. He wondered if the dissonance would make a difference.

Down in the vault Quirk opened his eyes. He heard music blaring through the walls and recognized the tunes. The Savages were engaged in full warfare. He knew the sounds. His guitar floated in front of him, doing fast circles. He opened his eyes wider in time to see the guitar throw out a blue protective field around the three of them. Then he saw another blue arm streak out from the guitar into the wall going through it. He tried to make sense of it, but he seemed paralyzed for the moment. He fought the paralysis, but the guitar held him in place. Quirk cussed, "What the hell....."

Chapter 55

The music war raged on. The Magi had a two-way bluish white lightning attack; a red-white front mounted by Mist, Leslie's scalding blue-red power bursts coming from her outstretched arms. Razor shooting hot blue-white beams, Bayou shooting brilliant red and orange beams.

The Magi was surrounded, except for the portal.

Razor was blind now, but feeling the guitar evil radar focus, he guessed at the point where the Magi was. It correlated to where he had seen him. The final move to his plan was now, and he knew this was going to be tricky. He felt lighter than he had ever felt, and the guitar was taking his entire finger picking moves to the next level, and amplifying energy beyond anything in recorded history.

Razor felt more power than he had ever felt and kept pouring energy into the bastard, waiting for the bomb. He felt more hair disintegrating off his body. His ears were still working, thank God, and he poured more on.

Bayou felt Razor's energy and synched with it. He too was beyond what he had ever produced before.

His eyes were watering, but so far, his body was taking the abuse. He reached for more power and felt the pick melt in his hand. He kept strumming with his bloody hand, seeking more power. Razor was undistinguished now, just a white flare centered, attacking the Magi. The power emanating from him fueled everyone else to dig deeper. Pure rage fueled all the Savages as they realized what the old man was doing. The son-of-a bitch was committing suicide somehow with the guitar. He kept pulling in more and more power, lighting the Magi up in a multicolor storm and loud cacophony.

Razor felt Bayou's power increase to his right. He was proud of his son. He could feel Bayou also sucking all the energy his guitar had to give him. He looked over and realized he was blind now. But he could feel the power and he knew those licks. Bayou had played them for years, so everything was muscle memory now.

Mist was synching the Bloodstone energy into the syncopation of the guitar rhythms. Something was wrong with Razor, but she couldn't help. Instead, she followed his lead and poured her whole mind into the Bloodstone. The Bloodstone understood her intentionality and unleashed all its reserves into the Magi.

Time slowed to microseconds and separated itself into momentary snatches of death foreplay. With all this energy something had to give, something had to die. Time froze, defying linear sequence.

Then she had the Bloodstone find the perfect sync all three ghost fighters hit the Magi with coordinated, concentrated beats of pure raw magic. The end was a few seconds away one way or the other. The universe rocked as the enemies prepared for the knockout blow. Mist was beyond thinking, but something flashed in her head.

Leslie had also caught the Razor message and looked up as the bomb came through their field of vision. It looked like it was starting to implode.

Mist also caught, out of her peripheral vision, the bomb coming through.

Bayou kept firing blue-white rays, bisecting the Magi with everything he had. He was screaming now in full fury.

Mist acted as Razor had instructed her. Leslie helped her guide the bomb straight into the portal. Leslie left her and teleported straight on top of the bomb.

With her remaining ghost energy, she tried to open a hole just big enough for the bomb to go through. The portal stayed closed. She increased her energy, trying to guide it in.

Razor heard Mist's thoughts and felt her panic. He attacked head-on, flying guitar first straight into the Magi. He levitated blindly into the mass of the now gorged shape of the ancient mystic.

The Magi was caught off guard. One event at a time he could have handled. The two concentrated guitar blasts together, and the entrance of some object from above, constructed confusion. He hesitated, not knowing which to deal with first.

Razor hit him, and the pain doubled the Magi over. He screamed as he felt his center being invaded by the good magic. The good and bad magic collided with an audible detonation.

Screaming, he grabbed Razor and the guitar with his right hand and threw him into the nearest wall. With his left he reached back and opened the portal.

Mist saw the portal opening and guided the bomb straight into it.

As the portal closed, she sent Leslie all her remaining energy. Leslie turned back, and with both hands shot out blue beams closing the portal opening as the bomb exploded. It was then the nuclear bomb blasted purgatory to purgatory.

Chapter 56

The President asked, "What the hell happened?"

One of the senior advisors said, "We have radiation. Some of the radiation made it, but 99% of the effect was nullified."

Hold on.

They watched as many sensors set up to monitor the Institute showed energy fluctuations all over the scale.

"Plus, we have collateral damage to the pro-ghost fighters. It appears to have killed all humans in the immediate area."

"It looks like the battle is still going," one said, not believing her eyes. "The radiation is clearing itself up."

Nothing in the universe could instantly reverse nuclear damage. Yet they had just witnessed it and the only conclusion was that somebody was in charge down there, the question was who?

Chapter 57

They all felt the effects.

The guitars and Bloodstone cocooned the ghost fighter forces. Then the Bloodstone reversed its normal light flow and drew energy from the radiation void into itself.

Mist was mystified, and too tired to do anything but hold it and let it work its magic. The light show was unlike anything she had seen. The Bloodstone was a black hole sucking in all the residual radiation.

No one knew what was happening and everyone froze in place.

Bayou was the first to guess. "Mist," he beamed, "it's sucking in the nuclear energy, making it safe for us."

Bayou's guitar was still fired up. He looked at the Magi, who had shrunk. The Magi was doubled over, smoke coming off his body. He had been directly in front of the portal and had taken a direct hit of the bomb blast. Yet he still tried to stand.

"Have mercy," he beamed to them.

Bayou looked over at the crumpled clump of what was left of Razor in the corner. He saw the '53 Esquire floating above Razor now floating over to him. He knew what that meant. "Leslie's dead, and now Razor." His rage was full, and he didn't even hesitate. Screaming at the top of his lungs with rage, he felt both guitars wrapped to him. “Dad,” he yelled, “Aghhhhhhhhh” and he disconnected from reality, letting nothing but emotion rule his movement.

He didn’t even see Cornelius and Quirk come into the room.

With that scream, he screamed again and again as he charged, and stopped in front of the Magi.

The Magi looked up in defiance. “Go ahead Human, kill me if you can. I feel my energies starting to increase.” Bayou took one last look at Razor and turned back to look at the Magi.

He smiled as he put both guitars on either side of the Magi’s head. He spoke loudly, as AC/DC used to sing, “For those about to rock, we salute you!” He screamed one more time and fired both guitars into the Magi’s head. He shot the guitars up and down the Magi’s body, still screaming, actually putting the guitars where they were making contact. Explosions kept buffeting Bayou, but he kept it up, remembering Razor. Finally, he quit.

With orange and black lightning, the Magi imploded. Bayou fainted, dropping unconscious into Quirk’s outstretched, tired, beat-up arms. Brothers in arms to the end.

Chapter 58

Cornelius reached deep. The first person he saw was Mist, fainting, and he used his powers to heal her. She woke up shrieking, "Dad, Dad!" ....., then Cornelius forced her to look him in the eyes. He beamed to her, "Mist, Mist, he's okay, Quirk has him, I'm going to him now."

Mist finally understood. She tried to set up, the Bloodstone started bleeding red drops. She understood and raised the Bloodstone to let the mystical drops fall into her eyes.

Cornelius ran to Bayou and started the same process.

Bayou had burnt his goatee, soul patch, and all facial hair off his face. He was burnt all over his body and his right and left hands had bones sticking through where he had kept playing in the rage attack.

The guitars circled Bayou's body, which wasn't a good sign. Where was Razor?

He couldn't think about that now.

He was exhausted but had to try again. He started using his powers, and felt Mist come up from behind him. She moved to his side and let the dripping Bloodstone drip into his eyes. It was then she realized something was wrong with his eyes. They were half the normal size. Bayou was blind.

She gave an involuntary gasp. Then the miracle happened.

Both guitars levitated up into playing positions and fired white light into the Bloodstone. Cornelius and Mist were both shocked. As they watched the Bloodstone took the energy, processed it somehow and a brighter red beam filled the inside. The drops came faster now into Bayou's eyes and mouth.

He stirred and greedily gasped the falling drops. As Cornelius, Quirk and Mist watched, his beaten up body started healing. The process took one minute.

Bayou sat up.

He gasped, "Thanks, everything is blurry. Where's Razor?"

Mist said, "Hold on Dad," she tilted his head back and let the drops continue to drip in for a few more seconds. Bayou was too tired to argue. After a few seconds, he rolled to his side. "I can see now, let's find and rescue Razor."

Chapter 59

Oswalt looked at the now working monitor and picked up the red phone.

The President saw it light up and against all hope picked it up. "Is that you, Oswalt?"

"Yes sir, according to the Monitors the Institute is secure."

The President let out a breath of relief and shouted the news to the watching observers.

"What do our sensors show?"

Advisor after advisor verified and validated the miracle. The Institute had a high body count, but no indication of psychic activity.

"Call off the next bomb ASAP." It had been scheduled to be dropped in ten minutes.

The most senior advisor came up. "Our satellites show absolutely no psychic interference of manifestations."

The President smiled, "How are you holding up, any casualties?"

Oswalt didn't say anything.

"Sir, I am not sure, let me get back with you." He hung up.

The President had that sour mouth feeling, when he knew that a price had been paid for their success. His mood changed, but he let the celebration go on.

"Notify the press," was all he said to the Vice President. Tell them we have won and details will be released shortly. Get a rescue, clean-up crew to Asheville immediately. Call FEMA, (the joke was that FEMA stood for Fix Everything My Ass), get the Purple Hearts and Medals of Honor ready. I think another or a few of the ghost fighters died in the service of mankind."

He thought, "Check with other countries to see if they want to contribute. Hell, they died beating hell for mankind's survival and that should be worth something. Run it through the system and come up with the best we can do for them."

Chapter 60

The Bloodstone and guitars had mysteriously picked out the good forces from the bad forces. All the ghost fighters had been protected from the radiation.

A few medics and doctors were huddled in one corner. It was the last place Bayou had seen Razor thrown in the heart of the battle.

They ran over.

Everyone parted as a sign of respect. Plus, you couldn't miss the two floating guitars circling Bayou and the old Martin Quirk had strapped to his back.

They all looked at Razor.

The doctor turned around. "Sorry," was all he said.

Bayou smiled. Razor would have liked that, no big speech; "sorry" kind of said it all.

Then a medic, still inspecting the body, turned to another. He looked at the doctor for a look of approval.

The medic, looking at the ghost fighters, talked while the assistant started writing.

"Cause of death is many. Take your pick. It looks like he died of broken neck, broken back, heart attack, 3rd degree burns. His clothes were totally burnt off and he was a mass of black with white streaks." The Bloodstone flashed to Razor's body, removing the smell that was accosting them.

They all just stared. Mist started crying.

Bayou turned around to her. "Mist did the Bloodstone flash right before Razor hit the wall? It did to me one time before when Leslie and he were hidden in the quantum stream."

"No Dad, I would have felt it." The tears now were coming down all their faces.

A bright light started to surround Razor's body. Everyone backed away. The guitars and Bloodstone stayed neutral, which was a good sign.

The light grew into three bodies.

Leslie stepped out; a vivid ghost appearing with two other apparitions next to her. They both looked very familiar to Bayou and Quirk.

She smiled at all of them.

Looking at Bayou, "Bro, the odds were against us, or as you would say, the earth had a better chance of being ejected out of the solar system than us winning., but congrats, you just won the celestial lottery," and she smiled. "I love you and you truly are a great brother. You truly are the last of the true romantics."

She winked, "I will tell William Wordsworth 'Hi' for you," knowing that Wordsworth was Bayou's favorite poet. Jade had turned him on to him.

Leslie looked at Cornelius. "The forces have destined you the Magi. Thank you for choosing to side with us. I wish I could have got to you earlier. I kept trying but the Magi was too strong for me to find you. At times I thought you were just a figment of my imagination. My advice is to get active and keep unlocking the arcane secrets of true paranormal activity. We need a person to proactively create documents, spells, and anything we can use to fight evil.

Never fear evil, where there is a shadow, there is a light. I know that you are using your power for good. Tell Jacob and Leah Hi, and I wish I had had the chance to meet them."

She confessed, "The ghost fighters will need you. There are many more little Magi's, but I don't see another attack for five years and no one else is close to being as powerful as the ones before were. By that time, you guys should be powerful enough to put them down with little effort and I predict that mankind will be safe for a long time."

Leslie turned to Mist.

"My niece, the Bloodstone is in good hands. I see that you will leave a legend in history with it. Your power grows every day. It's funny, with your attitude and adaptability you are the perfect ghost fighter. I will give you my favorite poem." as she quoted it Mist remembered seeing it among her few possessions they had come across when they went through after Leslie's death.

"You have brains in your head.

You have feet in your shoes.

You can steer yourself

Any direction you choose."

Dr Seuss.

She reached over and laid a ghost kiss on Mist's cheek.

They both had tears in their eyes.

"Mist, use the Bloodstone to help reveal real versus fake reports. It can do that, and save precious resources that Oswalt will start complaining about soon." They both laughed.

The crowd parted and Oswalt, Steve and Jade Johnson and J.D. appeared, depositing themselves in the inner circle around Razor.

J.D. walked over and put her arm around Quirk and had that fierce mad look on her face. Quirk had some explaining to do, about why he left her there. Quirk smiled at her, and her look disappeared.

Leslie said to Quirk and J.D., "Have a happy marriage! Retire and see the world. Quirk, the Institute needs a spokesperson out there to let people know. The pro-ghost forces didn't just happen. We could have prevented it. I need you two to fight that fight."

She smiled, "I will miss your version of Desperado, and you sang it better than the Eagles ever did."

She turned to face Steve and Jade Johnson.

She looked at to the floating 1953 Fender Esquire and pointed her finger at it. A blue light appeared and connected to the guitar. She froze for a second like she was talking to it.

The guitar broke away from the other guitar.

They all stared as it floated over to Steve Johnson. "Put it on," she ordered. "Steve Johnson, you are now the newest ghost fighter."

She gave a knowing look at Mist and Cornelius. "Do it," was all she said.

Steve couldn't believe what was about to happen. He had spent twenty years of his life trying to resurrect Bayou and this magical guitar. For most of his life he had stared at this guitar. He had given more thought to it than he cared to admit. Now he was about to be rewarded for all his work. Fate had a way of tying up loose ends. For every ending there is a new beginning.

He accepted what was about to happen. She had been part of his adventure; she knew her man and the prices he had paid in resurrecting Bayou and the guitar. His Bayou imprint was there forever but he had learned control. The guitar would be a natural symbiosis with its new master.

He was different than Razor, but after all the fights he had been in, plus the Bayou imprint, he could use Razor's guitar probably better than anyone alive. He was the natural successor.

Jade took pleasure, knowing this was what he had always secretly wanted. Ever since he had tried to use it in the Woosley Heights second battle she knew he had been embarrassed by not being able to activate it. The Bayou imprint gave him the knowledge and skills, but he had never been able to access the guitar.

Everyone stepped back as Cornelius and Mist both laid hands-on Steve Johnson's head. Jade let go of his hand and he looked at her with no trace of fear. The Bloodstone was pulsating bright red.

The guitar was now strapped across his chest in classic playing fashion. It hung a little low, seeing how he was smaller than Razor.

Mist and Cornelius went into a trance. Repeating what they that had done with Quirk, they unleashed Mist's Bloodstone power with Cornelius's Magi power. The combination of power curtailed all movement in the room. Everyone felt frozen; Jade had forgotten the Bloodstone could do that.

Red and white light flowed into Steve's closed eyes. He sensed biological protocols connecting from his brain to the guitar. It was a rapture of incredible music initiation. He heard music like he had never heard it before. It was incredible; the Universe was operating on string theory at least from a musical perspective. He could feel it. Jed would never believe this. He stayed upright as the mystical connections solidified.

After a minute the red light died down.

Everyone was quiet, as Steve opened his eyes.

He felt the power. He could feel it, feel the universal harmonies. He strummed an E chord and the guitar lit up, giving approval to its new owner.

Jade felt her eyes brim. He looked happier than she had ever seen him. All the sacrifices he had made, and now he was the newest guitar ghost fighter.

Leslie beamed at him. "The cosmic balance is once again achieved."

She looked at Oswalt.

"You made the tough choice. You could have aborted the bomb, but you made a great decision even at the cost of your own and our lives. You will go down in history. Great leaders are the ones that rise to the occasion and make the tough choices. You never quit. Thank you for all your support."

Their mutual soft smiles said it all. Mutual respect, people doing what had to be done.

Finally, she turned to Razor.

Everyone consciously stepped back, even Bayou, who had moved as close to Razor as he could.

A bright light came from above and Razor stood in front of them looking exactly like he did before they went into the final battle.

Razor, ***the*** Razor was now a ghost. He looked down at his body and immediately surveyed the scene below him. Everyone knew the look. He was still in battle mode. After he surveyed the situation, he shocked everyone. He smiled and spoke.

"Damn, folks, had I known that death felt ***this*** good I would have kissed my ass goodbye a long damn time ago."

A muted, reverent chuckle spread through the gathered, despite themselves.

Razor looked around and started barkin' orders. Evidently, old habits die harder than the body.

"Cornelius, take that power and use it offensively. When in doubt, trust your instincts. I like that about you. You got good instincts, son."

His gaze wandered to Steve and Jade. Steve was strapped with the old warrior's 53 Esquire around his back.

"Ahh," Razor's voice was growing quieter by the moment, "the guitar made a good choice. That guitar is a good one, Steve, and couldn't have chosen a better caretaker. You have the experience to reciprocate. I'm not worried anymore. Jade, do your best to keep him out of trouble." The graveled voice chuckled from the depths of a cave.

He looked at Quirk and J.D. and smiled. "Wellllll," he imitated Quirk's famous trademark, "There is no substitute for guts, keep 'em in line, my brother from another mother...and you, you foxy flaxen haired beauty. Damn, you are a beautiful woman. Quirk, you'll have your hands full." A raspy full-throated roar slipped from the fading father's last breaths.

Mist, he smiled at his granddaughter, "Remember, a clear conscience is usually the sign of a bad memory."

Even dead, he was still Razor, testing her critical thinking. It had been a game they played well.

Bayou, he looked over, "Son" and he paused.

"Son", he began again. The lump in his throat more evident with every breath...Son, when they bury me, make sure the preacher won't talk a second past fifteen minutes. If the pious bastard starts down the path of recruitment, shut him the hell up. I don't want no religious recruiting. So, I'll come out of my grave if he tries that bullshit and you ain't seen a haint like the one you'll see from me! I hate that shit!"

Bayou smiled, "Speech number twelve again." Bayou had long ago numbered his dad's speeches. This was a familiar one, the old number twelve, the famous "after I die speech". He waited for the acceleration, rest of it. "They can't let a person die with dignity!"

They heard muted laughter from the agents standing around. Even dead, Razor was giving hell about his funeral. The old man was always remarkable in his direct approach. He could give one helluva of a speech. Tell 'em this: "He was a good one, worked hard, took care of family and friends alike, in good times and bad. Killed the damned demons when they needed reacquainting with their bastard master, caught more fish than the law allowed, and loved to cook. Then play Wayfaring Stranger and I am a Pilgrim and then put me in the ground."

Razor continued the message, "If it costs too much, cremate me and put my ashes out in the trout stream of the Nantahala Gorge.

Oswalt grinned. The man would be a national hero and the world would pay for his grave. But that was Razor, always have a contingency. He had told Oswalt many times, if everything is coming your way, you're probably in the wrong lane.

Razor continued going the speech twelve ending, the natural gravity coming into place. Bayou counted down, 5, 4,3,2,1.

Razor looked at him right on time and looked at his ghost hand where his watch was.

"Here it comes," Bayou thought and grinned.

"That total funeral service should wrap up in fifteen minutes, son".

A bright circle started opening above them.

Razor looked at the two guest apparitions besides Leslie and changed his demeanor.

Chet Atkins and Merle Travis, two of Razor's biggest influences, looked at him.

Merle said, "Nice to meet you Razor, Chet and I thought we would come down and invite you to a jam session we are starting in a few minutes."

Razor smiled a big smile.

Leslie said, "Oh Razor, Pierre is also waiting for you. He had a big meal cooked up for you and said you won't believe the kitchens up in heaven."

Razor looked around one last time at everyone. There wasn't a dry eye. Everyone had a smile, seeing how happy he was. A true send-off of a legendary ghost fighter.

Then in his characteristic manner, he laughed and said, “Then, what the hell are we waiting for?” and walked straight into the white portal not looking back. Chet and Merle followed.

Leslie took one last look. “Don’t worry, I’ll try to keep him out of trouble!” She smiled and laughed, the way she used to when she was alive. She turned and followed them into the white portal. The circle of light closed and disappeared.

Epilogue

Quirk and J.D.'s marriage made all the news. Everyone had shown up. They were a good-looking couple, and it was a celebrity-filled ceremony with even the President making an appearance. Many nations sent gifts and other contributions.

The graphic scenes of the battle had been played and analyzed. The majority opinion was that the Institute had saved the world.

The Institute had remained the way it was, and a philanthropist had donated a new, bigger building.

The old building was a major tourist draw. A wall like the Vietnam Veteran's Memorial had been erected to remember the agents who had died in the battle. The truth was it could have been a lot worse.

A movie had been sponsored, made and produced by the best of the old Bayou Savage movie biographers. It was about the group of agents who had been cut off in the retreat and died giving the ghost fighters a chance to defend the world from the Magi.

It had been called "The Institute Crucifixion, The Doomed Squad!" Everyone was happy when Adam Constantine had been chosen to play the lead actor. Many of the actors were former agents who had been there in the battle.

The biggest attraction at the destroyed Institute site was the Razor Savage tombstone where they had laid the old warrior to rest, per his instructions.

Bayou and crew had been a little scared when the old preacher went over the fifteen-minute mark. They nervously looked the grave and motioned for the old man to hurry up.

The big and most photographed feature was the twenty-nine-foot statue showing Razor with his guitar fighting the Magi. The sculptor had been hand-picked by Mist. She had wanted, like Bayou, to give the old man the true credit he deserved.

The statue had tuned out well and was a good replication of what Razor had done as he sacrificed himself in battle.

Oswalt gave speeches along with the rest of the ghost fighters.

He was still the Institute Director, but the President was putting pressure on him to be a Secretary of Paranormal Defense, a newly made position. Steve Johnson was the next in line, if Oswalt took the position. Steve and he had talked it over and it looked like a foregone event.

Jade won a Nobel Prize for her historical coverage of the original Quirk recordings when they had first arrived. She also had been promoted to Director of Risk Management. Her job was to run the History, Public Relations, and Human Resources departments. It was great that she and Bayou had worked together, and she indoctrinated the concepts of quality engineering into her operations.

All the ghost fighters won the Nobel Prize for contributions to the peace of the planet. They attended and became parade crazed after a while. No wonder, everyone wanted to see them. They were the most awarded fighters in history.

Bayou, Quirk and Steve Johnson had recorded a few songs and donated all the monies made for contributions to the families who lost agents in the Magi battle. Quirk's voice had won him male vocalist of the year.

Steve and Bayou had become famous in music magazines for their twin matching leads. Bayou mentioned in interviews that the Allman Brothers band had been a big influence. This led to a big trend in post religious war studies and reviving that old rock and roll.

Bayou had revived his interest in magic. He started performing live stage and closeup magic around the world. Sometimes Mist would help. In his shows he talked about and gave a quick historical review of Houdini, David Copperfield, and the other legendary musicians.

He also exposed fakirs and mediums and showed how they did their tricks, yet never revealed how he did his own. His famous response was when someone interviewing him, ask him how he did it and did he use true magic, he responded, "No, anyone could do this with training," and could the interviewer keep a secret. When they said "yes", he would respond with those bright blue eyes and a twinkle, "So can I, so can I!"

Jade wrote a best-seller about what happened in the battle, to fight the twisted versions being produced and downloaded by the media. The Institute had filed many lawsuits and was winning. It was a battle to keep the truth of the events from being distorted.

Cornelius was now in charge of all ghost fighters' training. Quirk had worked with him, documenting and sharing all his tribal knowledge. Quirk wasn't worried, in his opinion he felt Cornelius was a natural warrior and always thought of terms of the Art of War. Cornelius had gone beyond the call of duty and enrolled himself into Special Forces training branches around the world. He caught on fast and was highly respected. The gift he brought was his love of technology with a love of combat.

In his one-of-a kind Institute ghost fighting training, he used his powers to duplicate ghost feats. The Institute's fighters were thought to be the best of the best due to the unique nature of their training. Oswalt had tons of requests for getting in and "getting in" was a serious honor. The ghost fear psychological exam had a pass rate of under twenty-five percent. You had to be truly elite to get in, and that was just the mental aspect.

Mist traveled the world, using the Bloodstone to solve mysteries that no one could solve. She was in high demand from all law enforcement agencies. The tougher they were the better. She had a talent for being unconventional. She had learned a lot of forensic investigation techniques from hanging around with Jed, now Director of Science at the new Institute. He accompanied her on mystery solving when he had the chance, and they were making a name for themselves. Jed's wife considered Mist like a daughter, and they were Mist's second family.

One Year Later

It was Razor Savage's birthday. If he had lived, he would have been 277 years old. Bayou, Steve Johnson, and Quirk were playing guitars at Bayou's cabin. Jade, J.D., Oswalt, Jed and his wife, Adam Constantine and Mist were listening and singing along.

Bayou and Quirk had brought along the last of Razor's special moonshine. The white lightning was loosening up the singing voices and each was giving a special memory of Razor during the breaks. Most memories were humorous, and all laughed.

If Razor had been there, he wouldn't have denied any of it, and said his reactions had been based on common sense and that if they had been in the same situations, they would have done the same thing.

It was the end of the night, and most had drifted off to bed. Quirk looked over at Bayou, "Your turn to lead one, son."

Bayou looked at Steve and knew that he would know the next song. It was a permanent part of the Bayou imprint lodged in Steve's brain. A song Bayou had been raised on; a song he had heard Razor play ever since he could remember.

He opened "Eight More Miles to Louisville" and all three guitar players kicked it hard, in memory of Razor.

When it was finished, they put their guitars down and finished the last of the moonshine. They passed the Mason jar around like a holy relic.

Quirk asked, “Bayou, what would Razor be doing if he were here? Still alive I mean. We all went our own ways, but what do you think Razor would have done?”

Bayou didn’t even hesitate. “Pierre and he would have opened a cooking school. Pierre would have taught French cuisine and Razor would have taught how to make southern cuisine. Razor’s recipes are still in my house, scanned on my computer.”

Steve said, “You know, his recipe for cornbread, the sour, not sweet kind is to kill for, and his gravy and biscuit recipes are Jade’s favorite.”

It hit all three of them at the same time as the epiphany it was.

Three months later the book was released. “Razor Savage’s Book of Southern Cooking, For People Who Love Real Food.”

Quirk threw in his special recipes and asked all the other ghost fighters for their favorites.

The book became the hugest best seller in cooking history and stayed on the top ten cookbooks for six more years.

Somewhere Razor Savage was smiling!

Made in the USA
Columbia, SC
25 February 2025